continued . . .

Something from the Nightside

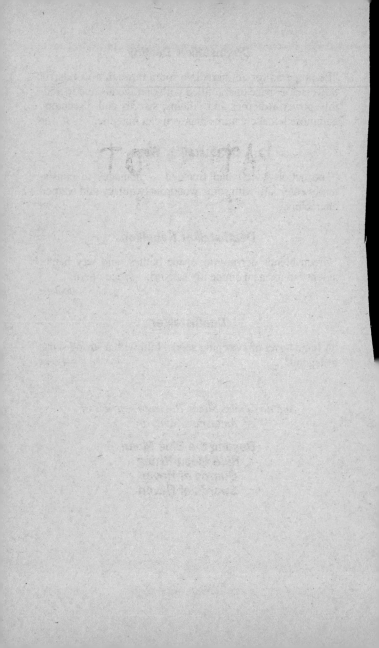

PATHS NOT TAKEN

SIMON R. GREEN

ACE BOOKS, NEW YORK

THE BERKLEY PUBLISHING GROUP
Published by the Penguin Group
Penguin Group (USA) Inc.
375 Hudson Street, New York, New York 10014, USA
Penguin Group (Canada), 90 Eglinton Avenue East, Toronto, Ontario M4P 2Y3, Canada
(a division of Pearson Penguin Canada Inc.)
Penguin Books Ltd., 80 Strand, London WC2R 0RL, England
Penguin Group Ireland, 25 St. Stephen's Green, Dublin 2, Ireland (a division of Penguin Books Ltd.)
Penguin Group (Australia), 250 Camberwell Road, Camberwell, Victoria 3124, Australia
(a division of Pearson Australia Group Pty. Ltd.)
Penguin Books India Pvt. Ltd., 11 Community Centre, Panchsheel Park, New Delhi—110 017, India
Penguin Group (NZ), Cnr. Airborne and Rosedale Roads, Albany, Auckland 1310, New Zealand
(a division of Pearson New Zealand Ltd.)
Penguin Books (South Africa) (Pty.) Ltd., 24 Sturdee Avenue, Rosebank, Johannesburg 2196, South
Africa

Penguin Books Ltd., Registered Offices: 80 Strand, London WC2R 0RL, England

This is a work of fiction. Names, characters, places, and incidents either are the product of the author's
imagination or are used fictitiously, and any resemblance to actual persons, living or dead, business
establishments, events, or locales is entirely coincidental.

PATHS NOT TAKEN

An Ace Book / published by arrangement with the author

PRINTING HISTORY
Ace mass market edition / September 2005

Copyright © 2005 by Simon R. Green.
Cover art by Jonathan Barket.
Cover design by Judith Murello.

ISBN: 0-441-01319-8

ACE
Ace Books are published by The Berkley Publishing Group,
a division of Penguin Group (USA) Inc.,
375 Hudson Street, New York, New York 10014.
ACE and the "A" design are trademarks belonging to Penguin Group (USA) Inc.

PRINTED IN THE UNITED STATE OF AMERICA

10 9 8 7 6 5 4 3

My name is John Taylor. You can frighten people with that name, in certain places. I operate as a private eye, though I've never held a license or owned a gun. I wear a white trench coat, if that's any help. I'm tall, dark of eye, and handsome enough to get by. I have a gift for finding things, whether they want to be found or not. I help people, when I can. I like to think I'm one of the Good Guys.

I operate in the Nightside, that sick magical city within a city, London's best-kept secret. It's always night in the Nightside, always three o'clock in the morning, the hour of the wolf, when most people die and most babies are born. That part of the night where it's always darkest just before the dawn, and the dawn never comes. Gods and monsters walk openly along rain-slick streets, basking in the sleazy glow of hot neon, and every temptation you ever lusted after in the darkest reaches of your heart is right there to be found, for a price. Most often your soul, or someone else's. You can find joy and horror in the Nightside, salvation and damnation, and the answer to every question you ever had. If the Nightside doesn't kill you first.

I have something of a reputation on those dark streets, and not in a good way. My father drank himself to death after finding out my mother wasn't human after all. A mysterious group of Enemies have been trying to kill me ever since I was a small child. There are those in the Nightside who see me as a King in waiting, and others who have named me Abomination. To the Authorities, that faceless group who like to think they run things, I'm just a rogue agent and an unrepentant pain in the arse.

Only recently I found out my mother was a Biblical myth: Lilith, Adam's first wife, driven out of Eden for refusing to accept any authority other than her own. She created the Nightside, thousands of years ago, to be the one place on Earth free from the eternal battle between Heaven and Hell. She's been away; but now she's back. And everyone's waiting for the other shoe to drop.

I once saw a possible future for the Nightside. In it everyone was dead, the whole world a wasteland. And all of it was my fault, because I went looking for my mother. I swore an oath to die rather than let that happen.

But, of course, nothing's ever that simple—in the Nightside.

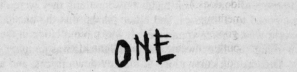

ONE

There Are Reasons Why I Never Go to My Office

There's never enough time in the Nightside, which is odd, because you can buy everything else. I had much to do and enemies on my trail, so I went walking through the streets of the Nightside, and was surprised to see the streets cringe away from me. People, and others, were giving me even more room than usual. Either the news about my mother's identity was already getting around, or they'd heard that the Authorities had finally declared open season on me, and no-one wanted to be too close when the hammer came down.

The night sky was brilliant with stars, laid out in constellations never seen outside the Nightside, while the full moon was a dozen times larger than most people are used to. The air was hot and sweaty like a fever room, and all around gaudy neon blazed come-ons for every kind of sin and temptation. Music drifted out the propped-open doors of every kind of club, from the slow moaning of saxophones to the very latest throbbing bass beats. Crowds surged up and down the pavement, faces alight at the prospect of getting their hands on something they weren't supposed to. Pleasures, and other things, that the outside world would never approve of. It was three o'clock in the morning, just like always, and the Nightside was jumping.

Dreams and damnations at marked-down prices, and a little shop-soiled.

I was on my way to visit my office. I'd never been there before, and was quite looking forward to seeing what it looked like. My teenage secretary Cathy (she adopted me after I rescued her from a house that tried to eat her, and no, I didn't get a say in the matter) set up the office for me after I came into some serious money. (I tracked down the Unholy Grail for the Pope. I also started an angel war in the process, but that's the Nightside for you.) Cathy ran my office and my business with frightening efficiency, and I was happy to let her do it. Being organised has always been an alien concept to me, along with regular exercise, clearing up after myself, and remembering to do the laundry.

But this night I was considering a course of action that was dangerous in a whole bunch of ways that were new even to me, and I felt the need for some serious research and advice. If I was going to get at the truth about who and what my mother really was, I was going to have to go back through Time, to the very beginnings of the Nightside, more than two thousand years ago. And that meant talking to Old Father Time, that immortal incarnation who was scarier and far more powerful and more dangerous than I would ever be.

Still, forewarned was hopefully fore-armed, and I had some truly powerful computers on my side. They were supposed to be Artificial Intelligences from some potential future, on the run from something they preferred not to talk about. Cathy picked them up in a really good deal, the details of which she preferred not to discuss. Business as usual, in the Nightside. The AIs put up with being owned and used because they were datavores, information junkies, and they'd never seen anything like the Nightside.

Time travel, up and down the line, was a common enough occurrence in the Nightside, but far too arbitrary to do anyone any good. Timeslips could spring up anywhere, without warning, offering brief access to the past or any number of potential futures. No-one knew how or why Timeslips operated, though down the years people had come up with some really disturbing theories. All the Authorities ever did was set up barriers and warning signs around the affected areas and wait for the Timeslips to disappear again. There was a Really Dangerous Sports Club, whose members would come running from all directions to dive into a Timeslip, just for the thrill of it. Danger junkies, for whom the thrill of setting themselves on fire and jumping off high buildings just didn't do it for them any more. They must like what they find at the other end of their rainbow, because none of them ever come back to complain.

There was only one person in the Nightside powerful enough to send someone through Time with any degree of accuracy, and that was Old Father Time. A Power and a Domination so mighty, his services could not be bought or commanded by anyone, very definitely including the Authorities. You had to approach him in person, in the Time Tower, and convince him that your trip was . . . worthwhile. And given my chequered reputation, I was going to have to be very persuasive. I was relying on Cathy and her computers to come up with the necessary ammunition.

(The Authorities did operate their own Time Tunnel for a while, back in the 1960s, but apparently it was never very accurate, and was shut down under something of a cloud.)

I finally tracked down the address Cathy had given me, and was surprised to find my office was located in a reasonably up-market area. There were more business offices than establishments, and the streets boasted a much better class of sinner. Rent-a-cops lounged around in gaudy private uniforms, but somehow always found something else to be interested in whenever I looked in their direction. My office was in a tall high-tech building, all gleaming steel and one-way windows. I gave my name to the snotty simulacrum face embedded in the front door, and Cathy buzzed me in. I sneered at the face and swaggered into the oversized lobby like I owned it.

An elevator with a really posh voice took me up to the third floor, invited me to have a really nice day, and complimented me on my trench coat. I strolled down the brightly lit corridor, checking the names on the doors. All very professional, very impressive, big names and big money. I'd clearly come up in the world. The door to my office turned out to be solid silver, deeply scored with protective signs and sigils. I nodded approvingly. Security can be a life-and-death matter in the Nightside, and sometimes even more serious than that. There was no bell, or handle, so I announced myself loudly, and after thinking about it for a moment, the door swung open.

I entered my office for the very first time, looking suspiciously about me, and Cathy came forward to greet me with her very best winning smile. Most people are charmed by that smile, because Cathy is a bright, good-looking blonde teenager bubbling over with life and high spirits. I, on the other hand, was made of sterner stuff, so I nodded briefly and went right back to glaring around me. My new office was bigger than some of the places I've lived in, broad and spacious and absolutely packed with all the latest conveniences and luxuries, just as Cathy had promised. It was bright and cheerful and open, representing Cathy's personality and absolutely nothing of mine. A long way from my last office, a pokey little room in a seedy building in a really bad area of London. I'd run away from the Nightside some years ago, to escape the many pressures and dangers involved in being me, but I'd never been very successful in the real world. For all my many sins, I belonged here in the Nightside, with all the other monsters.

I cautiously decided that I approved of this new office, with its colourful walls, deep pile carpet, and enough room to swing an elephant. But it had to be said that Cathy had not been entirely truthful about everything. To hear her talk she was the soul of tidiness, with a place for everything and everything in its place. In fact, the office was a mess. The great oaken office desk was so buried under piles of paper that you couldn't even see the in- and out-trays, and more folders were piled up on every other flat surface. Large cuddly toys observed the chaos from assorted vantage points. Polka-dot filing cabinets lined one wall, and shelves of reference books covered another. We rely a lot on paper in the Nightside. You can't hack paper. On the other hand, you can't get fire insurance for love or money. Mysterious pieces of high tech peered out from under each other, crammed together in one corner as though in self-defence. I finally looked back at Cathy, and she hiked up the wattage of her smile.

"I know where everything is! Honestly! All I have to do is put out my hand, and . . . It may look like a mess—all right it is a mess—but I have a system! Have I ever lost anything? Anything that mattered?"

"How would I know?" I said dryly. "Relax, Cathy. This is your territory, not mine. I could never run my business as well as you do. Now why don't you pretend to be my secretary and fix me a pot of industrial-strength coffee while I do battle with these super-intelligent computers of yours."

"Sure, boss. The AIs are right there, on the desk."

I looked where she indicated and sat down behind the desk, after clearing some folders off the chair. I considered the simple steel sphere before me. It couldn't have been

more than six inches in diameter, with no obvious mark-
ings or controls or . . . anything, really. I prodded it tentatively with a fingertip, but it was too heavy to move.

"How do I turn the thing on?" I said, somewhat plaintively. I've never been good with technology.

"You don't," the steel sphere said sharply, in a loud and
disdainful voice. "We are on, and fully intend to stay that
way. You even think about trying to shut us down, and we'll
short-circuit your nervous system, primitive."

"Aren't they cute?" beamed Cathy, from the coffeemaker.

"Not quite the word I had in mind," I said. I glared at the
sphere, not wanting to appear weak in front of my own
computers. "How am I supposed to work you, then? There
don't appear to be any operating systems."

"Of course there aren't! You don't think we'd trust an
over-evolved chimp like you with operating systems, do
you? You keep your hands to yourself, monkey boy. You tell
us what simple things you want to know, and we'll supply
you with as much information as your primitive brain can
handle. We are wise, we are wonderful, and we know everything. Or, at least, everything that matters. We are plugged
into the Nightside in more ways than you can imagine, and
no-one suspects a thing. Ah, the Nightside . . . You've no
idea how far we had to come to reach this place, this time.
Such a glorious extravaganza of data, of mysteries and
enigmas and anomalies. Sometimes we orgasm just thinking about the possibilities for original research."

"We are definitely heading into the area of too much
personal information," I said firmly. "Tell me what you
know about Time travel in the Nightside, with special reference to Old Father Time."

"Oh, him," said the sphere. "Now he is interesting. Let
us consider for a moment. You go count some beans or
something."

Cathy came bustling over to pour me a mug of very
black coffee. The mug bore the legend PROPERTY OF

NIGHTSIDE CSI, but I knew better than to ask. Cathy led a busy and varied private life, and the less I knew about it the happier I felt. I took a sip of coffee, winced, and blew heavily on the jet-black liquid to cool it. Cathy pulled up a chair and sat down beside me. We both looked at the steel sphere, but apparently it was still considering. I looked at Cathy.

"Cathy . . ."

"Yes, boss?"

"There's something I've been meaning to talk to you about . . ."

"If it's about that sexual harassment suit, I never touched him! And if it's about me maxing out all your credit cards again . . ."

"Wait a minute. I've got more than one credit card?"

"Oops."

"We will come back to that later," I said firmly. "Right now, this is about me, not you. So for once in your teeny-bopper life sit still and listen. I thought you ought to know; I've made a will. Julien Advent witnessed it, and I've left it with him. The way things have been going lately, I thought it might be wise. So, if anything does happen to me . . . Look, I always meant for you to inherit this business. It's as much yours as mine, these days. I just never got around to putting it in writing. If anything should . . . go wrong, you go and see Julien. He's a good man. He'll take care of everything, and see that you're protected."

"You've never talked this way before," said Cathy. She was suddenly serious, older, almost frightened. "You're always so . . . sure. Like you could take on anyone, or anything, tie them up in knots, and walk away laughing. I've never seen you back down from men or monsters, never seen you hesitate to walk into any situation, no matter how dangerous. What's happened? What's changed?"

"I know who my mother is now."

"You really believe that crap? That she's Lilith, the first

woman God created? You believe in the Garden of Eden and all that Old Testament stuff?"

"Not as such," I admitted. "To be fair, my mother did say it was all a parable, a simple way of explaining something much more complicated. But I do believe she's incredibly old and unimaginably powerful. She created the Nightside, and now I think she's planning to wipe the whole place clean and start over. I may be the only one who can stop her. So, I'm planning a trip back through Time, in the hope of finding some information and maybe even weapons I can use against my mother."

"All right, I'll go with you," Cathy said immediately. "I can help. The office can run itself without me for a while."

"No, Cathy. You have to stay here, to carry on if I don't come back. My will leaves pretty much everything to you. Use it as you see best."

"You can't lose," said Cathy. "You're John Taylor."

I smiled briefly. "Even I've never believed that. Look, I'm just being . . . sensible, that's all. Seeing that you're provided for."

"Why me?" said Cathy, in a small voice. "I never expected this. I thought you'd want to leave everything to your friends. Suzie Shooter. Alex Morrisey."

"I've left them some things, but they're only friends. You're family. My daughter, in every way that matters. I've always been so proud of you, Cathy. That house would have destroyed anyone else, but you fought your way back, made yourself strong again. Made yourself a new life here in the Nightside, and never once let this damned place tarnish your spirit. I'm leaving it all to you because I know I can trust you to carry on the good fight, and not screw it up. If this is . . . too much for you, you can always sell the lot and move back out to London. Go home, to your mother and father."

"Oh shut up," said Cathy, and she hugged me tightly. "This is home. And you're my father, in every way that matters. And I . . . have always been so very proud of you."

We sat together for a while, holding each other. She finally let go and smiled at me, eyes bright with tears she refused to shed in front of me. I smiled, and nodded. We've never been good at talking to each other about the things that matter, but then, what father and daughter are?

"So," she said brightly, "does that make me Lilith's grand-daughter?"

"Only in spirit."

"At least take some serious backup with you on this trip. Shotgun Suzie, or Razor Eddie."

"I've put word out for them," I said. "But last I heard Suzie was still running down an elusive bounty, and Razor Eddie hasn't been seen since doing something really unpleasant in the Street of the Gods. It must have been really appalling, even for him, because for a while you couldn't move outside the Street for gods running around crying their eyes out."

"Time travel," the sphere said suddenly, and we both jumped a little. The artificial voice sounded distinctly smug. "A fascinating subject, with more theories than proven facts. You probably have to be able to think in five dimensions to appreciate it properly. We won't talk about Timeslips, because their very existence makes our head hurt, and we don't even have a head. The only reputable source for controlled travel in Time is the Time Tower. Which is not natural to the Nightside. Old Father Time brought it here from Shadows Fall, just over a hundred years ago, saying only that he thought it would be needed for Something Important."

"Shadows Fall?" said Cathy, frowning.

"An isolated town in the back of beyond, where legends go to die when the world stops believing in them," I said. "A sort of elephants' graveyard for the supernatural. Never been there myself, but apparently it makes the Nightside look positively tame. And boring."

"I'll bet they have great clubs there," Cathy said wistfully.

"If we could stick to the subject at hand," the sphere said loudly. "We will not discuss Shadows Fall because it makes the head we don't have hurt even worse than Time-slips. Some concepts should be banned, on mental health grounds. Let us discuss Old Father Time. An enigmatic figure. No-one seems too sure exactly what he is. An incarnation, certainly, and immortal; but not a Transient Being. Some say he is the very concept of Time itself, given a human form to interact with the human world. Why this was ever considered necessary, or even a good idea, remains unclear. Humans do enough damage in three dimensions, without giving them access to the fourth. Anyway; the one thing everyone agrees on is that he is extremely powerful and even more dangerous. The only person ever to tell the Authorities to go to Hell on a regular basis and make it stick. You don't argue with someone who can send you back in Time to play with the dinosaurs. Well, not more than once, anyway. Old Father Time is a native of Shadows Fall, and still lives there, but he commutes into the Night-side when he feels like it.

"It takes a *lot* of power to move someone through Time. All the Nightside's major players working together would have a hard time sending anyone anywhen with any degree of accuracy. That's if you could get them to work together, which you almost certainly couldn't. So the only way to travel safely through Time is via Old Father Time's good offices, by convincing him that your trip is in everyone's best interests. Lots of luck selling him that one, Taylor. Right; that's it. Anything else we might have to say would only be guesswork. So off you go, run along, and be sure to give Old Father Time our warmest regards before he throws you out on your ear."

"You know him?" said Cathy.

"Of course. How do you think we got here in the first place?"

I was about to follow that one up with a whole series of probing questions when we were interrupted by a polite knock at my door. Or at least as polite as any knock can be when you have to hammer on solid silver with your fist just to be heard. I looked sharply at Cathy.

"Are we expecting anyone you might have forgotten to tell me about?"

"There's no-one in the diary. Could it be Walker? Last I heard, the Authorities were seriously upset with you."

"Walker wouldn't bother to knock," I said, standing up and staring at the closed door. "If he even thought I was in here, he'd have his people blow that door right off its hinges."

"Could be a client," said Cathy. "They do turn up here, from time to time."

"All right," I said. "You open the door, and I'll stand back here and look impressive."

"I wish you'd let me keep guns in here," said Cathy.

She moved warily over to the door and spoke the Word that opened it. Standing outside in the corridor, and looking more than a little lost, was an entirely ordinary-seeming man in a smart suit and tie. He peered hopefully at Cathy, then at me, but didn't look particularly impressed. He was average height, average weight, somewhere in his forties, with thinning dark hair shading into grey. He edged into my office as though expecting to be ordered out at any moment.

"Hello?" he said tentatively. "I'm looking for a John Taylor. Of Taylor Investigations. Have I come to the right place?"

"Depends," I said. Never commit yourself to anything until you have to. My visitor didn't seem too obviously dangerous, so I came out from behind my desk to greet him. "I'm Taylor. What can I do for you?"

"I'm not entirely sure. I think . . . I need to hire your services, Mr. Taylor."

"I'm rather busy at the moment," I said. "Who sent you to me?"

"Well . . . that's rather the point. I don't know where this is, or how I got here. I was hoping you could tell me."

I sighed heavily. I knew a setup when I saw one. I was being made a patsy, I could feel it; but sometimes the only way to deal with cases like this was to walk right into the trap and trust that you're bad enough to kick the crap out of whoever it was behind it.

"Let's start with your name," I said. "If only so I know whom to bill."

"I'm Eamonn Mitchell," my new client said nervously. He ventured a little further into my office, looking about him dubiously. Cathy gave him her best welcoming smile, and he managed a small smile in return. "I appear to be lost, Mr. Taylor," he said abruptly. "I don't recognise this part of London at all, and ever since I got here . . . strange things have been happening. I understand you investigate strange things, so I'm come to you for help. You see . . . I'm being haunted. By younger versions of myself."

I looked at Cathy. "You see? This is why I never come to the office."

TWO

Paths Not Taken

So we sat Eamonn Mitchell down, after I cleared off a chair, and Cathy poured some of her life-saving coffee into him, and bit by bit we got the story out of him. He relaxed a little, once he realised we were prepared to take him seriously, no matter how strange his story seemed. But he still preferred to talk mostly to his coffee mug rather than look either of us in the eye.

"My . . . hauntings weren't exactly ghosts," he said. "They were quite solid, quite real. Except . . . they were me. Or rather, myself at a younger age. Wearing clothes I used to wear, saying things I used to say, used to believe. And they were angry with me. Shouting and pushing, haranguing me. They said I betrayed them, by not becoming the kind of man they'd intended and expected to become."

"What kind of person are you, Mr. Mitchell?" I said, to prove I was paying attention.

"Well, I work for a big corporation, here in London. I'm quite successful, I suppose. Good money . . . And I'm married, with two wonderful children." And then nothing would do but to interrupt his story to get out his wallet and produce photos of his wife Andrea, and his two children, Erica and Ronald. They seemed nice enough, good ordinary people just like him. He smiled fondly at the photos, as though they were his only remaining life-line to a world he knew and understood, then reluctantly he put them away again. "I was coming home from work this evening, on the tube, checking over some last bits of paperwork. I was mentally counting off the stops, as usual, and when it got to my turn I got off the train. Only when I looked around, it wasn't my stop. I'd disembarked at a station I'd never seen before, called *Nightside*. I turned round to get back on the train, but it was already gone. I hadn't even heard it leave. And the people on the platform with me . . ." He shuddered briefly, looking at me with large, frightened eyes. "Some of them weren't people, Mr. Taylor!"

"I know," I said reassuringly. "It's all right, Mr. Mitchell. Tell us everything. We'll believe you. What happened next?"

He drank some more coffee, his lips thinning from the bitterness, but it seemed to brace him. "I'm ashamed to say I ran. Just pushed and forced my way through the crowd, up out of the station and onto the street. But things were even worse there. Everything was wrong. Twisted. Like walking through a nightmare I couldn't wake up from. The streets were full of strange people, and creatures, and . . . things I couldn't even identify. I don't think I've ever been more scared in my life.

"I didn't know where I was. Didn't recognise any of the street names. And everywhere I looked there were shops and clubs and . . . establishments, offering to sell me things I'd never even thought about before! Awful things . . . After that I stared straight ahead, not looking at anything I didn't have to. All I could think of was to get to you, Mr. Taylor. Somehow, I had your business card. It was in my hand when I got off the train. It had your address. I nerved myself to ask some of the more ordinary-seeming people for directions, but no-one would talk to me. Finally, a rather shabby and intense gentleman in an oversized grey coat pointed me in the right direction. When I looked back to thank him, he'd already disappeared."

"Yeah," I said. "Eddie has a way of doing that."

"All the way here, it felt like someone was following me." Mitchell's voice dropped to a whisper, and his knuckles whitened as he gripped his coffee mug. "I kept looking back, but I couldn't see anyone. And then a man jumped out of an alleyway and grabbed me by the shoulders. I started to cry out, thinking I was being mugged, but then I saw his face, and my throat closed up. It was my face . . . only younger. He grinned nastily, enjoying the shock he saw in my face. His fingers were like claws digging into my shoulders.

"Did you think you'd get away with it? he said. *Did you think you'd never be called to account for what you've done?*

"I didn't understand. I told him I didn't understand, but he kept shouting into my face how I'd betrayed everything we ever believed in. And then someone pulled him away, and I thought I was being rescued, but it was another me! Older than my attacker, but still younger than I am now. You can't imagine how terrifying it is to see your own face, looking right at you with hate in its eyes. He was shouting, too, about the waste I'd made of my life. His life. And then there were more of them, these doppelgangers, all of them from different periods in my life, pulling and yelling at me and at each other, fighting each other to get to me. A whole crowd of shouting, struggling people, and all of them me!

"I ran away. Just put my head down and ran, while they were distracted with each other. I never thought of myself as a coward before, but I couldn't face all those other versions of me, saying such hateful things, blaming me for doing something . . . terrible." He took a deep breath, and looked at me with a strained smile. "Tell me the truth. Please. Am I in Hell? Have I died and gone to Hell?"

"No," I said quickly. "You're still very much alive, Mr. Mitchell. This isn't Hell, it's the Nightside. Though sometimes you can see Hell from here. Basically . . . may I call you Eamonn? Thank you. Basically, Eamonn, you have stumbled into a place you have no business in. You don't belong here. But not to worry; you have fallen among friends. I'll get you back where you belong."

Eamonn Mitchell actually crumpled in his chair, as relief flooded through him. Cathy had to grab his coffee mug as it slipped from his fingers. She patted him comfortingly on the shoulder. And then my solid silver, reinforced, security-spelled office door banged open, catching us all by surprise, and two more Eamonn Mitchells stormed in. It was quite clearly the same man, at different ages. The youngest looked to be about twenty, probably still a student, with a SAVE THE WHALES T-shirt, bright purple bell-bottoms, long hair, and an unsuccessful beard. He would have seemed ridiculous if he hadn't looked so angry and so dangerous. The other man was maybe ten years older, in a sharp navy blue suit, clean-shaven, with seriously short hair. He looked just as angry, and perhaps even more dangerous because he was more focussed, more experienced. I decided to think of them as Eamonn 20 and Eamonn 30, and my client as Eamonn 40, just to keep my head straight. I moved to stand between the newcomers and my client, and they transferred their angry gaze to me.

"Get out of our way," said Eamonn 20. "You don't know what this bastard's done."

"Get out of our way, or we'll kill you," said Eamonn 30.

"Oh, Security!" said Cathy.

A closet door I hadn't noticed before sprang open, and a huge and impressively hairy hand shot out of the closet and wrapped itself firmly around both the invading Eamonns. They struggled fiercely against the great gripping fingers, but with their arms pinned to their sides, they were both quite helpless. They shouted and cursed until I strolled over and gave them both a brisk warning slap round the back of the head. A thought struck me, and I looked back at Cathy.

"Can I ask what's on the other end of this thing's arm?"

"I find it best not to ask questions like that," Cathy said, and I had to agree with her.

I gave the two intruders my best intimidating glare, and they glared right back at me. Proof, if proof were needed, that they were newcomers to the Nightside. Anyone else would have had the sense to be scared.

"Look," I said patiently. "You are currently being held by a hand big enough to give all of us seriously worrying thoughts about what it might be attached to. A hand that will do whatever I tell it to. So not only are you not going anywhere anytime soon, but if I were you, I'd be giving some serious thought about what might happen if I don't start getting some answers out of you. Words like *crunch* and *squish* should be echoing uneasily through your heads. So, why not tell me what it is you're doing here and what you have against my client? There's always a chance we can work this out peacefully. Not a very big chance, admittedly, this is the Nightside after all; but I feel we should make the effort."

"He betrayed me!" said Eamonn 20, almost spitting out the words, his face dark with rage. "Look at him! Just another faceless drone in a suit and tie. Everything I ever hated and despised. I was never going to be him! I had dreams and ambitions, I was going to go places and do things; become someone who mattered, doing things that mattered! I was going to change the world . . . live a life I could be proud of . . ."

"Dreams are nice," said Eamonn 30, his voice cold but controlled. "But we wake up from dreams. I had drive and ambition. I was going places, going to make something of myself. Be a mover and shaker in the business world. I never intended to settle for being just another cog in the machine, like him! Look at him! Middle-aged middle-management, filling in his days till his pension."

"I was going to be an ecowarrior!" said Eamonn 20. "Fight the good fight for the environment! No compromise in defence of Mother Earth!"

"Causes!" sneered Eamonn 30. "Just more dreams, more illusions. I'd had enough of living on pocket change and good intentions. I was going to be rich and powerful, and force the world to make sense!"

"So," I said to Eamonn 40. "What happened?"

"I fell in love," he said, in a quiet, almost defiant voice. "I met Andrea, and it was like finding the one part of my life that had always been missing. We married, then the children came along; and I was never happier. They became my life. Far more important than the vague dreams and ambitions of my younger days that I never would have achieved anyway. Part of maturity is learning to recognise your own limitations."

"That's it?" said Eamonn 20. "You threw away my dreams for some bitch and a couple of snotty-nosed brats?"

"You got old," Eamonn 30 said bitterly. "You found the world too hard to cope with, so you settled for suburbia and apron strings."

"Neither of you has ever been in love, have you?" said Eamonn 40.

Eamonn 20 snorted loudly. "Women? Love them and leave them. They just get in the way."

"I had more important things in mind," said Eamonn 30. "Marriage is a trap, an anchor holding you back."

"I can't believe I was ever you," said Eamonn 40. "So small, so limited. Thinking of no-one but myself. For all your great dreams and ambitions, can either of you say you were ever really happy? Content? Satisfied?"

There was a strength and conviction in his voice that gave his younger selves pause, but only for a moment.

"You won't get away with this," said Eamonn 20. "We have been given power; the power to change things. To change you! To remake our life into what it should have been."

"Probability magic," said Eamonn 30. "The power to rewrite history by choosing among alternate timetracks. You're a mistake, a stumble that should never have happened."

"I'm going to undo all your decisions," said Eamonn 20. "Snuff you out with my magic!"

"My magic is more powerful than yours!" Eamonn 30 snarled immediately. "My future will prevail, not yours!"

And then somehow they'd both worked a hand free, and each of them was brandishing a magic wand. I was so surprised I just stood there for a moment, and gaped. No-one's used a wand in the Nightside for centuries. Wands went out with black cats and pointy hats. (All right, the Faerie Court still use them, but the Fae have always been weird.) And then Cathy and I had to jump for our lives as both the younger Eamonns started blasting probability magics at each other, and around my office in general. Beams of pure chance energy shot out of the wands, spitting and crackling on the air, full of the power that runs through rolling dice or a tossed coin, power to change the outcome of any decision in favour of the magician's will. Except these were a couple of amateurs with wands, so all they could do was unleash the magic and let it run wild, changing whatever it touched. I pushed Cathy to safety behind the heavy oak desk, then realised Eamonn 40 was still sitting in his chair, staring open-mouthed at what was happening. I scuttled across the carpet on all fours, keeping my head well down, hauled Eamonn 40 off his chair, and drove him to safety behind the desk with encouraging words and harsh language.

Both the younger Eamonns turned their attention to the giant hand still holding them. They blasted it repeatedly with their wands, and there was a flurry of coruscating energies as the hand changed colour several times, then was suddenly and quite definitely female. Right down to the pink nail varnish. The fingers snapped open, and the hand shot back into its closet, probably in shock. The two younger Eamonns staggered free, blasting everything they could see with their wands, searching for Eamonn 40. They might have done some serious damage if they hadn't been compelled to spend most of their time dodging each other's magics.

Everything touched by the crackling beams changed its nature immediately. A Spice Girls poster on the wall suddenly featured Twisted Sister. The bullet-proof glass in my office's only window was abruptly replaced by a stained-glass effort featuring St. Michael slaying the dragon. With an Uzi. The coffeemaker became a Teasmaid, and a big bunch of flowers in a vase started snapping at each other with pointed teeth. One beam hit the steel sphere of the future computers dead-on, but it shrugged off the magic, announcing loudly *We're protected, monkey boy.*

Eamonn 40 stuck his head out from behind the desk to see what was going on, and a sputtering beam of change magic only missed him because Cathy dragged him back out of the way. Unfortunately, she left one hand in plain view a moment too long, and a second beam hit it. And Cathy was suddenly Colin. A tall, good-looking young man in the very latest Versace. He looked at me, wide-eyed, and for once in my life I didn't have a thing to say.

Colin stood up to yell obscenities at the two Eamonns, and was immediately hit by another beam, changing him back to Cathy. She dropped back down out of sight with a muffled shriek. We looked at each other again.

"Don't ever ask," said Cathy.

"I wouldn't dare."

"You have to Do Something about these two idiots!"

"I will. I'm thinking."

"Think faster!"

"I could still disinherit you, you know."

Fortunately, I already had an idea. The two younger Eamonns were still trying for a clear shot at Eamonn 40 while dodging attacks from each other. I waited till they were on opposite sides of my office, then I charged out from behind the desk, yelling at the top of my voice. They both turned their wands on me, I hit the deck, and two change beams hit each other head-on. The resulting clash of probabilities was too much for local causality to bear, and both Eamonns vanished, as probability decided they'd never been given the bloody wands in the first place.

The universe does like to keep itself tidy, whenever possible.

Cathy rose cautiously up from behind the desk, which now seemed to be made of an entirely different kind of wood, and after checking that everything really was all clear, she hauled Eamonn 40 up beside her. His eyes were stretched so wide it had to be painful, and he was visibly shaking. Cathy eased him into a chair, patted him comfortingly on the head in an absent-minded sort of way, and winced as she looked round my haphazardly transmuted office.

"It's going to take forever to get everything looking nice again. Though I do like the new poster. And I know I'm going to have to go through every damned folder to check that the contents haven't been changed. John, I want whoever is responsible for this nonsense strung up by the balls!

If I have to work late, I want someone to suffer! Who the hell would be dumb enough to equip complete amateurs with change magics?"

"Good question," I said. "There must be more to our new client than meets the eye."

"Wouldn't be difficult," Cathy sniffed. A thought struck her, and she considered the still-dazed Eamonn 40. "I don't know if we can really class him as a client, boss. He couldn't afford our rates, these days. I mean, look at him."

"Someone sent all these Eamonns into my life, to mess up my day," I said. "That makes it personal."

Cathy rolled her eyes dramatically. She got away with it because she was a teenager, but only just. "So, it's another freebie, is it? The money you got from the Vatican won't last forever, you know. Not with the rent we're paying on this place. You need to take on some proper-paying cases, and soon. Before someone large and professionally unpleasant turns up here to cut off your credit with a meat-axe."

"My creditors can take a number," I said. "I've got far more powerful people mad at me, at the moment. I think . . . I'll take Eamonn to Strangefellows. If nothing else, it should prove safer territory."

"Strangefellows?" Cathy said dubiously. "Given the shape he's in, I'm not sure he's ready to cope with that much weirdness in one dose."

"Sink or swim," I said briskly. "I've always believed in shock treatment for someone in shock. Take a look round while I'm gone and see how much actual damage the wands did. Keep anything that's been improved and throw out the rest. Are we insured?"

Cathy gave me a hard look. "What do you think?"

"I think I need several large drinks, followed by a really large drink as a chaser. Come along, Eamonn, we are going to pay a visit to the oldest bar in the world."

"Oh, I don't drink much any more," said Eamonn 40.

"Why am I not surprised? We're going anyway. I have a

strong feeling that even more alternate versions of you will be turning up soon, and I'd rather they made a mess of someone else's place." I paused and looked about me. "Cathy . . . didn't you once tell me we had an office cat?"

She shrugged. "The future computers ate it. It wasn't a very good cat anyway."

I took Eamonn 40 by the arm and ushered him firmly towards the door. Some conversations you just know aren't going to go anywhere good.

THREE

Oblivion

Strangefellows is the oldest bar in the world, and not for the faint-hearted. You find it up a back alley that isn't always there, under a small neon sign with the bar's name in Sanskrit. The bar's owner doesn't believe in advertising. If you need to find the place, you will, though whether that's a good or bad thing is open to debate. I hang out there from time to time, mostly because it's full of people with even worse problems than mine, so no-one bothers me. Strangefellows is a seedy place, bordering on sleazy, with good booze, bad service, and really distressing bar snacks. The atmosphere is unhealthy, the mood is changeable, and most of the furniture is nailed to the floor so it can't be used in hand-to-hand combat. I've always felt right at home there.

The bar's current owner, Alex Morrisey, did experiment

with going up-market, but it didn't take. You can give a bad dog all the makeovers you like, but it'll still hump your leg when you're not looking.

Rather than risk freaking Eamonn 40 out by walking him through the streets again, I hailed a horse and carriage to take us to Strangefellows. He seemed somewhat reassured by the solid and uncomplicated nature of the transport, only to get upset all over again when the horse asked me for the destination. Eamonn sat bolt upright beside me in the carriage with his arms folded tightly across his chest and refused to say a single word for the rest of the journey. I had to half cajole and half bully him out of the carriage when we finally stopped, and he stood very close to me as I paid off the driver. He stared determinedly at the ground as I guided him towards Strangefellows, so he wouldn't have to see what was going on around him. Some country mice have no place in the big city.

"Why are you doing this?" he said suddenly, still not looking at me. "Why are you helping me? Your secretary was right; I can't pay you. At least, not the kind of money you're used to, for dealing with . . . things like this. So why are you so ready to get involved with my problems?"

"Because I'm interested," I said easily. "Someone's gone to a lot of trouble to introduce you and all your chaos into my life, and I want to find out who, so I can thank them appropriately."

"So . . . you're using me, for your own reasons."

"Well done," I said. "You see—you're already learning to think like a Nightsider."

He looked at me sharply for the first time. "I'm not stupid, Mr. Taylor. I may be out of my depth, but I still know a shark when I see one. You're using me, as bait in a trap. But, if it takes enlightened self-interest to get you on my side, I can live with that. Just how good are you, Mr. Taylor? Can you really sort out this mess I'm in?"

"I'll give it my best shot," I said. "And I really am pretty good at this. I may be . . . any number of things, but I never let down a client."

We came to the bar and I took him inside, holding him firmly by the arm so he couldn't turn and bolt. Strangefellows can have that effect on people. We descended the metal stairway into the bar proper, and everyone looked round to see who was coming. The place was packed with the usual unusual suspects. Two glowing nuns in white habits were sitting at the bar, Sisters of the Holy Order of Saint Strontium. They were drinking tall glasses of sparkling water, though it probably wasn't sparkling when they ordered it. A cyborg with jagged bits of machinery poking out of him kept sticking his finger into a light socket and giggling. A vampire was drinking a bloody Mary, and from the look on her face Mary was really getting into it. Ms. Fate, the Nightside's very own transvestite-costumed adventurer, a man who dressed up as a super-heroine to fight crime, was shaving his legs with a Bic before going out on patrol. A couple of tourists stood in one corner, with cameras raised. Someone had had them stuffed and mounted, for a joke.

I got Eamonn 40 to the bar with only minimum force, sat him down as far from the radioactive nuns as possible, and nodded to the bartender and owner, Alex Morrisey, who glowered back at me. We're friends, I suppose, but we've never been very demonstrative. It would probably help if I remembered to pay my bar tab now and again.

Alex Morrisey was a tall streak of misery who always wore basic black, down to designer shades and a stylish French beret perched on the back of his head to hide his growing bald patch. He was in his late twenties, but looked ten years older. Running a bar in the Nightside will do that to you. His permanent scowl had dug a deep notch above his nose, and he only smiled when he was fiddling your change. He'd been married once, and was still bitter about it. Basically, Alex was pissed off at the entire world, and didn't care who knew about it. Order a cocktail from him at your peril.

He was descended from Merlin Satanspawn, who was buried in the cellars under the bar, after the fall of Camelot. Merlin occasionally manifests through Alex, and everyone sensible runs for cover. Being dead doesn't stop you from being a major player in the Nightside.

"What are you doing here, Taylor?" said Alex. "Trouble follows you around like a stalker. I've only just finished refurbishing the place after your last visit."

"I'm fine, thanks for asking," I said. "You're looking very yourself. Bring me many drinks, and have several for yourself."

"How about Mr. Ordinary?" said Alex.

Eamonn 40 was sitting sullenly beside me, keeping his back stubbornly turned on all the more outrageous elements in the bar. I asked him what he'd like to drink, and he said he'd have a dry white wine. I gave Alex a hard look, and he reluctantly poured Eamonn 40 a glass of the better stuff. Alex hated to waste a good vintage on people he didn't think were capable of appreciating it.

"I have a mystery to solve," I said briskly. "Someone has been messing about with my client's time-line, yanking other versions of him out of alternate timetracks, to harass and maybe even kill him. They've also been messing about with me, by dumping him and his problems in my lap. I hate it when people start interfering with Time. As if the Nightside wasn't complicated enough as it is."

"You take far too narrow a view of things, my dear Taylor," said a lazy, affected voice. "Where you see problems, other more robust intellects see possibilities."

I looked around, carefully not letting myself be hurried, and standing at my side was one of the Nightside's few other private investigators, Tommy Oblivion. There was a time I was the only PI in the Nightside, but my successes had encouraged others to throw their hats into the ring. One such was Tommy Oblivion, the existential detective, who specialised in cases that might or might not have actually happened. One of the most persuasive men I'd ever met, Tommy could tie logic in square knots and have people swearing black was white and up was down, just to get rid of him. He was a tall, studiedly effete fellow in starkly coloured New Romantic silks. (Unlike most of us, Tommy had a great Eighties. Being existential probably helped.)

He had long, limp black hair, a long horsey face with a toothy smile, and long-fingered hands he liked to flap around while he was talking. Tommy liked to talk. It was said by many, and believed by most, that Tommy Oblivion could talk his own firing squad into shooting each other to get away from his relentlessly reasonable voice. He thrived in areas of moral obscurity, uncertain reality, and cases so complicated you couldn't pin anything down even if you used tent pegs. And yet Tommy was very good at getting answers to the kinds of questions people in authority didn't want answered. Tommy had a gift for getting at the truth. Not a very nice gift, perhaps, but then, that's the Nightside for you.

I had a feeling there was something I should remember about Tommy Oblivion, something important, but I couldn't pin it down.

"Hello, Tommy," I said resignedly. "Keeping busy?"

"Who can say? But I'm almost certain I would like a drink. My usual, Alex."

Alex scowled at him. "You always say that, and you always order something different."

"Of course," said Tommy, smiling brightly. "I have a reputation to maintain. I think I'll have a Buck's Fizz."

"You really shouldn't tease Alex," I said, as Alex slunk away, muttering. "He's quite capable of slipping something in your drink that will have you throwing up meals you ate six months ago."

"I know," said Tommy. "It's my way of living dangerously. Now then, a little bird tells me you're contemplating
a journey back in Time."

"My, what big ears you have, grandma. Why would you
be interested, Tommy?"

"Because I'm desperate to go travelling in Time, but
I've never been able to persuade Old Father Time to let me.
The old poop. Apparently he regards me as a somewhat
frivolous character."

"Get away," I said. "And after you've made a whole ca-
reer out of being flippant, foppish, and dropping other people right in it."

"How very unkind."

"I notice you're not denying it."

"I wouldn't dare. Image is everything these days. But
even you would have to admit I do get results, in my own
distinctive and somewhat lateral way. The point is . . . I
know I had a point with me when I came in here . . . ah yes,
the point is, I was wondering whether I could prevail on
you to put in a good word for me when you talk with Old
Father Time."

"Oh, I've got a very good word for you, Tommy," I said.

Perhaps fortunately, that was when the unpleasantness
started. Two sets of heavy feet came crashing down the
metal stairs into the bar, and everyone turned to look.
Sometimes I think Alex only had those stairs installed so
no-one could sneak into his bar unnoticed. I was sort of expecting it, but even so my heart sank as two more Eamonn
Mitchells stormed into the bar, brandishing wands. Eamonn 40 made a sad, trapped sound, and clutched at my
arm. I murmured something soothing, carefully detached
his hand from my arm, and moved to put myself between
him and the newcomers.

One of the new Eamonns looked to be a prosperous
businessman in his fifties, overweight with good living.
The other man was older, at least in his sixties, and looked

like a street person. Malnutrition-thin, and wrapped in ragged charity shop clothes. I immediately tabbed them Eamonn 50 and Eamonn 60, and let my hands drift towards certain useful objects in my coat pockets. Much more than the earlier alternates in my office, these two looked desperate and dangerous. They stalked through the crowded bar, ignoring the strangeness to all sides, their hot angry gazes fixed on the Eamonn behind me. I stepped forward to block their path, and they stopped and smiled nastily at me. All around people were getting up from their tables and backing away, so as not to get caught in the cross-fire. Ms. Fate put his disposable razor back into her utility belt and produced a steel throwing star. I caught his eye, and shook my head slightly. I've always felt it important to handle my own messes.

"You must be Taylor," said Eamonn 50. Even his voice sounded fat and self-important. "We were warned you might try to interfere. This is none of your business. Get out of our way, or we'll fix it so you were never born."

I had to smile. "You might find that harder than you think," I said.

"Then maybe we'll fix it so you were born crippled, or diseased," said Eamonn 60. His voice was harsh and painful, as though he didn't use it much any more. "We'll kill you, Taylor. Kill you nasty, if you try and stop us doing what we have to do."

"What is it you want?" Eamonn 40 said from behind me. He was scared, but he kept his voice firm.

"I want you to make the decisions that will lead to me, and my life," said Eamonn 50. "I worked hard to get all the good things that life has to offer. All the comforts, and the pleasures. I won't risk losing them now, just because you don't have the balls to go for the brass ring. I'll fix you. Make you make the right decisions. Make you become me."

"Is that what you want?" I asked Eamonn 60.

"I don't want to be me," he said flatly. "No-one should

have to live like I do. I never wanted this. Never wanted to sleep in shop doorways and beg for food from people who walk right past without making eye contact. I've been given the chance to undo the decisions that stupid bastard made, that led to him becoming me; and I'll destroy anyone who interferes."

"Kill you all," said Eamonn 50. "Destroy you all."

"Hold everything," I said, holding up one hand politely. "Can I check something? Have either of you ever been married . . . and in particular, have either of you ever met a woman named Andrea?"

The two new Eamonns looked at each other, confused, then they shook their heads angrily.

"You're trying to confuse us," said Eamonn 50.

"No, really," I said. "Her arrival in my client's life is what changed everything. Changed him. So your being here is already redundant. He was never going to become either of you."

"He will if we force him to," said Eamonn 50. "If we re-make him with our magics. Cut the woman out of his life, like a cancer."

"You could kill him with your meddling," I said. "You could destroy yourselves."

"Death would be a release," said Eamonn 60.

"Excuse me," said Eamonn 40, from behind me. "Could someone please explain where all these others mes are coming from?"

"Alternate timetracks," Tommy Oblivion said briskly. "Possible futures, lives that might have been, the wheels of If and Maybe. Our lives are determined by the decisions we make, or fail to make, and these . . . gentlemen are the men you might have become if you'd made certain specific decisions. Can't say either of them looks particularly attractive, but that's probably why your enemies chose to empower them. Can I ask what's happened to my Buck's Fizz?"

"But how did they get here?" said Eamonn 40, a little desperately.

"Someone's been meddling," I said. "Somebody really powerful, too, to be able to manipulate probability magics."

"Has to be a major player," said Tommy. He'd gone behind the bar to get his own drink, as Alex was quite sensibly keeping his head down. "Messing about with Time and timetracks is a serious business. So serious that the few who do work with probability tend to come down really heavily on anyone new trying to invade their territory. No-one wants some dilettante threatening the carefully maintained status quo."

"But I don't have any enemies!" said Eamonn 40. "People like me don't have enemies! I'm no-one important!"

"You are now," said Tommy, sipping daintily at his drink with one finger carefully extended. "Someone's gone to a lot of trouble over you, old man." He looked at me thoughtfully. "Could it be the Jonah, perhaps?"

"Dead," I said.

"Count Video?"

"Missing, presumed dead," I said. "Last seen running through the streets with his skin ripped off, during the angel war."

Tommy shrugged. "You know the Nightside. People are always making comebacks. Just look at your good self."

"God, you people love to talk," said Eamonn 50. "I came here to fix this stupid, short-sighted version of myself, and nothing and no-one is going to stop me."

"Nothing you do here will change anything that matters," said Tommy. "Every version of you is as valid as any other. Every timetrack is just as real, and as certain. Changing or adapting this younger version won't make your existence any more or less likely. If anyone told you otherwise, they lied."

"I don't believe that," said Eamonn 60. "I can't believe that."

"You'd say anything, to try and stop us," said Eamonn 50.

Both men let fly with their wands, beams of probability magic crackling as they shot through the air. I dived out of the way, dragging Eamonn 40 along with me. Tommy ducked gracefully down behind the bar, still holding on to his drink. A change beam hit the oak bar and ricocheted harmlessly away. The bar's main furnishings and fittings were all protected by Merlin's magic. Both the new Eamonns fired their wands furiously in all directions as I dodged back and forth across the bar, hauling Eamonn 40 along with me. A haze of change magic filled the air as the wands' beams transmuted everything they touched in arbitrary and unpredictable ways.

The vampire who'd been feeding on his bloody Mary got hit by a beam and swelled up like a tick, engorging with more and more blood as he drained Mary dry, before exploding messily and showering everyone around him with second-hand blood. The empty husk of Mary crumpled to the floor like a paper sack. Some of the newer chairs and tables fell apart as they were brushed by probability beams, reduced in a moment to their original component parts. So was one of Baron Frankenstein's creatures, as all his stitches came undone at once. Body parts rolled across the floor, while the head mouthed silent obscenities. Lightning bolts struck down out of nowhere, blackening bodies and starting fires all over. Bunches of hissing flowers blossomed from cracks in a stone wall. An old Victorian portrait began speaking in tongues. People collapsed from strokes and cerebral haemorrhages and epileptic fits. Some simply blinked out of existence, as the chances that created them were abruptly revoked.

A ghost girl was suddenly corporeal again, after years of haunting Strangefellows, and she sat at the bar crying tears of happy relief, touching everything within reach. Bottles stacked behind the bar changed shape and colour and contents. And a demon long kept imprisoned under the floor-boards burst free from its pentacle, as its containing wards were suddenly undone. Burning with thick blue ectoplasmic flames, it turned its horned head this way and that, cherishing centuries of hoarded frustrated rage, before lurching forward to kill everything within reach of its clawed hands. The bar's two muscular bouncers, Betty and Lucy Coltrane, jumped the demon from behind and wrestled it to the floor; but it was clear they wouldn't be able to hold it for long.

By then I'd dragged Eamonn 40 to safety behind the huge oak bar and was running through my options, which didn't take me nearly as long as I'd hoped. Alex glared at me.

"Do something, dammit! If Merlin has to manifest through me to sort out this mess, I can't speak for the safety of your client. You know Merlin's always favoured the scorched-earth policy when it comes to dealing with problems."

I nodded reluctantly. I know a few tricks, and more magic than I like to let on; but in the end it always comes down to my gift. I have a gift for finding things, a third eye in my mind, a private eye that can see where everything is, but I don't like to use it unless I have to. When I raise my gift, the sheer power involved means I blaze like a beacon in the dark, and my Enemies can see where I am. And then they send terrible agents like the Harrowing, to kill me. They've been trying to kill me for as long as I can remember.

But needs must, when the devil drives . . .

Tommy leaned in beside me. "It's a paradox," he said urgently. "Just their being here, mutually exclusive futures in a time-line that couldn't possibly produce them. Use that against them."

So I reached deep inside my mind and powered up my gift, and found how unlikely it was that Eamonn 50 and Eamonn 60 should be there, in that place and in that time. And having found that tiny, precarious chance, it was the easiest thing in the world for me to blow it out like a candle. Both men vanished in a moment, because it was impossible for them to be there.

I shut down my gift, and quickly re-established all my mental defences. My Enemies were usually wary of attacking me on Merlin's territory, but they'd been growing increasingly desperate of late. It was all very quiet in the bar. Patrons slowly emerged from their hiding places, looking around rather confusedly. Since the two older Eamonns had never been there, the attack had never happened, but all the changes enforced by the probability wands remained. Magic trumps logic every time. We all took turns kicking the crap out of the released demon, until Alex reactivated the old spell that put it back under the floor-boards again, then we set about extinguishing the various fires that were still burning. Betty and Lucy Coltrane gathered up all the scattered parts of the Frankenstein creation and stacked them behind the bar, until one of the Baron's descendants should drop in for a drink again.

All in all, we'd got off pretty lightly. Playing around with probability magic is always dangerous. Time doesn't like being messed around with, and it plays dirty. That's why Time travel is so very carefully regulated.

Alex looked at what had been done to all the bottles behind his bar and tugged bitterly at tufts of his hair. "Those bastards! I'm going to have to check every bottle individually to find out what's in them now. Could be anything from demon's urine to designer water. And I could probably sell demon's urine . . . You're a jinx, Taylor, you know that? If I had any sense, I'd have shot you on sight the moment you walked in."

Eamonn looked at me worriedly, but I smiled at him reassuringly. "Don't worry; that's just Alex being Alex. He doesn't really mean it."

"Yes I bloody do!"

"All right, he probably does really mean it, but he'll get over it. He's a friend."

"Then I'd hate to meet one of your enemies," muttered
Eamonn.

"I think some of you already have," I said. "I think someone's using you, in all your many versions, to get at me."

"But why use me?" said Eamonn plaintively.

"Good question," I said.

I led him over to a table in the furthest corner of the bar,
and we sat down. Tommy Oblivion sat down with us. I gave
him a thoughtful look, and he laughed a little nervously.

"We did seem to work rather well together, old man. I
thought perhaps I could help you out on this case of yours.
It does seem to be my sort of thing. For a reasonable percentage of the fee, of course."

"Oh, of course," I said. "This is business, after all. Tell
you what; you can have half of what I'm getting. How's
that?"

"More than reasonable, my dear sir! Never let it be said
that John Taylor is not a prince among men!"

Since I wasn't expecting to make a penny out of this
case, I was quite happy to share the penny I wasn't getting
with Tommy Oblivion. I could be existential, too, when it
suited me. He smiled happily at me, and I smiled back.

"Look, is it over now?" said Eamonn. "Can I go home
now? I really don't like it here."

"I'm afraid not," I said. "I could escort you safely out of
the Nightside, but the odds are our mutual enemy would
find some way to bring you back and start this up all over
again."

"Oh God . . ." Eamonn sat slumped in his chair, a small
ordinary man struggling to cope with problems he should
never have had to face. I felt sorry for him. The Nightside
is hard enough to deal with when you choose to come here.

"Don't worry," I said. "I'm on the case. I will find out
who's doing this to you, and I will make them stop."

"And if Taylor says that, you can take it to the bank,"
said Tommy, unexpectedly.

"Talk to me, Eamonn," I said. "Tell me about yourself, about your life. There must be a clue in it somewhere."

But Eamonn was already shaking his head. "I'm nobody. Or at least, nobody important. Just a minor cog in the great machinery of a big corporation. I do the necessary, everyday work that keeps the wheels turning."

"All right," I said. "Who do you work for?"

"The Widow's Mite Investment Corporation. It's a big company, with branches and offices worldwide. I've worked in the London branch almost twenty years now, man and boy. It's interesting work. We're a fund-raising company, persuading other companies to invest their money in worthy and charitable ventures. That's organised charities, of course, along with small start-up businesses that show promise, and some lobbying groups, for recognised Good Causes. We raise a lot of money, and take a reasonable percentage for ourselves along the way. I say *ourselves*, but of course I don't see any of the money. It's just when you work for a company for twenty years . . . Anyway, mine may not be a particularly challenging job, not what I expected my life would be, but . . . that's life. Few people ever really achieve their dreams or ambitions. We also serve, who keep the wheels of civilisation turning. Because the world couldn't get by without us. And anyway, all I've ever cared about is providing for my family. They are my dreams and ambitions now."

And nothing would do but that he get his photos of the wife and children out again, to show to Tommy. He made all the correct polite noises while I frowned, thinking. I was still pretty sure Eamonn was bait in a trap for me, but I was beginning to think there was rather more to it than that.

"What made you come to John Taylor for help?" said Tommy, as Eamonn carefully put away his photos again.

"I found his business card in my hand when I arrived in the Nightside."

"That's how I knew someone had to be playing us," I said. "I don't have a business card. Never saw the need. Everyone here knows who I am."

"I have a card," said Tommy. "Or, at least sometimes I do. It depends."

I knew better than to pursue that. "What matters," I said firmly, "is that someone is interfering in Eamonn's life, and mine. And I won't have that. Anyone wants to come after me, they can do it to my face. I'm used to it. I won't have them attacking me through innocents."

"I've heard of the Widow's Mite company," said Tommy. "They have a branch here in the Nightside."

Eamonn looked at us with something very like horror. "My company has a branch in this . . . hellhole?"

I shrugged. "Most big companies do. Can't say I've heard anything particularly good or bad about the Widow's Mite . . . What say we go and pay them a visit?"

"What if they won't let us in?" said Eamonn.

Tommy and I shared a smile. "We'll get in," I said.

"They couldn't have anything to do with . . . all this," said Eamonn. "They just couldn't. They've always treated me well. Offered me promotions . . . though of course I could never take them. It would mean leaving my family for long periods. You can't really believe a reputable company like the Widow's Mite is behind this!"

"Sure I can," I said. "Big corporations aren't always the bad guys; but it's the sensible way to bet."

FOUR

Time for Straight Talking

We left Strangefellows and went walking through the Nightside, with Eamonn in the middle. He felt safer that way. He was taking more notice of his surroundings, but it was clear he didn't approve of anything he saw. The inhuman elements scared him, and, if anything, the temptations available scared him even more. There was nothing in the Nightside he wanted, and what might have seemed magical or fantastical to others just disturbed him. He wanted nothing to do with any of it.

"I have to get home," he said miserably. "I'm never late getting home. Andrea and the children will be so worried. They'll think something's happened to me."

"Well, something has," I said reasonably. "Just think of the great story you'll be able to tell them when you get back."

"Oh no," he said immediately. "I could never tell them

anything about . . . this. It would only frighten them. It frightens me."

"Will you please relax," said Tommy, a little irritated. "You're with me and John Taylor; the two most proficient private investigators in the Nightside. You couldn't be safer if you were wrapped in cotton wool and body armour. We'll sort out your little problem for you. After all, I have a marvellous deductive brain, and Taylor is the only man in the Nightside that everyone else is afraid of."

"Somehow I don't find that particularly reassuring," said Eamonn, but he managed a small smile nonetheless. "I do appreciate your efforts on my behalf. It's only that . . . I don't belong here."

I couldn't help but agree with that. The Nightside isn't for everyone. Dragging Eamonn into our endless night was like throwing a small child to the wolves. I was starting to feel protective about him, and increasingly angry at whoever had decided to put him through this ordeal.

"We'll get you through this," I said. "Once we talk to the people at the Widow's Mite, I'm sure they'll tell us everything we need to know."

"Taylor is very good at getting answers out of people," Tommy said blithely. "Even if he has to prise them out with a crow-bar."

I gave him a hard look. "You're really not helping, Tommy."

"Couldn't we hail a taxi?" Eamonn said plaintively. "I think I'd feel a lot safer off the streets."

"Best not to," I said. "Not everything here that looks like traffic is. There are taxis, but most of them charge unusual and distressing payments for their services. Hell, even the ambulances run on distilled suffering, and motorbike messengers snort powdered virgin's blood for that extra kick. All kinds of things use that road, and most of them are hungry. We're better off walking. Besides, we'll be harder to locate in the crowds."

"The more you explain things, the worse I feel," said Eamonn. "I'd hate to see your Tourist Information office." It was a small joke, but a brave effort under the circumstances.

We made our way into the business sector, and Eamonn did seem to relax a little as more and more business suits appeared in the crowds around him. Admittedly some of the suits were worn by demons, and some weren't being worn by anyone at all, but he was pleased to see something familiar at last. Rent-a-cops were thick on the ground, and gave me suspicious looks as we passed, but they all kept their distance. They weren't paid enough to mess with me. In fact, I had heard a rumour that the rent-a-cops' union was trying to get a clause inserted in their contracts that said they were all entitled to go off sick if I so much as entered their territory. It's little things like that that make life worth living. We finally came to the Widow's Mite building and stopped before the main entrance to look it over. For the first time, Eamonn actually looked angry rather than upset.

"This shouldn't be here," he said flatly. "Not *here,* in this place. It puts our whole moral probity at risk. I can't believe top management knows about this. We raise money for charities. Important charities. If top management knew about this branch, the same top management that decides which charities get the money we raise . . ."

He broke off suddenly, as he realised where his argument was going. "Go on," I said. "If they know about this, and approve . . ."

"Then their judgement in deciding where the money goes would have to be equally suspect," Eamonn said unhappily. "And possibly I've spent twenty years persuading people to give money to unworthy causes. If Widow's Mite has a branch here, I have to wonder . . . where all that money has been going, all these years."

"You see?" I said. "Only a few hours in the Nightside, and already you're much smarter than you were. Let's go inside and make some trouble."

I knew a big corporation like the Widow's Mite would have to be protected by some major magical security, but even so I was startled when the two great stone statues on either side of the door suddenly came to life. Tall, idealised figures carved out of the very best marble turned their heads with a slow, grating sound, and their blank eyes fixed unerringly on me. Eamonn almost jumped out of his skin, and even Tommy took a step back. I held my ground. The more worried you are, the less you can afford to show it. Both statues stepped ponderously down from their pedestals to stand between us and the door. They loomed threateningly over me, huge, hulking, marble forms, cold and implacable as the stone from which they were carved. They would kill without conscience, do any terrible thing they were ordered to, because there was nothing in them to care about the soft, fragile living things they hurt. Stone endures, but it has no soul. Tommy looked at me to see what I was going to do, and I looked right back at him. I had a few useful tricks up my sleeve, but I was interested to see what the famous existential detective could do. He smiled easily and approached the two statues.

"Do be reasonable and stand aside, chaps. We have business inside."

"None shall pass," said the statue on the left, its voice like grating rocks.

"Now that is interesting," said Tommy. "How is it you're able to talk, considering you almost certainly don't have any vocal cords?"

The statue looked at him blankly. "What?"

"Well, I mean, I don't see how you're even able to move, old thing. Being solid stone and all. It's not as if you have any musculature, or even joints. How can you even think to act, when you have no brain? How can you be living, when no part of you is living matter? You're quite clearly stone, and nothing but stone, and therefore you cannot be alive, or think, or act."

The statues had clearly never considered this before, and impressed by Tommy's relentless logic, they stepped back up onto their pedestals and reverted to unmoving statues. I kicked the one on the left, just to be sure, but it didn't budge. I grinned at the bewildered Eamonn.

"That's Tommy's gift—to ask the unanswerable question, to raise doubts on any matter and confuse any situation beyond retrieval. He could talk all four legs off a donkey, then persuade it to fly him home. Demons from Hell have been known to run screaming from his appalling logic. Which is kind of scary, when you think about it."

"How very kind," Tommy drawled. "I think we can all learn a lesson here, you know. It doesn't always have to end in violence."

"Bet it will," I said.

"Well of course," said Tommy. "You're here."

We slammed the door open and stalked into the lobby, which was very grand, very luxurious, with a polished wooden floor and original masterpieces adorning the walls. Various people in sharp business suits saw us coming, and decided they were urgently needed somewhere else. Anywhere else. I headed straight for the reception desk, Tommy and Eamonn in tow. It was a big lobby, and long before we got to the desk the far doors banged open, and a whole bunch of armed men came running in. They fanned out to form a big semicircle blocking us off from the desk, pointing all kinds of guns in our direction. I stopped and considered them thoughtfully. They gave every appearance of being the real deal, wearing body armour rather than the gaudy uniforms of rent-a-cops, and they held their guns like they knew what to do with them. I stood very still, with Tommy and Eamonn both trying to hide behind me. There really were a hell of a lot of guns trained on us. The men behind them stood rock-solid, perfectly concentrated. They were professionals, ready to shoot us down at the bark of an order. I felt like shouting *Boo!* to see what would happen.

"That's far enough, Taylor," said the officer in charge. His voice was sharp and cold, military to the core. "We were warned you might be coming. This whole building is secured. There's nowhere you can go where my men won't open fire on you, on sight. Put your hands in the air. Slowly."

"Of course," I said. I raised my hands. Tommy and Eamonn had already raised theirs. "I like your guns," I said. "Very impressive. Pity they don't have any bullets in them."

The officer looked at me. "What?"

And I smiled as I opened my empty hands, and a steady stream of bullets fell from my palms to clatter and jump on the polished hardwood floor. The security guards watched wide-eyed as the bullets kept falling, then several of them tried to open fire anyway. But by then, of course, it was far too late, and the guards all looked very unhappy as their guns just made forlorn clicking noises. The last few bullets tumbled from my palms, and I lowered my hands. I was still smiling. Not a very nice smile, perhaps, but that's the Nightside for you. The security men looked mournfully at the officer in charge, who looked at me and tried a smile of his own. It wasn't very successful.

"Go away," I said to him. "Go away terribly quickly, or I'll show you all a similar trick, involving your inner organs and a whole lot of buckets."

The security force disappeared from the lobby with impressive speed, probably to go and tell upper management that I'd been nasty to them. A few looked like they were going to cry. Eamonn looked at all the bullets scattered across the floor and prodded a few with the toe of his shoe, to be sure they were real.

"You see?" I said to Tommy. "It doesn't always have to end in violence."

"It's still the sensible way to bet when you're involved," Tommy said darkly.

"Someone's going to have to clear all this up," said Eamonn.

We took the elevator to the top floor, overriding the security locks with a hairpin and an enchanted screwdriver, and the doors opened obligingly onto upper management territory. The corridor before us was completely empty. I strolled past a series of doors, Tommy and Eamonn trotting along in my wake, checking off the names on the doors until I came to a brightly polished brass plate bearing the title BRANCH DIRECTOR, and the name MR. ALEXANDER. I looked enquiringly at Eamonn, but he just shook his head.

"I don't know the name, but then, I wouldn't. I don't normally have dealings with people on this rarefied level." He looked at me uncertainly. "I'm really not sure we should disturb someone like him over something like this."

"Really?" I said. "I'm sure. I live to disturb people like him."

"And you do it so well," said Tommy.

I slammed the door open without knocking, and strode in like I owned the place. Tommy took Eamonn by the arm and tactfully eased him in. It was clearly an outer office, complete with uncomfortable chairs to wait on and an ice queen secretary sitting barricaded behind her desk. Really thick pile carpeting, tasteful prints on the walls, and hidden speakers playing classical Muzak. The air was subtly scented, probably with the smell of new currency. I looked at the secretary, and knew we weren't going to be friends. She looked like a fashion model with a business degree, tall and blonde and supernaturally slender, with a cold gaze that could give an Eskimo the shudders. I headed for the desk, giving her my best intimidating smile, and she didn't budge an inch.

"Good evening," she said, in a tone that doubted it was. "Do you have an appointment?"

"I'm John Taylor," I said cheerfully. "I don't do appointments."

"I'm afraid Mr. Alexander only sees people by appointment." She didn't sound sorry. "Mr. Alexander is a very busy man."

She indicated a heavy, old-fashioned appointments book, with every entry handwritten. I snapped my fingers at it and it burst into flames, crumbling quickly into ashes. The secretary didn't flinch a bit.

"Nice trick," said Tommy. "Flashy, but effective."

"Thank you," I said. "I've been practising. You should see what I can do with an elephant." I put both hands on the desk and leaned forward so I could glare right into the secretary's face. "Tell Mr. Alexander that John Taylor is seeing him right now, if he knows what's good for him. Or I'll do something distressing to this office. Suddenly and violently and all over the place."

"Mr. Alexander doesn't see anyone without an appointment," said the secretary, every word chipped out of ice. She stood up, and I straightened up with her to keep the glare going. She was taller than I'd thought, and up close there was an uneasy, animal presence to her. She glared right back at me, and her eyes were very dark. "I am here to ensure Mr. Alexander isn't bothered by unsuitable people. Go now. While you still can."

"Anyone ever tell you you're cute when you're angry?" I said.

And then I stepped back abruptly, as her body stretched and swelled, bones cracking loudly as they lengthened, fur covering her skin as she burst out of her clothes. Her face elongated into a wolf's muzzle, and sharp claws appeared on her hands and feet. Great muscles swelled under the dark grey fur. By the time the change was complete, the werewolf was eight feet tall, broad-shouldered and narrow-waisted, with a long, slavering muzzle packed with viciously sharp teeth. She breathed heavily, presumably with anticipation, as she moved unhurriedly out from behind the desk. Her clawed feet dug deep furrows in the carpet.

"Go on, Taylor, sweet-talk her some more," said Tommy. "Since it worked so well the last time."

"Ah hell," I said. "All these corporate types are guarded by watchdogs of some kind. Don't suppose you've got any silver with you, have you?"

"Don't you?" said Tommy.

"Nothing big enough to do any damage. You want to try your voice of reason? Maybe persuade her she isn't really an eight-foot-tall engine of destruction?"

"She doesn't look like the type to listen to reason," said Tommy. "Eamonn? Eamonn, don't you dare faint on me."

"Nice doggy," said Eamonn, in a far-away voice.

"Okay, he's off with the faeries," I said. "Come on, Tommy, maybe you could get her to roll over onto her back, so I could tickle her tummy?"

"You try it," said Tommy. "Eamonn and I will watch from a safe distance."

The werewolf lunged forward, and Tommy and I jumped out of the way, Tommy dragging the dazed Eamonn with him. We moved quickly to hide behind the secretary's desk, and the werewolf tossed it aside with one sweep of a powerful arm. I looked quickly about me. It was a small office, and the werewolf was between us and the door. There was nowhere to run, and she knew it. Her wolfish grin lengthened, showing even more teeth, and she flexed her clawed hands languorously, anticipating dragging them through yielding human flesh. She lunged forward impossibly quickly, her front paws slamming into my chest and hurling me to the floor. She straddled me, sticking her long muzzle right into my face, her jaws opening wide to show a crimson tongue lapping unhurriedly over huge, pointed teeth. Her rank animal smell was almost overpowering. I gagged, fighting for breath, and that gave me an idea. Using a variation on my little trick for taking bullets out of guns, I took all the air out of her lungs. The werewolf straightened up suddenly, her eyes bulging, then she collapsed on the churned-up carpet, kicked a few times as she fought for air that wasn't there, and finally was still. I relaxed the spell, and she started breathing again, but I didn't think she'd be waking up again anytime soon. I kicked her in the head a few times, just to be sure. Tommy winced.

"Oh please," I said. "She would quite definitely have killed all of us."

Tommy sniffed. "Why did you wait so long to take her out?"

"Just biding my time," I lied.

"You could have let her die," Tommy said thoughtfully. "But you didn't. Why not?"

"Because I'm trying to be one of the Good Guys, these days. Let's go see Mr. Alexander."

I walked over to consider the inner door, while Tommy took Eamonn firmly by the arm. My client's eyes were clear again, but he still didn't want to look at the werewolf's unconscious body. I used the smallest part of my gift to check the door for hidden security magics, but to my surprise there didn't seem to be any. It was only a door. I shrugged, opened it, and walked through, with Tommy and Eamonn right behind me.

The inner office was luxurious enough, but Mr. Alexander turned out to be a surprisingly anonymous guy, sitting behind his oversized desk. Just another business suit and tie, carrying more weight than was good for him, with thinning hair and a salt-and-pepper beard. He smiled easily at all of us, though he must have heard the commotion in his outer office. We arranged ourselves before his desk, and Mr. Alexander nodded to each of us in turn, finishing with Eamonn, who stepped forward suddenly.

"Why?" he said bluntly. "Why me, why . . . all of this?"

"Because we're very disappointed in you, Eamonn," said Mr. Alexander, his rich, deep voice kindly but firm, like the headmaster who only wants what's good for you. "Your work has always been perfectly adequate, but you could be so much more. We pride ourselves on spotting people who could do great things for the Corporation. People who could go right to the top. We offered you promotion often enough, but you always turned us down. We don't take kindly to having our offers thrown back in our face, Eamonn. So we decided sterner measures were in order."

"We?" I said.

"The Corporation, of course."

"Of course," I said. "Spread the blame widely enough, and no-one's really guilty."

"We expect our employees to live their lives for the Corporation," said Mr. Alexander, ignoring me to concentrate on Eamonn. "But you always held back. You wouldn't give us one hundred per cent."

"My wife and family have always been more important to me than my job," said Eamonn, and his voice was firm and unimpressed. Werewolves might throw him, but he knew where he was with Mr. Alexander. "I only work here, that's all."

"And there we have the problem, in a nutshell," said Mr. Alexander, smiling smugly. "We like our employees to think of the Corporation as their family. Their first loyalty should always be to us. Our needs should be their needs. How else can we survive and prosper in this competitive age? You showed such promise, Eamonn. We all thought so. You could have gone right to the very top. I'm getting old, you see, and an obvious successor has yet to appear.

So I chose you, or, to be more exact, I chose the man you could be, with a little input from us. A little persuasion from outside."

"Finally," I said. "You do like the sound of your own voice, don't you?"

"I called in a specialist," said Mr. Alexander, still ignoring me. "You can find any kind of specialist, in the Nightside. And he brought you here, to act as a lodestone for all the other versions of you, from other time-lines. So you could fight it out, survival of the fittest and all that, until one man was left. One strong and dominant Eamonn Mitchell, suitable to be my successor."

"Why involve me?" I said, a bit sharply.

"Because I was asked to," said Mr. Alexander, turning the full force of his smile on me for the first time. "Walker came to see me, representing the wishes of the Authorities. He'd heard about my little plan, but then, Walker hears about everything. He had a favour to ask, and of course, one doesn't say no to Walker. It seems the Authorities want you kept busy and distracted for a while, Mr. Taylor, while they decide precisely how they're going to deal with you."

"The Widow's Mite isn't what I thought it is," said Eamonn. "Is it?"

Mr. Alexander nodded approvingly at the first clear stirrings of anger in Eamonn's voice. He leaned back in his expensive chair, lacing his fingers across his bulging waistcoat, looking distinctly pleased with himself. "Here in the Corporation, we pride ourselves on taking the Long View. We back causes and businesses and people whom we believe most likely to bring about the kind of future we desire. A future where we hold the purse strings on all those who matter. Where we are in charge; because whoever controls the world's finances, controls the world."

He leaned forward suddenly, holding Eamonn's eyes with his. "It's not too late, you know. You could still agree to enter the fast track, to be personally groomed by me. I'd call off the dogs, and everything would go back to normal. You'd have to adjust your thinking in certain ways, of course, learn to see the world as we do . . . but eventually all the riches of the world would be yours."

"I already have everything that matters," said Eamonn, his voice calm and even. "My wife and my children. How many times do I have to say this? I am happy, and content. Can you say the same, for all your wealth and power? Get thee behind me, Mr. Alexander; I will not sell my soul to your Corporation. You have nothing I want or need."

Mr. Alexander sighed heavily, leaning back in his chair as though suddenly bored with the whole business. "Well, if you won't do what's necessary of your own free will, I'll have to replace you with another you who will. Allow me to present my specialist—Count Video."

And just like that Count Video was there in the office with us, as though he'd always been there, but we hadn't noticed him. The man himself, wrapped in shifting plasma lights, tall and pale and ghostly in his tattered black leathers, his colourless skin studded with silicon nodes and sorcerous circuitry. Heavy black stitches and metal staples held his skin in place. Whoever had reattached it, after it was flayed from him during the angel war, had done a good job. Though his face did look a bit taut, his thin-lipped mouth pulled into a constant mirthless grin. His hands twitched at his sides, eager to weave binary magics and rewrite probabilities. He did so love to show off what he could do. Count Video had no natural gift for change magic; he'd made himself the way he was through dedicated research into the more insane areas of quantum physics, and a little help from a Transient Being.

He's supposed to have had sex with a computer. The things a scientist will do for knowledge.

And to further complicate things, the last time I'd seen Count Video had been in a vision of a possible future where I destroyed the Nightside. He had been one of the

Enemies trying to hunt me down and kill me here, in the Past, before I could do whatever terrible thing it was that brought about the end of the Nightside, and the world.

"Hello, Tristram," I said. "You're looking . . . well, a lot better than the last time I saw you."

"Hello, John," said Count Video, sitting easily on one end of Mr. Alexander's desk. "Not many people get to see me these days. Everyone thinks I'm dead, and I like it that way. Operating in secret, in the shadows, behind the scenes. You see, after what happened to me during the angel war, I had something of an epiphany. No more messing around with magical theory and forbidden knowledge; I wanted all the good things the world has to offer, and I wanted them now, while I was still able to appreciate them. So now I work secretly, for the highest bidder, and I don't care what I do as long as it pays well. Does that make me sound shallow? Well, I find having your skin ripped off concentrates the mind wonderfully on what really matters."

"Tell me what you've been doing to Eamonn," I said. "You know you want to."

"Don't mind if I do," said Count Video, settling himself comfortably as he switched to lecture mode. "For everyone else, alternative timetracks are only theory. But to me, every time-line is as real as any other. I see them all, flowing past me like so many rivers, and I can dip a toe into any of them I please. Sometimes I go fishing, and pull out all kinds of strange and useful things. Like all those variant editions of Eamonn Mitchell. All the people he was and might have been, if only things had gone a little differently. I scattered them across the Nightside, armed them with wands charged by my probability magic, and sent them after your client. Most never got to him, of course. The Nightside is such a dangerous and distracting place."

"Yes, but why *wands*?" I said.

Count Video shrugged. "When dealing with amateurs, keep it simple."

"And there's no way I can persuade you to walk away from this?" I said.

"Not at what I'm being paid. And you needn't look at me that way, John. You're not powerful enough to stop me, and you know it. I have seen your futures, and in most of them you're dead."

"Most isn't all," I said. "And you really should have looked more closely at my past, Tristram. I'm not what everyone thinks I am."

He heard the threat in my voice and stood up abruptly, pulling his power about him. Plasma lights sparked and scintillated all around him, and the sorcerous circuitry embedded in his flesh glowed with an eerie light. Anyone else would probably have been impressed. But for all his magic, Count Video was really quite limited. All his power came from the terrible technology implanted in his body by the Transient Being known as the Engineer, and Tristram had never really appreciated its potential. He used it to see possible futures, like a video junky flipping endlessly from one channel to another. That was how he got his name. And with all those other Eamonns out there in the Nightside, draining his energy, he had to be running low on power by now. All I had to do was keep him busy, and his clockwork would run down.

Assuming he didn't manage to kill me first, of course.

He laughed suddenly, a happy, breathless sound. He flexed his hands, and the whole office disappeared in a moment, replaced by a craggy mountainside under an erupting volcano. The heat was overwhelming, the air almost too hot to breathe. Lava streams flowed down the cracked mountainside, cherry red and steaming, and blazing cinders flew through the air. But my gift was strong in me, too, and I could See the office behind the volcano. I found my way back to the office, and the volcano timetrack disappeared, snapped off in a moment, like the changing back of a channel. I took a step towards Count Video, and the office was gone again, and we were standing on a bare stone plain, surrounded by huge iron monoliths. Lightning cracked down repeatedly from an overcast sky, and slow misshapen things emerged from behind the monoliths, dragging themselves across the grey plain towards us. But I found the office again, and the plain and everything on it disappeared. I took another step towards Count Video.

He actually spat at me, shaking with rage. "How dare you set your will against mine? I'll find a time-line where you have no gift! Where you were born crippled, or blind, or maybe never born at all!"

And while he was ranting I stepped forward and kicked him in the balls. His mouth dropped open, his eyes bulged, and he folded up and collapsed, to lie twitching on the floor.

"I guess they must have sewed those back on as well," said Tommy.

"It seemed likely," I said. "When we're finished, I think I'll drag him out of here and find a passing Timeslip to drop him into. That should keep him busy for a while."

"Still trying to be the Good Guy?" said Tommy.

And that was when Count Video reared up just long enough to fire one last blast of change magic at me. I threw myself to one side, and the crackling change flew on to hit Mr. Alexander squarely on the chest. There was a bright flare of light, and suddenly Mr. Alexander looked . . . different. Physically unchanged, he looked calmer and kinder and more relaxed with himself. He smiled at me, and it was a warm, generous smile. Somehow I knew he was a better person now, someone he might have been if things had gone a little differently.

"I'm so sorry," he said, and we could all tell he meant it. "How can I ever apologise to you all?" He came out from behind his desk and insisted we all help Count Video to his feet, then settle him into the expensive chair behind his desk. He even poured Count Video a stiff whiskey from a bottle of the good stuff he kept in a desk drawer. Finally, he looked at me, and at Tommy, and finally Eamonn, before shaking his head ruefully.

"Please relax, all of you. It's over. The man who started this nonsense is gone, hopefully never to return. I intend to do things differently. I shall put a stop to this operation and see that none of you are troubled again. I feel . . . so much easier in myself now. You have no idea how much stress is involved in being the bad guy. Most of that man's memories are going, fading away like a bad dream, and I'm happy to see them go. Let me reassure you, Eamonn; I will make the Widow's Mite into the kind of Corporation we can both be proud of. And you are free to be . . . whatever you want to be."

Tommy looked at me. "This is really spooky. I feel like I've wandered into *A Christmas Carol*."

Mr. Alexander patted Count Video fondly on the shoulder. "Take it easy, dear boy. You can leave whenever you want. Your work here is over."

"The hell it is," Count Video said painfully. "This isn't over until I say it's over."

Mr. Alexander took a cheque from his wallet and gave it to Count Video. "Here. Payment in full, for services rendered."

Count Video considered the cheque in his hand, then looked at me. I raised an eyebrow, and he winced.

"All right, it's over."

He lurched to his feet, shrugging off a helping hand from Mr. Alexander, and walked painfully over to the door. He pulled it open, then looked back at me.

"I'm not finished with you, Taylor."

"I know," I said. *In the future, you will be one of my Enemies, and try to kill me, for the good of the Nightside.*

And that was it, really. We all had a nice sit-down and a chat with the new and improved Mr. Alexander, who couldn't do enough for us. He even presented all of us with generous cheques of our own. Eamonn had to be persuaded to accept his, but Tommy and I had no problem with it. We certainly weren't going to be paid by anyone else.

"Don't you love a happy ending?" I said to Tommy.

"Well, it depends what you mean by happy, and by ending," the existential detective began.

"Oh shut up," I said.

We all said our good-byes to Mr. Alexander, and left the Widow's Mite building. Tommy and I escorted Eamonn back through the Nightside streets to the underground station, so he could finally return to London and his precious family. We did try to interest him in trying some of the Nightside's tamer delights, just for the experience, but he refused to be tempted. He was going home, and that was all he cared about. We finally stood together outside the entrance to the tube station.

"Well," he said. "It's been . . . interesting, I suppose. Thank you both for all your help. I don't know what I would have done without you. But I trust you'll forgive me if I say I hope I'll never see you again."

"Lot of people feel that way about me," I said, and Tommy nodded solemnly.

"It was strange," said Eamonn. "Seeing all those other mes, the people I used to be, and the men I might have become. They were all very passionate about who they were, and what they wanted, but none of them seemed particularly happy, did they? I'm happy, in my quiet little life. I have my Andrea, and my children; and perhaps that's what true happiness is. Knowing what really matters to you."

He smiled briefly, insisted on shaking hands one last time, then he went down the steps into the Underground, and in a moment he was lost to sight among the crowd—a man going home, like so many others.

"There goes, perhaps, the wisest of us all," I said to Tommy, and he nodded. I considered him thoughtfully. "I am planning a trip through Time, all the way back to the very beginnings of the Nightside. We seem to work well enough together. If I can talk Old Father Time into this, would you like to come along?"

"What's the catch?" said Tommy.

I had to smile. "The catch? The catch is, it's hideously dangerous, and we'll probably end up killed!"

"Ah," said Tommy Oblivion. "The usual."

FIVE

A Parade of Possibilities

The Nightside is a dark and dangerous place, but I've always felt at home there, like I belonged. If only as one more monster among many. So it came as something of a surprise to me when Tommy Oblivion and I went walking through the crowded streets and found the tenor of the times was definitely changing. The crowd was jittery, like cattle before a thunderstorm, and the air was hot and close as a fever room. The raised voices of the club barkers and the come-on men sounded that little bit more desperate, and everywhere I looked the Merchants of Doom—the shabby men with burning eyes, preaching and prophesying and bellowing their proclamations of Bad Times coming—were out in force. One man barged sullenly through the crowds, wearing a sandwich board with the message THE END BLOODY WELL IS NIGH. I had to smile. Many of the self-styled prophets recognised me, and made the sign of the cross at me. Some made the sign of the extremely cross, and shook hand-made charms and fetishes at me.

And then the crowd immediately ahead suddenly scattered, falling back every which way as a manhole cover slid jerkily to one side. Thick blue smoke belched up from underneath the street, lying low and heavy on the ground like early-morning mist. People recoiled from the stench, coughing and rubbing at smarting eyes. Even at a distance the smell was distressing, dark and organic, like dead things pushing their way up out of newly turned earth. And up out of the manhole squeezed and crawled a whole series of faintly glowing creatures, so twisted and misshapen it was hard to be sure they were even all the same species. Their flesh was a grubby white shot with raised purple veins, mobile and half-melting, slipping and sliding around their underlying structure. They might have been human once, long ago, but now the only real resemblance left was in their puffy faces, blue-white like spoiled cheese and speckled with rot. Their eyes were huge and dark, and they did not blink. More and more of them spilled out onto the pavement, and everywhere people pushed back to give them plenty of room. And every single one of these creatures headed straight for me.

I stood my ground. I had a reputation to maintain, and besides, it's never wise to turn your back on an unknown enemy. They looked too soft and squishy to do me any real harm, but I didn't underestimate them either. Defenceless things don't tend to last long in the Nightside, and these things looked like they'd been around for a while. The smell grew steadily worse as they slumped across the ground towards me. I gave them my best cold glare and slipped one hand into my coat pocket, where I kept several items of a useful and destructive nature. Tommy stood his ground, just behind me.

"Do you know what those things are?" he said quietly.

"Disgusting, with a side order of utterly gross," I said. "Otherwise, no."

"What do you suppose they want with you?"

"Nothing that involves getting too familiar, hopefully. I've just had this coat cleaned."

The glowing creatures lined up in ranks before me, bobbing and pulsating, their corrupt flesh oozing all over each other; and then, at some unheard signal, they all bowed their dripping heads to me.

"Hail to thee, proud Prince of Catastrophe and Apocalypse," said the creature closest to me, in a thick gurgling voice. It sounded like someone drowning in their own vomit, and close up the smell was almost overwhelming. "We hear things, in the dark, in the deeps, and so we come to pay homage. Remember us, we pray thee, when thou dost come into thy heritage."

They hung before me for a while, bobbing their raised heads and sliding across one another, as though waiting for some response. I said nothing, and eventually they all turned away, slithered back across the enslimed pavement, and disappeared back down the manhole. The last one pulled the manhole cover back into place over them, and the blue ground fog slowly began to disperse, though the rotten smell still lingered on the air. There was a pause, then the watching crowd dispersed, everyone going about their business as though nothing unusual had occurred. It's not easy to shock hardened Nightsiders. Tommy sniffed loudly.

"You know, old horse, I wouldn't work in the sewers here for any amount of money. What do you suppose that was all about?"

"I don't know," I said. "But it's been happening more and more recently. Word about my mother's identity must be getting around."

Tommy considered the manhole cover thoughtfully. "Is it possible they know something you don't?"

"Wouldn't be difficult. Let's go."

We walked on, leaving the smell and the blue mists behind us. Everyone seemed to be moving just a little faster than normal, and the pace of life seemed that little bit more frantic. As though everyone had the feeling time might be running out. The club barkers were out in force, striding up and down outside the entrances to their members-only establishments. Bouncers whose job it was to throw the customers in. They shouted their wares, tempting and cajoling the passing trade like there was no tomorrow. *Come in and see the lovely ladies!* one checker-suited man shouted at us as we passed. *They're dead and they dance!* I wasn't tempted. There were street traders, too, dozens of them, selling all kinds of goods at all kinds of prices. One particularly furtive specimen in a knockoff Armani jumpsuit was selling items from possible futures, all kinds of junk sold by people who'd blundered into the Nightside via a Timeslip and needed to raise some quick cash. I paused to inspect the contents of the open suitcase. I've always been a sucker for unique items.

I knelt and rooted through the stuff. There was a Betamax video of the 1942 *Casablanca*, starring Ronald Reagan, Boris Karloff, and Joan Crawford. A thick paperback gothic romance, *Hearts in Atlanta* by Stephanie King. A plasma energy rifle from World War IV. (Batteries not included.) A gold pocket watch with butter in the works, and a cat that could disappear at will, leaving behind nothing but its smile. It said its name was Maxwell, but not to spread it around.

And that was just the stuff I recognised. Many of the items acquired from future travellers turn out to be technology so advanced or obscure that what they're for or even what they do is anybody's guess. Buyer beware; but then that's business as usual in the Nightside.

There was a tiny armchair, backed by a big brass wheel, with a bent cigar sitting in it, some kind of glowing lens, and a small black box that shook and growled menacingly when you tried to turn it on. The trader was very keen to hawk a philosopher's stone that could turn lead into gold, but I'd encountered it before. The stone could transmute the elements all right, but the changing atomic weight meant you ended up with extremely radioactive gold. A man kneeling beside me held up a phial full of a shimmering rainbow liquid.

"What does this do?" he challenged the trader, who grinned cheerfully.

"That, squire, is your actual immortality serum. One sip, and you live forever."

"Oh come on!" said the doubtful buyer. "Can you prove it?"

"Sure; drink it and live long enough to find out. Look, squire, I only sell the stuff. And before you ask, no, I don't do guarantees. I don't even guarantee I'll be here tomorrow. Now if you're not going to buy, make room for someone who will." He looked hopefully at me. "How about you, sir? You look like a man who knows a bargain when he sees one."

"I do," I admitted. "And I also know the Borealis Accelerator when I see it. One sip of that stuff will make you immortal, but I have read the small print that usually accompanies the phial. The bit that says, *Drink me and you'll live forever. You'll be a frog, but you'll live forever.*"

The other customer quickly dropped the phial back into the suitcase, and hurried away. The street trader shrugged, not bothered. He knew there'd be another sucker along in a moment. "Well, how about this, squire? A jet pack you strap on your back. Fly like a bird, only without all that onerous flapping of arms. It glides, it soars, and, no, it doesn't come with a parachute."

A young man pushed forward, eager to try it out, and I made room for him. The trader haggled cheerfully over a down payment, then strapped the hulking steel contraption to the young man's back. The two of them studied the complicated control panel for a while, then the young man shrugged and stabbed determinedly at the big red button in the centre. The jet pack blasted up into the night at speed, dragging the young man along with it, his legs kicking helplessly. His voice came drifting desperately down.

"How do I steer the bloody thing?"

"Experiment, squire, experiment!" shouted the trader, and he turned away to concentrate on his other customers.

One of them had already picked up a small, lacquered box, whose label boasted it could contain an infinity of things. I decided to step back. The customer opened the box, and, of course, it swallowed him right up. The box fell to the ground, and the trader picked it up again, scowling.

"That's the third this week. I do wish people wouldn't try things without asking." He held the box upside down and shook it hard, as though hoping the customer might fall out again.

Tommy and I decided to leave him to it. From some way down the street came a loud crash; the sound of a jet pack returning to earth. There's one born every minute, and a hell of a lot of them end up in the Nightside.

And then suddenly everyone was running and shouting and screaming. People streamed past me, pushing and shoving each other out of the way. It didn't take me long to see why; and then I felt like running and screaming myself. Walker had finally lost patience with me. In the growing empty space where the crowd had been, dark shapes were heaving and sliding across the street, flowing like slow dark liquid across the pavement and walls. Dark as midnight, dark as the gaps between the stars, dark as a killer's thoughts, the huge black shapes spilled silently down the street towards me. Two-dimensional surfaces sliding across the three-dimensional world, changing and expanding their shapes from one deadly form to another. They had hands and claws and barbs, and horribly human faces. Anyone who didn't get out of their way fast enough was immediately swallowed up and absorbed in the dark depths of their bodies.

"What the hell are they?" asked Tommy, so shocked he actually forgot to sound effete.

"The Shadow Men," I said, looking around for an escape route, but the shadows had already cut us off, approaching now from all sides at once. "They're Walker's enforcers. You can't fight them, because they're not really here. That's just their shadows. They can swallow up anything and take it back to Walker. But you're never the same after you've been in that darkness. If the stories I've heard are true . . . I think I'd rather die than be taken by the Shadow Men."

"Why didn't Walker send the Reasonable Men after you?" said Tommy, sounding more than a little desperate. "I could have out-reasoned them." He tried to hide behind me, but the Shadow Men were coming at us from every direction. "This is not good, Taylor, this is seriously not good. I may have one of my turns. This isn't fair! I thought Walker always sent the Reasonable Men after people he was upset with!"

"Normally, he does," I said. "But I killed them all."

"Impressive," said Tommy. "But perhaps a little short-sighted. Do something, Taylor! These things really are getting terribly close!"

"Thank you, Tommy, I had noticed. Stop gripping my arm like that, you're cutting off the circulation. Now try and panic a little less loudly; I'm thinking."

"Think quicker!"

We were standing alone by then. Everyone else was keeping well back, giving the Shadow Men plenty of room to work in. No-one wanted to get involved, but many were watching interestedly from what they hoped was a safe distance. Quite a few were placing bets. Everyone wanted to see what would happen when the infamous John Taylor went head to head with the appalling Shadow Men.

The dark shapes glided forward, not hurrying, now that they had their prey cornered. They could take on any shape, because they had no texture or substance, but they had a taste for the shapes that terrified. Their faces were blank, heads without eyes that could still see you, like childhood nightmares. Their more abstract shapes were designed to disturb and unsettle. Just looking at them for too long could make you feel sick, right down to your soul. They oozed forward, savouring our helplessness.

"What are they made of?" Tommy asked, as much for the comfort of the sound of his own voice as anything.

"They're living shadows," I said. "Anti-life. No-one knows exactly what they are, or how Walker bound them to his will, to serve the Authorities. Most likely rumour is that they came through a Timeslip from a far future, where the sun has gone out and an endless night has fallen over all the Earth. And the Shadow Men are all that live in that terrible dark."

"I wish I hadn't asked," said Tommy. "So? How do we fight them?"

"Actually, I was hoping you'd have some ideas," I said, glancing quickly around me. "I don't know anyone who's ever beaten a Shadow Man."

"Well try something, dammit!"

I looked at all the gaudy neon signs surrounding us, and muttered a few Words of Power under my breath. Immediately every sign flared up simultaneously, the bright letters and shapes blazing fiercely against the night. The signs sparked and buzzed loudly, the sheer force of the light driving back the dark like a Technicolor dawn, but it didn't even slow the advance of the Shadow Men. One by one the signs overloaded, exploding or sputtering out in showers of sparks, shutting down all the length of the street. And the night that returned was even darker than before.

I reached into my coat pocket and pulled out three salamander eggs I'd been saving for a rainy day. I threw them at the nearest Shadow Men, and they exploded like incendiaries, blazing up with incandescent light and heat. The Shadow Men rolled right over them, swallowing them up in a second.

I breathed deeply, trying to steady myself, and looked at Tommy.

"I have an idea," he said, reluctantly. By now he was standing so close to me he was practically pushing me over. "But I have to say, it is rather . . . risky."

"Do it," I said. "I'm not going into those Shadows alive."

Tommy frowned, concentrating, and I could feel his gift activating, as though suddenly there was a third person standing there with us. The Shadow Men were all around us now, almost close enough to touch us. I could feel my heart hammering in my chest, and I could hardly get my breath. Tommy spoke slowly, thoughtfully, as though saying the words aloud made them certain, incontrovertible.

"I deal in probabilities. In the nature of shifting reality. I persuade the world to see things my way. And since there is a small but very real chance that we could have got to Time Tower Square before the Shadow Men could find us . . . I believe that is what really happened."

And in the blink of an eye, we were somewhere else. The dark street was gone, replaced by the quiet cul-de-sac that was Time Tower Square. Tommy let out his breath in a long, shuddering sigh.

"That's it. We are here. All previous possibilities are now redundant, never happened."

His gift shut down, like a dangerous animal reluctantly going to sleep. I looked carefully around me, but all the shadows in the Square were only shadows. A few people were strolling up and down, intent on their own business. They hadn't noticed anything, because there had been nothing to notice. We'd always been there. I looked respectfully at Tommy Oblivion.

"You can persuade reality itself to go along with your wishes? That's one hell of a gift you've got there, Tommy. Why aren't you running things in the Nightside?"

"Because using my gift that way diminishes me," Tommy said tiredly. "Every time I use it, the less real I become. Less certain, less anchored in reality. Use the gift too much, and I'd become too unlikely, too impossible to exist."

It was clear from his voice that he didn't intend to discuss the matter any further, so I turned away and studied the Time Tower. It didn't look like much, just a squat stone structure of maybe three storeys, brooding ominously over a backwater square. The few people passing by gave it plenty of room, though. The Tower had *serious* layers of protection to ensure that only Old Father Time had control over Time travel. It was said by some, and believed by many, that you could blow up the whole world and the Time Tower would still be standing there, unaffected. Most people couldn't even find the place if they approached it thinking bad thoughts.

Just an old stone building, with no windows and only the one, anonymous, door. But the last time I'd been here, during the angel war, I'd seen an angel crucified against the stone wall of the Tower, with dozens of cold iron nails hammered through its arms and legs, and its severed wings lying on the ground beneath it. They play for keeps in the Nightside, and especially in Time Tower Square.

I'd never travelled purposefully in Time before. Just the thought of what I was planning to do unnerved me, but I had to do it. More and more I was convinced that all the answers to all my questions could be found at the very beginning of the Nightside, in that moment when it was created by my missing mother, for reasons of her own. My mother, who might or might not be that Biblical myth known as Lilith. I only had her word for it, after all. I needed to *know,* to be sure.

The only thing I did know for sure, concerning my mother, was that she had been banished from the Nightside once before, long and long ago, thrown out of reality and into Limbo for centuries. Maybe I could learn how to do that again. I was sure I could learn all kinds of things by observing how and why my mother created the Nightside, all those millennia ago. If I could persuade Old Father Time to send me all the way back to that fateful moment, there had to be all kinds of useful information there, and maybe even weapons I could use against my mother. There had to be. I had to stop her bringing about that awful future I'd seen in the Timeslip, the future where I destroyed the Nightside and maybe all the world, too, because of who my mother was.

"Bang, you're dead," said a familiar cold voice.

Tommy and I both looked round sharply as Suzie Shooter stepped unhurriedly forward out of a concealing shadow. My old friend Suzie, also known as Shotgun Suzie and *Oh Christ it's her, run.* The most deadly and efficient bounty hunter in the Nightside, and certainly the most pitiless. She'd track a bounty all the way down to Hell itself if the money was right. She looked icily impressive, as always, a tall blonde Valkyrie in black motorcycle leathers, heavily adorned with steel chains and studs, complete with knee-length boots with steel-capped toes, and two bandoliers of bullets criss-crossing her impressive chest. Grenades dangled from her belt. Her face was striking rather than pretty, with a strong bone structure and a determined jaw, and the coldest blue eyes I ever saw. She kept her long hair back out of her face with a leather band, fashioned from the skin of the first man she ever killed.

She was covering us both with her pump-action shotgun, and I didn't like her smile.

"Hello, Suzie," I said. "You're looking very fit. Been busy?"

"You know how it is," said Suzie. "So many people that need killing, and so little time." She lowered her shotgun. "You're getting soft, Taylor. Was a time I wouldn't have been able to sneak up on you like that."

"I've been somewhat preoccupied," I said, trying for dignity. "Killed anyone interesting recently?"

She shrugged easily and slipped her shotgun over her shoulder and into the holster hanging down her back. "No-one that matters. There's a lot of hysteria around. People saying the End Times are coming, like we haven't heard that before. But it's definitely good for business. Lot of people out there determined to pay off old scores while they've still got the chance. I've been looking for you, Taylor."

"Oh yes?" I said. Suzie might be an old friend, but it wasn't always wise to drop your guard around her. She only separated her business and private lives when it suited her. Five years ago I ran away from the Nightside, away from all the troubles and unanswered questions of my life, and I left with a bullet in my back from Suzie's gun.

"I've been hearing rumours about you," Suzie said lazily. "Disquieting rumours. About you and your mother, and what's going to happen now she's revealed herself at last . . . I went to Strangefellows, but you'd already been and gone. I could tell you'd been there; they were still clearing up the wreckage. So I asked around, and after bruising my knuckles a few times, I learned you were planning a trip through Time. So I came here and waited. I've decided that if you're determined to do this incredibly risky and stupid thing, you're going to need serious backup. And they don't come any more serious than me."

"True," I said. "But this isn't for a client or a case, Suzie. This is personal."

"So no money, then. Ah, what the hell. I owe you one, Taylor."

Tommy's ears pricked up, sensing gossip. "Really? How intriguing . . . Do tell."

"Don't go there," I said.

Suzie drew her shotgun in a blur of motion and stuck both barrels up Tommy's nose. "Right."

"Of course," said Tommy, standing very still. "None of my business, I'm sure."

Suzie put her shotgun away again. "I don't normally do warnings. I must be mellowing."

"It had to happen eventually," I said.

"Everyone's so touchy these days," said Tommy, fingering his nose gingerly.

"Who is this person?" said Suzie.

"This is Tommy Oblivion, the existential detective," I said. "He's coming along. He has a very useful gift. Don't break him."

The two of them studied each other dubiously. I looked at Suzie, and the cold hand that had gripped my heart the moment I set eyes on her squeezed a little more tightly. The last time I saw Suzie Shooter, it had been a version of her from the future. The bad future I encountered in the Timeslip. The future Suzie had been terribly injured, and rebuilt by my Enemies to be an engine of destruction. A weapon they sent back through Time to kill me, before I could do whatever terrible thing it was that would lead to their destroyed future. And the awful thing was, that future Suzie had volunteered for everything that had been done to her. Looking at her now, so whole and hale and hearty, so alive . . . I couldn't bear to think of her being hurt and used in such a way. Not because of me.

"You don't have to come along, Suzie," I said, abruptly. "This one is going to be dangerous. More so than anything you've ever faced. And there really isn't any money involved . . ."

"Not everything is about money," said Suzie. "You need me, Taylor. You know you do."

"The odds are stacked against us . . ."

"Cool," said Suzie. "You always know how to give a girl a good time, Taylor."

I looked at her for a long moment. "You do know I would stand between you and all harm, don't you, Suzie?"

She stirred uncomfortably. "What brought that on? You start getting sentimental, and I'll shoot you myself. You need to be razor-sharp and dangerous for Time travel."

I nodded. Suzie wasn't very good at emotions, for good reasons. So I had to be strong for both of us. And there and then I swore to myself that I would die before I let her become the terrible thing I'd seen from the future. I nodded briskly to her and changed the subject.

"Did you ever find that elusive bounty of yours, Big Butcher Hogg?"

Suzie grinned unpleasantly. "I got a good price for his head. And an even better price for his heart, lungs, and kidneys."

Tommy looked at me. "Is she joking?"

"I find it better not to ask," I said.

"It's a good thing I'm here," said Suzie, glaring disparagingly at Tommy. "I heard you nearly got your head handed to you on your last case. See what happens when you try to get the job done without me? I mean—Sinner, Madman, and Pretty Poison as your backup? What the hell were you thinking?"

I shrugged. "I needed someone scary, and you weren't around."

She sniffed loudly. "Is it true about your mother? That she's Lilith?"

"Looks that way."

"I had to look her up," Suzie admitted. "I only knew the name from an old Genesis song. I hate it when the world starts going Old Testament on my arse; those guys are hard-core." She looked like she was about to say something else, then shook her head sharply. "Come on, we need to get moving. If I can track you here, you can bet your enemies will, too. There's a lot of people in the Nightside who want you dead, Taylor. Even more than usual."

"Anyone interesting?" I said.

Suzie started counting them off on her fingers. "First up, we have Sandra Chance, the consulting necromancer. She's mad at you because you destroyed that revolting old Power, the Lamentation, on your last case. (And when you've got the time, I'd really like to know how you did that. The Lamentation was seriously creepy.) Anyway, it seems she had some kind of relationship with it, and she's sworn a blood oath against you."

"Bad news there, old thing," said Tommy. "You're not even safe in your grave, when that demented little filly is out to get you."

"Shut up," I said. I find a little effete goes a long way.

"Then," said Suzie, glaring at Tommy, "there are all the very well connected families of the thirteen Reasonable Men you killed. These grieving families have been putting out some serious paper on you, backed up by very serious money. Enough to tempt every bounty hunter in the Nightside. The families want you dead, and they aren't at all fussy about the details. They did try to hire me."

I raised an eyebrow.

"I was busy," said Suzie.

"But for the right money you'd take me down?"

Suzie smiled briefly. "For the right price I'd take God down. But I'd have to be paid a hell of a lot to go up against you, Taylor."

"Well," I said. "That's reassuring. Who else is after me?"

"Walker, for the Authorities, but then you probably already know that."

I nodded. "He sent the Shadow Men after me."

It was Suzie's turn to raise an eyebrow. "You defeated the Shadow Men?"

"Not as such," I said. "We ran away."

"Finally getting smart in your old age," said Suzie. "I wouldn't go up against the Shadow Men for all the gold in Walker's fillings. In fact, a trip through Time is probably the safest thing you could do right now. Even Walker has no power over Old Father Time." She glanced disparagingly at Tommy again. "You sure you want to drag him along with us, Taylor?"

"Yes," I said firmly. "I have a use for him."

"Oh good," said Tommy. "Am I going to like it?"

"Probably not," I said.

"Some days you shouldn't get out of bed in the morning," said Tommy. He glared at Suzie. "I don't think we should take her along, actually. She has a reputation for sudden and unexpected violence and a complete disregard for things like consequences. And unthinking acts in the Past can have terrible consequences. Change things too much in the Past, and the Present you return to might have nothing in common with the Present you left from."

"I thought you were desperate to go Time travelling," I said.

"Not necessarily this desperate."

"I'm going, and so are you," Suzie said briskly. "Now shut your face, or I'll rip your nipples off." She turned her cold gaze on me. "He may be annoying, but he does have a point. Time travel really is a last resort. You sure there's no-one else in the Nightside you could talk to about your mother?"

"The only other person who knew my mother, and is still around, is Shock-Headed Peter," I said. "And he's crazy."

"How crazy?" said Tommy.

"Crazy as in, criminally insane. He murdered three

hundred and forty-seven people before the Authorities finally caught up with him. That's three hundred and forty-
seven victims that they're sure of . . . Walker once told me,
very much off the record, that the real number was probably in the thousands. That's a pretty respectable body
count, even for the Nightside. They never did find any of
the bodies. Or any trace of forensic evidence. Just the victims' clothes . . . The Authorities have him locked up in the
nastiest and most secure dungeon in the Nightside."

"Why didn't they execute him?" said Suzie, practical as
ever.

"They tried. Several times. It didn't take. I'll talk to him
when I've tried absolutely everything else first."

"I would," said Tommy.

And that was when the Shadow Men found us again.
Somehow they'd tracked me half-way across the Nightside
in a matter of minutes, without even a trail to follow. They
came slipping and sliding across the open Square, great
black shapes with long reaching arms, and the few people
in the Square ran screaming from them. I would have liked
to do the same, but once again they'd silently surrounded
me, blocking me off from every exit. They'd even been
careful to get between me and the Time Tower. They
moved in slowly from all sides like a creeping black tide,
taking their time. They wanted to savour this. And I had
nothing left with which to fight them.

Suzie Shooter had her shotgun in her hands again. She
blasted the nearest Shadow with both barrels, and the darkness absorbed the blast without even a ripple. Suzie swore
dispassionately.

"I have silver bullets, blessed bullets, cursed bullets,
and a couple of grenades I stole from some Satanic terror-
ists. Any of them do any good?"

"No," I said. I was having trouble breathing, and I could
feel cold beads of sweat popping out on my forehead. I

didn't want to go out like this. Swallowed up by the dark, reduced to some broken, screaming thing. "Tommy?"

Give the man his due, he tried. He stepped forward and tried to reason with the Shadow Men. But his voice was uncertain, and I could feel his gift sputtering on and off. The Shadow Men oozed forward, taking their time, black lakes of evil intent. They didn't listen to Tommy. They didn't care about his logic, they didn't care about anything but dragging down the man who'd dared defy them. They had come for me, and not even Walker's orders would have turned them aside by then.

So I did the only thing left to me, and fired up my gift. I didn't want to. I blaze so very brightly in the dark when I open up my mind to find things, and my Enemies can See exactly where I am. They might send the Harrowing after me again, or worse still, the future Suzie. But I had no choice. I opened up my inner eye, my private eye, and used my gift to find the Time Tower's defences. I could See the many layers of magical protection radiating from the squat stone structure, like a dark rainbow, and it was the easiest thing in the world to reach out and grab them, and pull them to me.

I only meant to use them as a screen, to hide the three of us from the Shadow Men, but the Tower's defences had other ideas. They slammed into me, a cascade of terrible forces far beyond mortal ken, and I cried out as horrible pain racked my whole body. The defences forced their way into me, and focussed through me; then they leapt out to blast all the Shadow Men in the Square with a brilliant, incandescent, and overwhelming light that shone from me like a balefire against the night.

I screamed again and again as the power burned in and through me, and the light shone brighter, brighter, filling the whole Square. And everywhere the living Shadows fell back, shrivelling up and fading away under the onslaught of that terrible light. Suzie and Tommy had their heads turned away and their hands pressed over their eyes, but I don't think it was helping them much. They were crying out, too. The light rose up one last time, and the Shadow Men were gone, all gone, small patches of darkness blasted away by a light beyond bearing. The Tower's defences looked out through my eyes, checking that the Square was secure, then they withdrew, yanking themselves out of me with painful abruptness. I fell forward into my knees, shaking and shuddering. And all I could think was;

I don't think I'll try that again.

Suzie knelt beside me, not touching me, but giving me what support she could through her presence.

"I didn't know you could do that," said Tommy. He was looking dazedly about him. "You destroyed the Shadow Men! All of them! I didn't think anyone could do that!"

"I'm full of surprises," I managed to say, after a while.

"I'll say," Suzie said dryly. "First the Reasonable Men, now the Shadow Men. Soon Walker won't have anyone left to send after you."

"Sounds like a plan to me," I said.

I rose shakily to my feet and wiped the sweat off my face with a handkerchief that had seen better days. Tommy actually winced at the sight of it. I put it away, and we all looked at the Time Tower. Suzie looked at me.

"Why do they call it a Tower when it manifestly isn't?"

"Because that isn't the Tower," I said. Even my brief contact with the Tower's defences had been enough to fill my head with all kinds of information I hadn't possessed before. "That building is how you access the Tower, which isn't exactly here, as such. Old Father Time brought the Tower with him from Shadows Fall, but it's only connected to the Nightside by his will. It exists . . . somewhere else. Or maybe somewhen else. That stone thing only contains the Tower's defences. And trust me when I say you really don't want to know what powers them. I know, and I'm seriously considering scrubbing out my frontal lobes with steel wool."

"All right," said Tommy, in the tone of voice usually reserved for calming the demented and potentially dangerous. "How do we get to the Tower?"

"Through the door," I said. "That's what it's for."

I led the way over and tried the brass door handle. It turned easily in my hand, and the door swung open. This was a good sign. If Old Father Time didn't want to talk to you, the handle wouldn't budge. Inside the door was an elevator, with only the one button on its control panel. The three of us stepped inside, and I hit the button. The door swung shut, and the elevator started moving.

"Hold everything," said Suzie. "We're going *down*."

"The Tower exists at one hundred and eighty degrees to our reality," I said. "To reach the top of the Tower, we have to go all the way down."

"Am I the only one who finds that distressingly ominous?" said Tommy.

"Shut up," I said kindly.

Four mirrored walls surrounded us. As the elevator fell and fell, our reflections began changing. First a detail here and there, and then the changes accelerated, until the mirrors were showing us possible versions of ourselves, from alternate timetracks. Facing me was a female version of myself, looking very stylish in her long white trench coat. Another mirrored wall showed Suzie a male version of herself, looking like a berserker Hells Angel. A third wall showed a Punk version of Tommy, complete with a tall green Mohawk and safety pins through his face. The images changed abruptly, and suddenly all three of us were wearing masks and capes and gaudily coloured spandex. We had muscles and square chins and attitude to spare.

"Cool," said Tommy. "We're super-heroes!"

"More likely super-villains," Suzie said. "And I never

had breasts that big in my life. They're bigger than my head . . ."

Another change, and suddenly I was wearing black leather trousers and bondage straps across my shaved chest. Suzie was wearing a scarlet basque with all the trimmings, black stockings and suspenders, and makeup by Sluts R Us. Tommy was a surprisingly convincing crossdresser. None of us had anything to say. Another change, and we were Pierrot, Columbine, and Pantaloon. All three of us had a distinctly melancholy air, despite the bright costumes. The next change was . . . disturbing. I was a vampire, Suzie was a zombie, Tommy was a mummy. All of us were dead, but still continuing. Our pale and rotting faces had a grim, resigned look.

And then all the images faded away, leaving four mirrored surfaces showing no reflections at all. We looked at each other. Tommy actually reached out a hand to touch my arm, to make sure I was still there. Suzie tapped on the nearest mirror with a knuckle, and immediately all four walls showed a single terrible figure. It was the Suzie I'd seen from the bad future. Half her face had been destroyed, blackened and crisped around a seared-shut eye. One side of her mouth was twisted up in a permanent caustic smile. Her long straggly hair was shot with grey, and her leathers were battered and torn. She looked hard-used and horribly tired, from fighting evils I couldn't even imagine. And worst of all, her right forearm and hand were gone, replaced by that awful old weapon known as the Speaking Gun, which could destroy anything, anything at all. It had been plugged directly into what was left of her elbow.

Future Suzie stared out of all four walls, madness and fury and cold, cold determination blazing from her one remaining eye.

"Stop that," I said, and I don't think my voice had ever been colder or angrier. "Stop that now."

Tommy and Suzie looked at me sharply, but the future

image snapped off, and all four mirrors were reflecting us as we were. And, God willing, always would be.

"What the hell was *that*?" said Tommy.

"Just a possibility," I said, looking at Suzie. "Nothing more."

Suzie looked hard at me. I'd never been able to lie successfully to her.

The elevator fell and fell, descending in a direction we could only guess at. It started to get cold, and our breath steamed on the air before us. There were voices outside the elevator, drifting, inhuman voices, thankfully indistinct. I don't think any of us would have wanted to hear them clearly. But finally the elevator eased to a halt, and the door disappeared. And standing before us, in a brightly lit steel corridor, was Old Father Time himself. He seemed human enough, as long as you didn't look too closely into his eyes. He was a gaunt man in his late fifties or early sixties, dressed to the height of mid-Victorian elegance. His long black coat was of a fine but severe cut, over a dazzlingly white shirt and dark waistcoat, and apart from the gold watch chain stretched across his flat stomach, the only touch of colour in his garb was the apricot cravat at his throat. He had a fine-boned face with high cheekbones, old old eyes, and a mane of thick grey hair. He held his chin high, and looked us over with a sharp, considering gaze.

"About time you got here," he said. "I've been waiting for you."

"Interesting," I said. "Considering even I didn't know there'd be three of us until a while ago."

"Oh, I'm always expecting everyone, my boy," said Time. "Especially Kings in waiting, female bounty hunters, and dated dandies." He sniffed loudly at Tommy. "I really don't approve of you, you know. Time is complicated enough without people like you messing it about. No, no, don't bother to justify yourself. You're going with Taylor anyway. He's going to need you."

"I am?" I said.

"And he'll need you, too, my dear," Time said to Suzie. "Your presence is approved, because it is necessary. You will redeem him."

"She will?" I said.

"Follow me," said Old Father Time, and he set off down the steel corridor at a brisk pace. We had to hurry to keep up.

"What do you know about what's going to happen?" I said.

"Never enough to do any good," said Time, not looking around.

The steel corridor seemed to stretch away forever. The gleaming walls showed us blurred distortions of ourselves, but Time's image was always sharp and distinct. And only his feet made any sound on the metal floor.

"What was all that business with the changing images on the elevator walls?" Suzie said abruptly.

"Possible futures, variant timetracks," Time said airily. "I should never have given the elevator semi-sentience. It gets bored, and sometimes cranky. It's harmless. Mostly. And don't worry about the images; they don't mean anything. Usually."

"Talk to me about possible futures," I said. "How real are they? How definite? How can you tell . . . the likely ones?"

"You can't," said Time. "They're all equally real, and therefore equally possible." He was still striding along, not looking back. "However . . . That isn't as true as it used to be. There don't seem to be as many futures as there once were. As though one particular future is becoming increasingly probable. More and more powerful, replacing all the others. As though . . . events are conspiring to narrow us down to the one future. Which is fascinating, if a trifle worrying."

"Only a trifle worrying?" said Tommy.

"Oh, these things usually sort themselves out," Time said vaguely. "Except for when they don't."

We were suddenly walking through a forest of large, slowly turning metal pieces. Shapes and cogs and wheels working together as we walked through and between them. It was like moving inside the mechanism of a giant clock. A slow loud ticking came from everywhere at once, and every distinct sound had something of eternity in it. Old Father Time looked back briefly.

"Whatever you're seeing, it probably isn't really there. It's only your mind interpreting something so complex as to be beyond your comprehension. Your mind supplies you with familiar symbols to help you make sense of your surroundings."

"I've always liked Disneyland," said Tommy.

"So," said Time, carefully ignoring Tommy's comment, "you want to go back into the Past, do you? All the way back to the creation of the Nightside. An ambitious plan, if somewhat lacking in self-preservation."

"How do you know where we want to go?" Suzie said sharply.

"Because it's my business to know things like that."

"If you really are the living incarnation of Time itself," I said carefully, "do you know the truth about the Past? About everything that's happened? Do you know what's going to happen when we go back to the beginnings of the Nightside?"

"I only know what I'm allowed to know, to do my job," said Time. He still didn't look round, but his voice sounded sad, resigned.

"Allowed?" said Tommy. "Allowed by who?"

"Good question," said Old Father Time. "If you should happen to find out, do let me know. Assuming you come back from this trip, of course."

"What?" said Suzie.

Time stopped abruptly, and we almost ran into him. He

looked us over with his cold, crafty gaze. "Pay attention; this is important. Where you're going is much further back than most people go. And it is a very unstable moment in time, centred around a unique happening. I can send you there, but once you arrive you'll be beyond my reach. You'll be beyond anyone's reach. To put it bluntly, you'll have to find your own way back. I won't be able to help you. Knowing this, do you still wish to proceed?"

Suzie and Tommy and I looked at each other. I felt like the floor had been pulled out from under my feet. It had never occurred to me that this might be a one-way ticket.

"This changes things," said Suzie.

"Damn right," said Tommy. "No offence, old thing, but this isn't what I signed on for."

"I'm going," I said. "With or without you. I need to do this. I need to know the truth."

"Well," said Suzie, after a moment, "if you're dumb enough to do it, I guess I'm dumb enough to go along."

"You don't have to," I said.

"What are friends for?" said Suzie, and I don't think I've ever felt more touched.

"And I need to see the creation of the Nightside," Tommy said quietly. "I need to see one true, definite, and incontrovertible thing. So I'm going along, too. But I'm warning you now, Taylor; if we all end up stranded in the Past, I will dedicate what remains of my life to constantly reminding you it was All Your Fault."

"We're going," I said to Time, and he shrugged carelessly.

"I know," he said.

"There is a chance Walker and the Authorities will not approve of our taking this trip," I said. "Does that affect things?"

"Walker?" said Time, arching an eyebrow. "Appalling fellow. I wouldn't piss down his throat if his heart was on fire."

* * *

We came at last to the Waiting Room. Old Father Time asked us to wait there for him, while he checked that conditions were stable enough for our trip into the Past. I looked at him sharply.

"Conditions?"

He waved an elegant hand dismissively. "There are always storms and flurries in the chronoflow, and strangeness and charm run wild in the lower regions. And don't even get me started on quantum foam and superpositions. Sometimes I think the dinosaurs died out just to spite me. And despite all the traps I put down, there are still things that hunt and prey in the chronoflow, living like rats in the walls of reality. Just their passing can cause currents strong enough to carry away the most prepared traveller. Are you any happier for knowing all this?"

"Not really, no," said Tommy.

"Then stop bothering me with questions. Make yourselves comfortable here. I'll be back when I'm back."

He stalked out of the Waiting Room, head held high, hands clasped behind his back, as though already thinking about more important things. Suzie and Tommy and I looked at each other.

"Did you understand even half of what he said?" Tommy asked plaintively.

"Not even close," I said.

Suzie shrugged. "That's why he's Old Father Time, and we're not. I never bother with the backgrounds of cases, you know that, Taylor. Just find me someone I can shoot, and I'll be happy."

"You might want to start here," Tommy said nervously. "No-one seems at all happy to see us."

We looked around the Waiting Room. It could have been any doctor's waiting room, right down to the outdated magazines on the coffee table, but the people waiting were a strange collection, even for the Nightside. And all of them were scowling at us. They were waiting for their trips through Time to be approved, and they were all ready to get seriously unpleasant with anyone who looked to be getting preferential treatment. Suzie glared about her, and everyone started settling down again. Some of them even pretended to be interested in the magazines. Suzie has that effect on people.

Most of the people in Time's Waiting Room were from other time-lines, past and future. They'd arrived in the Nightside after stumbling into Timeslips, and ended up stranded here when the Timeslips collapsed. Old Father Time always did his best to find such temporal refugees a way home, but apparently it was complicated business. It took time. And so they waited in the Waiting Room, until either Time came through with the goods, or they got fed up with waiting and made new homes for themselves in the Nightside.

There were Morlocks and Eloi, sitting at opposite ends of the room. There were knights in full plate armour, with force shields and energy lances. They politely volunteered that they came from a world where Camelot never fell, and Arthur's legacy continued. They didn't say anything about Merlin, so I thought it best not to either. There were big hairy Vikings, from a time-line where they colonized all of America, conquered the world, and the Dark Ages never ended. One of them made disparaging remarks about Suzie, and unnatural warrior women in general, and Suzie punched him right between the eyes. His horned helmet flew the length of the room, and he took no further interest in the proceedings. The other Vikings thought this was a great joke and laughed uproariously, which was probably just as well.

There were even future people, tall and spindly and elegant, with animal grace and streamlined features, as though someone had decided to engineer a more efficient, more aesthetic form of humanity. They ignored everyone else, staring at something only they could see. Two hulking steel robots stood unmoving in a corner, watching everything with glowing crimson eyes. They came from a future where Man died out, and robots built their own civilisation. They talked in staccato, metallic voices.

"Flesh-based creatures," said one. "Obscene. Corrupt."

"Meat that talks," said the other. "Abominations."

The knights in armour powered up their energy lances, and the robots fell silent.

Old Father Time finally returned, smiled vaguely round the Waiting Room, then beckoned for the three of us to follow him. He led us through a labyrinth of twisting stone passages with a ceiling so low we all had to stoop. Smoking yellow torches blazed in iron braziers, and small things scurried back and forth across the shadowy floor. Time paid them no attention, so I tried not to either.

We ended up, quite abruptly, in a shimmering white room, a room so white it was blinding, overwhelming. We all winced and shaded our eyes, except for Time. The room had no details. Even the door we'd entered through had disappeared. The white light was so dazzling it was hard to be sure of the room's size or scale, the walls and ceiling so far away it was impossible to judge any distances. The white room felt like it went on forever, while at the same time the walls seemed to be constantly rushing in and out, contracting and expanding, regular as a heartbeat I could sense but not hear. Suzie and Tommy stuck very close to me, and I was glad of their human presence.

In the middle of the room, stark and alone, stood a single complex and rococo mechanism, its pieces and workings so intricate my mind couldn't grasp all the details. It didn't seem to belong in the white room. It looked like a dirty nail driven deep into white flesh. Its very presence was an insult. Old Father Time fussed busily over the mechanism, pushing back his sleeves to ease his arms deep inside it, making delicate adjustments only he understood, while muttering querulously to himself in a voice just below the level of understanding. Finally, he stepped back with a proud gesture and nodded vigorously. We could all feel the mechanism coming on-line, like a giant eye slowly opening and becoming aware of us.

I could feel the Time Winds blowing, hear their blustering roar tugging subtly at my soul. It sounded like the breathing of some long-forgotten god, rousing itself from sleep. It felt like the whole universe was turning around this single spot, this single moment. When the Time Winds blow, even the greatest Powers shudder and look to their defences. I wanted to turn and run, and keep running till I could forget everything I'd seen and learned and felt here, but I couldn't let myself be weak. This was what I'd come here for.

Old Father Time looked round sharply. "Be still, all of you! There are strange fluctuations in the chronoflow, distortions I don't understand. Something big is happening, or is going to happen. Or perhaps it has already happened, long ago, and the echoes are reverberating up through Time, changing everything. I should understand what's happening . . . but I don't. Which is in itself significant." He looked at me sharply. "Do you wish to postpone your trip?"

"No," I said. Suzie and Tommy said nothing.

Time spoke quickly, as though rushing to get everything in. "I have provided you with a process that will enable all of you to speak and understand any language or dialect you may encounter, and a glamour that will make you seem a part of whatever culture you may end up in. I wish I could be more specific, but where you're going, nothing is certain."

He was still talking, but now the roar of the Time Winds was drowning him out. I could feel them tugging at me, pulling me in a direction I could sense but not name. And then the three of us were falling, crying out to each other. The white room was gone, as though we'd dropped through it, like a stone through the bottom of a wet paper bag. We plummeted in a direction beyond understanding, wrapped in rainbows of colours I'd never seen before. We were falling, back, back towards something, somewhere, somewhen . . .

SIX

Past Very Much Imperfect

"I appear to be standing in a dead dog," said Tommy Oblivion. "And not in a good way."

The distress in his voice was clear, but I had my own problems. The world had slammed back into focus around me, but my head was still spinning. I was surrounded by darkness and leaning against a rough brick wall. The air was hot and sweaty, but it was the smell that hit me hardest. A thick and ripe organic miasma that hung heavily on the close air, and the stench of smoke and sweat and shit filled my head no matter how much I shook it. I pushed myself away from the wall and made myself study my new surroundings.

Tommy and Suzie and I were standing in a dark narrow alleyway, lit only by a burning human body in a hanging iron cage. The flames had pretty much died down, flickering sullenly around the blackened corpse. The walls of the alley were rough brickwork, stained black with soot, and the ground was packed earth covered with a rich mixture of fresh shit and other appalling detritus. Someone had painted *Dagon shall return!* on the wall, and pretty recently, by the look of it. Tommy had backed away from what was left of his dead dog and was banging his boots determinedly against the wall. Suzie stared slowly around her, frowning.

"Wherever we are, Taylor, I don't think it's where we were meant to be."

"You mean when we're supposed to be," I growled, simply to be saying something. "Obviously, something's gone wrong."

I headed for the end of the alley and the street noises beyond. There was light up ahead, and the sounds of some kind of civilisation. Suzie and Tommy hurried to catch up with me, the filthy ground sucking loudly at their feet. I stopped at the alley mouth, sticking to the shadows, and peered out into the street. Tommy and Suzie crowded in behind me. The street was busy, packed with mostly foot traffic, and if anything, the smell was even worse. There was a roar of constant chatter, intermixed with assorted animal noises, and the occasional crash of horse and oxen-drawn vehicles. We were definitely in the Past, but nowhere near far enough.

The buildings were mostly stone and timber, a mere two or three storeys high; basic blocky structures with a few lingering traces of Roman architecture. What style there was, was mostly Celtic with some Saxon, plus a whole bunch of stuff I didn't recognise. There were no pavements, only two thick streams of human traffic on either side of a deeply churned dirt road. The traffic in the middle wasn't moving much faster, being mostly horse-drawn

wagons, and rough carts pulled by equally rough people.
Hulking covered wagons groaned along, their heavy
wooden wheels sinking deeply into the muddy road. There
was mud and shit and filth everywhere, and flies hung in
thick clouds on the smoky air. Now and again a better-
dressed person would come riding through on a ca-
parisoned horse, driving everyone else out of the way. And
finally, a hunchbacked drover came along, riding a mule
and driving a herd of miniature mammoths. They were
about a foot or so high, cheeping cheerfully as they
ploughed through the mud.

"Aw, cute," said Suzie, unexpectedly. Tommy and I both
looked at her, and she stared us down with great dignity.

We looked out into the street again. "Judging by the architecture, I'd say we've ended up somewhen in the sixth
century," said Tommy. "The Roman Empire has declined
and fallen, and the dominant Celts are fighting a war
against invading Saxons." Suzie and I looked at him, and
he bristled. "I've read a lot about this period. It's really
very interesting."

"I don't care if it's downright fascinating, we shouldn't
be here," said Suzie. "We're at least five hundred years
short of when we were supposed to arrive. Somebody
screwed up."

"It can't be a mistake," said Tommy. "Old Father Time
doesn't make mistakes. In fact, he is famous for not making mistakes."

"He didn't," I said. "Somebody else interfered."

Rage blinded me for a moment, and I hit out at the wall
beside me, hurting my hand on the solid brick and not caring, almost relishing the pain. I tried to say something, but
the anger flooding through me clenched my teeth, and it
came out as a growl. Tommy started to back away. The
rage pulsed in my gut like a red-hot coal, bending me over
till I was glaring at the filthy ground. Hot, helpless tears
burned in my eyes, and I hit out at the wall again.

Suzie moved in close beside me, murmuring quiet words, bringing me back with her calm, steady presence. I was breathing hard and rough, as though I'd just been hit; but Suzie's reassuring presence slowly got through to me, and I straightened up again. I pushed the anger into the back of my head, to be released later, when I had someone to take it out on. I took a deep breath and nodded my thanks to Suzie. She nodded back. She understood.

I looked down the alley at Tommy, who stared back uncertainly. "It's all right," I said, in my best reasonable voice. "I got a little upset there, for a moment, but I'm all right now."

"Of course you are," said Tommy, moving slowly and somewhat reluctantly forward to join me. "It's just that you looked . . . very different there, for a moment, old thing. I'd never seen you look like that. Like you could kill the whole world and not give a damn."

I forced a short laugh. "You've been taking my legend far too seriously."

Tommy stared at me dubiously, then looked out at the street scene again. "Well, if nothing else, the sixth-century Nightside does seem rather more peaceful than the one we're used to."

Even as he was saying that, one hand gesturing at the slow-moving traffic, something huge and crooked, wrapped in flapping rags and long strings of cured entrails, came stalking down the middle of the road on tall stilt legs, towering over everything else. It had a head like a horse's skull, and long many-jointed arms that ended in vicious claws. It lurched down the street at some speed, cawing like a great bird, and everyone else hurried to get out of its way. One oxen-pulled wagon reacted too slowly, and the creature stamped it into the dirt road with one heavy leg. The wagon exploded under the pressure, throwing the driver forward, and the creature stamped on him, too, crushing him into bloody pulp. The oxen ran free, bellowing with fear, while the creature continued uncaringly on its way. A pack of child-sized bipedal rats rushed out of the alley mouth opposite us and swarmed all over the dead driver. They devoured the bloody mush with glee, stuffing it into their squeaking mouths with disturbingly human hands. In a matter of moments, there was nothing left of the driver but his bones, which the rats tidily gathered up and took with them as they hurried back into their alley mouth.

No-one paid any attention. The traffic kept moving, perhaps a little more urgently than it had before. On either side of the filthy road, men and women and others kept their heads down and pressed on, concerned only with their own business. Coming up the street from the other direction was a huge, flaming presence, taller than the surrounding buildings, burning so brightly it was hard to see what if anything was at the heart of the flames. It drifted through the crowds, crackling and smoking, but keeping its heat to itself. A giant millipede with a headful of snapping mouths scurried past, clinging to the sides of buildings. And a great ball of compacted maggots rolled sluggishly down the middle of the road, sucking up useful leavings from the churned-up mud. I looked at Tommy.

"Peaceful. Right. Come on, Tommy, you should know the Nightside is never peaceful for long."

"I take it we are still in the Nightside?" Suzie said suddenly. "I mean, for all we know this kind of shit is normal in the sixth century."

I pointed up at the night sky. Even through the drifting smoke, the crowded constellations of brilliant stars still burned like diamonds in the dark, and the oversized full moon looked down like a huge unblinking eye.

"All right," said Suzie. "Let's be logical about this. Who is there, powerful enough to intercept a journey through Time? Powerful enough to override Old Father Time himself and send us here? That's got to be a pretty short list."

"Just the one," I said, feeling the anger pulse briefly again. "Lilith. Dear Mother. I should have known she'd be watching me. I think perhaps . . . she's always watching me now."

"Okay," said Tommy. "That is seriously creepy. And I thought my family was weird . . . Why would Lilith want us here, in the sixth century?"

"To keep us away from the creation of the Nightside," said Suzie. "Must be something there she doesn't want us to see. Something we could use against her."

"Then why not block our trip completely?" I said. "No, I think she wanted us here. Now. She wanted me to see the Nightside as it was, before restrictions and controls and the Authorities moved it away from what she intended it to be. The only place on Earth completely free from the pressures of Heaven and Hell."

"Does Lilith exist here, now?" said Suzie.

"No. She would have been banished to Limbo by this time. I think."

"You think?" said Tommy. "I really think this is something you need to be bloody certain about, old boy, before we take another step! I demand to know exactly what the situation is before I'll even leave this alley!"

I raised an eyebrow. "Shame on you, Tommy Oblivion. I thought you existentialists didn't believe in certainties?"

"There is a time and a place for everything," said Tommy, with great dignity. "I vote for going home. Who else votes for going home?"

"Keep the noise down," said Suzie, and Tommy hushed immediately.

"We can't learn anything useful hiding in this alley," I said. "We need to get out and around, talk to people. Find out exactly when this is. I have a sneaking suspicion I know why Lilith chose the sixth century. This is, after all, the time of King Arthur and Merlin, when old gods and stranger powers still walked openly in the Nightside."

"Of course!" said Tommy, brightening up immediately. "Arthur and Camelot! The knights of the Round Table! The most heroic and romantic time in history!"

"Only if you're into poverty, bad food, and body lice," said Suzie. "You're thinking of the mediæval fantasies about Arthur, mostly written long after the fact by French aristos, who added all the knights in armour and damsels in distress. The real Arthur was only a barbarian warlord whose main innovation was using massed cavalry against the Saxons. This is a hard, dark, and brutal age, when most people lived short, squalid, and very hard-working lives, and the only people with a guaranteed future were the slaves." She stopped, as she realised Tommy and I were staring at her. "All right, I saw a documentary, okay? I like documentaries. Anyone here have a problem with that?"

"Perish the thought," I said. "If this really is the time of Camelot, I doubt they'd let the likes of us in anyway. What we have to find is a way out of here, and back in Time to where we need to be."

"We can't contact Old Father Time," said Tommy. "He really was very clear about that, remember? In fact, we have to face the extremely real possibility that we could be stranded here. Forever. I mean, who is there in this time with the sheer power necessary to send people through Time? One way or the other?"

"Merlin," I said. "The most powerful sorcerer of all. He still has his heart here, which means he's in his prime. Yes . . . Merlin Satanspawn could send us any damn when he wanted to."

"If we could persuade him," said Suzie. "Right now, he doesn't know us from a hole in the ground. He has no reason to help us. What could we offer him in return for his services?"

"News of the future," I said. "Like, for example, that someone is going to steal his heart."

"Hold everything," Suzie said immediately. "We're not supposed to make changes, remember?"

"Telling him things we know are going to happen would only help to reinforce our Present," I said. "We don't actually have to tell him about the witch Nimue."

"Does that mean we get to go to Camelot after all?" Tommy said hopefully. "I've read all the books and seen all the films. I love those stories! There must be something to the legends, or they wouldn't have survived so long."

"Camelot is a long way from the Nightside," I said. "Geographically and spiritually. If there really are knights of the Round Table, they wouldn't come to a place like this on a bet. Merlin, however, probably feels right at home here. I think we need to visit the Londinium Club, the oldest private members' club in the world. Merlin used to be a Member."

"You're packed with useful information, aren't you?" said Suzie.

I grinned. "How do you think I've stayed alive this long?"

And so we left the safety of the alleyway, and stepped out into the street. The air was thick with greasy smoke from all the burning torches in their iron holders, standing in for the hot neon of our time. We all braced ourselves, ready to react swiftly and violently if we were recognised and set on as obvious strangers who didn't belong, but no-one paid us any attention at all. Old Father Time's glamour was clearly working, making us look like everyone else. And the roar of voices around us sounded like perfectly normal colloquial English, even though it patently wasn't.

We barged through the crowds, showing them the same lack of respect they showed us. We didn't want to stand out. The street was packed with people, though a large percentage of them weren't human. There were elves in long, shimmering gowns, arrogant and disdainful. Demons out of Hell, scarlet imps with stubby horns and lashing tails, laughing nastily at things only they would find funny. A pack of tall bipedal lizards stalked through the crowd, wearing cured leather hides and brightly coloured scarves. The back of their jackets bore the legend *Dagon Rules* spelled out in silver studs. And even the humans were a pretty mixed bunch, representing races and cultures from all across the sixth-century world: Chinese, Indians, Persians, Romans, and Turks. It seemed like even here, the Nightside was still the place to be, to buy and sell all the dubious delights you couldn't get anywhere else. There were even a few obvious anomalies, people and others who clearly didn't belong in the sixth century. Since they didn't have Old Father Time's protecting glamour, they were probably dimensional travellers, or people who'd arrived accidentally, via Timeslips.

"Why are all the people here so much shorter, and well . . . ill-looking?" said Tommy.

"Poor diet," Suzie said briskly. "Vitamin deficiencies, never enough meat, or the money to buy it when there was. Plus no real medicines, and hard grinding work every day of your life, until finally you dropped in your tracks. I thought you said you were an expert on this period?"

"Only on the bits that interested me," Tommy admitted. "The romantic bits."

We carried on, sticking very close together. Everyone seemed to be carrying some kind of weapon. The smell was still appalling, and there was shit everywhere. There was no way of avoiding it, so we strode through it and tried not to think about the condition of our shoes. There were no drains, never mind sewers. And then everyone ducked as the whole street shook, and a massive dragon roared by overhead, like a low-flying jumbo jet. Most people didn't even look up. Just business as usual, in the sixth-century Nightside. I didn't like it. The streets seemed much darker here, without the usual gaudy neon. There were the torches, and oil-lamps, lanterns, foxfire moss, and more burning bodies in their hanging iron cages, but still the night seemed darker here, the shadows deeper.

There was none of the passion, none of the sardonic joie de vivre, of my time. Most of the people around us seemed to slouch along, as though afraid of being noticed. Perhaps with good reason. Things that weren't at all human lurked watchfully in most of the alley mouths we passed. I looked down one and saw a circle of possessed babies, fiery halos burning over their soft heads, drawing complex mathematical figures in the dirt at their feet and laughing in coarse adult voices. I looked away before they could notice me. A hooded monk stepped out into the road, gesturing angrily for the traffic to get out of his way. He disappeared abruptly as a hidden hole opened up beneath his feet and swallowed him up before he even had time to scream. Across the road, a dead woman in brightly coloured silks caught my eye and bumped a hip suggestively. Her eyes were very bright in her cracked grey face. No. I really didn't like this Nightside.

The dead woman was fronting a brothel, where women of all kinds, and some things that were only nominally female, called out to the passing trade with loud, carrying voices, coarse and raucous. Some of them were offering services even I hadn't heard of. I didn't feel inclined to investigate. Tommy was staring straight ahead and actually blushing, so of course the whores concentrated on him. He hunched his shoulders, and tried to pretend he wasn't there, which should have been easy enough for an existentialist. Next door to the brothel was a dark and spooky little shop selling reliquaries—the bones of saints, fragments of the True Cross, and the like. Special offer that week was apparently the skull of John the Baptist. Next to it was a smaller skull, labelled JOHN THE BAPTIST AS A CHILD. People weren't all that bright, back in the sixth century. The shop also boasted a large collection of furniture and wood carvings, supposedly produced by Jesus, or his father Joseph, or the rest of the carpenter's family.

Even in the sixth century, it seemed the Nightside traders knew the only rule that mattered, that there's one born every minute.

Inns and taverns of varying quality abounded everywhere, probably because you needed a lot of booze to get you through the strain of living in the sixth century. I'd been there less than an hour, and already I felt like biting the neck off a bottle. There were also lots of churches everywhere I looked, probably for much the same reason. Apart from the many already fragmenting Christian churches, there were also temples dedicated to Dagon, the Madonna of the Martyrs, the Carrion in Tears, and Lucifer Rising. (This last usually known as the Hedge Your Bets church.) There were also any number of Pagan and Druidic shrines, based around grotesque wood carvings and distressingly large phallic symbols. Religion was very up front and in your face in the sixth century, with preachers of every stripe haranguing the crowds from every street corner, preaching fire and brimstone and any number of variations on *My god will be back any time now, and then you'll be sorry!* The better speakers got listened to respectfully, and everyone else got pelted with . . . well, shit, mostly.

"Jesus is coming back a week this Saturday!" bellowed one preacher as we passed. "Repent now and avoid the rush!"

There were other, darker, forces abroad in the Nightside. Beings and Forces hadn't been forcibly segregated to the Street of the Gods yet. And so they walked in glory down the same streets as the rest of us, often surrounded by unearthly glows, radiating power and otherness. People hurried to get out of their way, and the slower-moving ones were often transfixed and sometimes physically transformed, just from sheer proximity to the Beings. One figure, a huge blocky shape with a great insect head, headed straight for us, only to turn aside at the last moment, actually stepping out into the road to avoid getting too close to me. It regarded me solemnly with its complex eyes, the intricate mouth parts moving slowly in what might have been a prayer.

"It sensed something about you," said Tommy.

"Probably that I'm in a really bad mood," I said. "I could have sworn the Londinium Club was around here somewhere, but it seems we're not necessarily where I thought we were."

"You mean we're lost?" said Tommy.

"Not lost, as such," I said. "Just . . . misplaced."

"We can't keep walking at random," Suzie said quietly. "Even with Old Father Time's glamour protecting us, you're still attracting attention, Taylor. Use your gift. Find the Londinium Club."

"You know I don't like to use my gift unless I have to," I said, just as quietly.

"Your Enemies aren't going to be looking for you in the sixth century," Suzie said sternly.

"We could ask people for directions," said Tommy.

"No we couldn't," said Suzie. "We want our arrival there to have the element of surprise. Use your gift, Taylor."

I thought about it. My Enemies had no reason to suspect I was here, sixteen hundred years in the Past, unless the future Suzie had told them about this little trip . . . but I couldn't keep thinking that way, or I'd go mad. So, I powered up my gift, opening the third eye deep in my mind, and Saw the world around me. There were ghosts everywhere, walking through the crowds and the buildings, pale, faded figures trapped in their temporal fugues, repeating the same endless circle of action and mourning. There were huge spirit forms, bigger than houses, striding through the material world as though they were all that was real and the rest of us only phantoms. Massive, winged things that were neither angels nor demons flapped overhead in great clouds, holding rigid formations. Unknowable forces moving on unguessable missions. I pulled my drifting thoughts together, concentrated on the Londinium Club, and found it in a moment. We weren't as far from it as I'd thought, only a few minutes' walk. Which made me think: did Lilith know that? Had she chosen where as well as when to drop me back into the world? Was I supposed to go to the Club, to meet someone or learn something? More questions with no answer.

I shut down my gift, carefully pulling my mental defences back into place. Just at the end there, I'd felt . . . Something, starting to take notice of my presence. Not my Enemies. Something of this time, big and dark and brutally powerful. Just possibly . . . Merlin Satanspawn.

I didn't mention this to the others. Just led them down the street, heading for the Londinium Club. But almost immediately our way was blocked by a ragged bunch of street thugs who appeared out of nowhere and had us surrounded in a moment. Ten of them, big and bulky swords for hire in scrappy chain mail and battered leather armour, with scarred faces and nasty smiles. They carried shortswords and axes, and long knives with blades so notched they were practically serrated. None of them topped five feet, but they all had barrel chests and arms bigger than my thighs. None of this lot had ever gone hungry. They were, however, filthy dirty, and they smelled awful. The leader was a swarthy man with a roughly cut mane of black hair. He smiled nastily, revealing several missing teeth.

"Well, well," he said easily. "Not often we gets nobility

in our part of town, do we, lads? So . . . clean, and well dressed. Slumming, are we, gents and lady? Looking for a bit of rough trade, perhaps? Well, they don't come much rougher than us, and that's a fact." His fellow thugs all laughed unpleasantly, some of them already looking at Suzie in a way I didn't like. If she killed them all, it would be bound to attract unwelcome attention. At least she hadn't drawn her shotgun yet.

"What do you want?" asked Suzie, and the leader looked at her uncertainly, taken aback by the cold, almost bored tone in her voice.

"What do we want, lady? What have you got? Just a toll, a little local taxation, for the privilege of passing through our territory."

"Your territory?" I said.

"Our territory, because we control it," said the leader. "Nothing and no-one moves through here, without paying us tribute."

"But . . ."

"Don't you argue with me, you tosser," said the thug, prodding me hard in the chest with a filthy finger. "Give us what we want, and we'll let you walk away. Piss us about, and we'll mess you up so bad people will puke just to look at you."

"How much is this going to cost us?" said Tommy, already reaching for his purse.

"Whatever coin you've got on you. Any goods we happen to take a liking to. And some quality time with this lady." The chief thug leered at Suzie. "I likes them big."

I winced on his behalf. I could feel Suzie's icy presence beside me, like the ticking of an activated bomb.

"That is a really bad idea," I said, in my best cold and dangerous voice. I relaxed a little as the thug turned his attention back to me. I could handle scumbags like him. I gave him my best hard stare. "You don't know who we are.

What we can do. So do the sensible thing and step aside, before we have to show you."

He laughed in my face, and his fellow thugs laughed with him. I was a bit taken aback. It had been a long time since anyone dared laugh in my face.

"Nice try, Taylor," said Suzie. "But they don't know your legend here. Let me deal with them."

"You can't kill them all," Tommy said immediately. "Kill them, and you kill all their potential future descendants. Who knows how many cumulative changes that could cause, back in our Present? Let me try my gift on them." He gave the leader his best winning smile. "Come, let us reason together."

"Shut your face, pretty boy," said the leader. He spat right into Tommy's face, and Tommy recoiled with a cry of disgust, his concentration shattered.

"So much for diplomacy," said Suzie, and she drew her shotgun with one easy movement.

The leader regarded the gun interestedly. "Whatever that thing is, it won't do you any good, lady. Me and the lads are protected, against all edged weapons and magical attacks. None of them can touch us."

Suzie shot the man in the face, blowing his head right off his shoulders. The body staggered back a few steps and collapsed. The other thugs looked at the body twitching on the ground, then slowly and reluctantly looked back at Suzie.

"Run away," I suggested, and they did. Suzie looked after them thoughtfully for a moment, then put her shotgun away again.

"There really wasn't any need for that," I said. "I could have dealt with them."

"Of course you could," said Suzie.

"I could!"

"You can deal with the next ones," said Suzie, as she set off down the street.

"I never get to have any fun," I said, following after.

"He's going to sulk now, isn't he?" said Tommy, hurrying to catch up.

"Oh, big time," said Suzie Shooter.

SEVEN

Some Unpleasantness at the Londinium Club

Only those personages of extreme power, prestige, or parentage can hope to gain admittance to the oldest private members' club in the world. Just fame, wealth, or knowing the right people won't do it. The Londinium Club was and is extremely exclusive, and the merely heroic or significant need not apply. There are those who say Camelot operated on a pretty similar principle. All I know for sure is that neither establishment would let me in without a fight.

We found the Londinium Club easily enough. It was a large, dignified building in a much more salubrious area of the Nightside. The traffic was quieter, the pedestrians were of a much-better-dressed class, and there wasn't a brothel anywhere in sight. Still a hell of a lot of shit in the street, mind. I stopped before the front door of the Club, and looked the place over. The exterior looked pretty much the same as the last time I'd seen it, back in my Present. Old, old stone decorated with sexually explicit Roman bas-reliefs, surrounding a large and very solid oak door. And when I say sexually explicit, I'm talking about the kind of images that would have made Caligula blush, and maybe dash for the vomitorium. Suzie regarded the designs calmly, while Tommy started searching his pockets for a paper and pencil, to make notes.

Standing in front of the main entrance was the Doorman, a solid and immovable presence whose function and delight it was to keep out the unworthy. He was protected against any form of attack, by Powers known and unknown, was strong enough to tear a bull in half, and was, supposedly, immortal. Certainly he was still around in my time, large as life and twice as obnoxious. The Doorman was a snob's snob, and he gloried in it. He was currently a short, stocky man in a purple Roman toga, with bare muscular arms folded firmly across an imposing chest. I half expected him to be wearing a sash saying THEY SHALL NOT PASS. He stood proudly erect, nose in the air, but his eyes missed nothing. He'd already noticed us.

"I could shoot him," said Suzie.

"Don't even think it," I said quickly. "The Doorman is *seriously* protected. And besides, we already know you didn't kill him, because I already met him, back in the Present, during my last case."

"I hate circular reasoning like that," said Suzie. "Let's shoot him anyway and see what happens."

"Let's not," I said, very firmly. "This is the kind of place where they have you impaled for being late with your membership dues. For once, our usual tactics of brute force and ignorance will not win the day. We're going to have to talk our way past him."

"Get to the front, Tommy," said Suzie. "You're on."

"I knew you were going to say that," said Tommy.

We approached the front door, and the Doorman actually

stepped forward to block our way, one meaty hand held out in warning.

"All right, that's as far as you go. You three are not at all welcome here. Ever. I still remember you from the trouble you caused the last time you were here, some two hundred years ago."

"Guess where we're going next," murmured Tommy.

"Shut up," I hinted.

"We must have made a pretty big impression on the man," said Suzie.

"You always do, Suzie," I said generously. I smiled at the Doorman. "Look, I know we're not actually Members, but we only want to pop in for a moment and maybe ask a few questions. Then we'll be gone and out of your life. Won't that be nice?"

"Members only means Members only," growled the Doorman. "Leave now. Or I will be compelled to use force."

Suzie started to reach for her shotgun. "No!" I said urgently. "When I said the Doorman was protected, I meant by everyone who's a Club Member. And that means he can draw on the powers of sorcerers, elves, and minor godlings to stop us."

"Ah," said Suzie. "So shooting him wouldn't work?"

"No."

"I've got these special grenades . . ."

"No!" I turned to Tommy. "You're up. Mess with the man's head."

Tommy Oblivion stepped forward, smiling confidently. The Doorman considered him warily.

"We're not from around here, old thing," Tommy said easily. "You probably already noticed that. In fact, we're not from this place, or this time. We're from the future. Some sixteen hundred years from now, to be exact. And in that future, my friends and I are Members of your Club."

"What?" said the Doorman. Whatever he'd been expecting to hear, that clearly wasn't it.

"We are Members, where and when we come from. Which means, technically speaking, we are also Members here and now. Once a Member, always a Member, right?"

The Doorman frowned as he thought about that. Thinking clearly wasn't what he did best. He brightened up as an idea came to him.

"If you're a Member," he said slowly, "you know the secret handshake."

Tommy raised an eyebrow. "There is no secret handshake, dear fellow. But there is a secret password, which I have written down on this piece of paper."

He showed the Doorman his empty hand. The Doorman looked at it closely, moving his lips as though reading, then nodded reluctantly and stepped back to let us pass. He was frowning heavily, as though his head hurt. The oak door swung open before us, and I led the way into the lobby beyond. Once the door was safely shut behind us, I looked at Tommy.

"You made him see something that wasn't there."

"Of course," said Tommy. "It's my gift to be convincing. Besides, in some alternate time-line we probably are Members. Or at least, I am."

I sniffed. "I still didn't get to do anything."

"You will, you will," Suzie said soothingly. "This place is bound to be packed with all the kinds of people you detest the most. I'm sure you'll find someone worth upsetting in some thoroughly appalling and vindictive way."

I sniffed again, unconvinced, and looked around the Club lobby. It still had some of the old Roman magnificence I remembered from my last visit, with gleaming tiled walls and marble pillars, but instead of thick carpeting on the floor there were only trampled rushes, strewn here and there in clumps, and the high ceiling had been covered in

thick Druidic designs that looked like they'd been daubed
with woad. The only lighting came from oversized oil-
lamps, and the perfumed air was hot and flat and a little
stale. There was a sense that the Club had declined somewhat from its original glory days in Roman times and had
yet to develop its own style. Certainly the Romans would
never have put up with this much mess. The rushes on the
floor looked like they hadn't been changed in days, and
there were smoke and soot streaks on the walls above the oil-
lamps. Stains here and there suggested spillages of all kinds.

A servant, or more probably a slave, given the iron collar bolted around his neck, came forward hesitantly to
greet us. Something about us clearly upset him because he
stopped dead in his tracks, and yelled *Security!* at the top
of his lungs. A panel slammed open in one of the walls, revealing a hidden alcove, from whose dark depths a hideous
crone emerged, spitting and cackling. She was clearly
some kind of witch, with stray magics sputtering and discharging around her clawed hands. She was a twisted figure in rags and tatters, with a heavy iron chain leading back
into the alcove from the slave collar around her scrawny
throat. She lurched towards us, her eyes wide with madness
and thwarted rage. I could feel the power building around
her as she muttered ancient words in a deep guttural voice,
and I knew that as soon as she oriented on us, we'd be in
deep shit.

So I raised my gift only long enough to find the spell
that kept her from breaking her chain and slave collar, and
removed it. The collar snapped open, and the chain fell
away from her. The witch broke off in mid spell, and
lurched to a halt. She kicked tentatively at the chain on the
floor, and it rattled helplessly. The witch grinned slowly,
revealing a handful of yellowed teeth, then she turned to
look at the slave who'd called her out of the alcove. He
turned and ran, but he was a grease spot on the floor before
he'd made half a dozen steps.

The witch raised her clawed hands and howled a ululating shriek of triumph and vengeance long desired. Vicious spells detonated on the air all around her, blasting holes in the walls and floor. Armed men came running from all directions, and the witch turned to face them with vindictive glee on her shrivelled face. Fires started, gale winds blew, and the armed men started exploding, blowing apart in showers of bloody gobbets.

"Happy now you've done something?" said Suzie.

"Very," I said.

Unnoticed in the general chaos, we strolled across the lobby and let ourselves into the dining room. We shut the door firmly behind us, and the din of the pandemonium shut off immediately. No-one looked up as we came in. Whatever the noise was, that was slaves' business and nothing to do with the Members. Most of them were reclining on couches to eat, in the old Roman style, giving their full attention to excellent food and drink, and good company. And probably paying more for that one meal than most people in the sixth century made in their entire lives.

Some of the diners still wore the old-fashioned Roman toga, but most wore simple tunics, with or without leather armour and trappings. The majority of the diners were human, but there were also quite a few elves, looking studiedly disdainful of their surroundings even as they gorged themselves on human delicacies, and a handful of gargoyles eating live mice and playing with their food in a quite distressing manner. The diners were being served by male and female slaves, some barely more than children, all of them wearing fixed, empty expressions. They were naked save for the iron collars round their throats, and all of them carried scars and whip marks.

"Slavery," said Tommy, his voice full of revulsion. "I knew about it, knew there were slaves even in King Arthur's time, but I never really . . . some of them are just kids!"

"This is the way things were," I said. "And will be, for centuries after. And get that look out of your eye, Tommy. I only freed that witch to provide a distraction. We start freeing slaves on a grand scale, and you can bet all the Powers here will rise up against us. We can't change a whole culture. That's not why we're here. And besides, we don't dare make any big changes if we want to return to our own Present, remember?"

"I remember," said Tommy. "But I don't have to like it."

There was an edge in his voice, a cold anger that hadn't been there before. I liked him better for it.

"Join the club," I said.

"I don't see any sign of Merlin," said Suzie, all business as usual. "And I'm pretty sure he'd stand out, even in this crowd. Want me to grab somebody and shake some answers out of them?"

"I think it might be better if I was to ask a few polite questions," I said. "On the grounds that I have at least heard of diplomacy."

A tall, elegant, and distinctly supercilious type was already heading in our direction, threading his way gracefully between the couches, bestowing smiles and sweet nothings on the people he passed. He wore a blindingly white tunic and no iron collar. He came to a halt before me, dismissing Suzie and Tommy with a mere flick of the eyes, and raised a painted eyebrow a carefully calculated fraction of an inch.

"I am the Steward," he said. "And you are very definitely not Members. Not ever likely to be. I don't know how you got in here, but you will have to leave immediately."

I smiled at him. "You know all that chaos and destruction that's currently going on in your lobby? All the fires and explosions and parts of deceased security people flying through the air? I did that."

"Take a couch," the Steward said resignedly. "I suppose you'll be wanting something to eat, before security

can put together a big enough force to restore order and
throw the three of you out of here? Today's specials are
larks' tongues in aspic and baby mice stuffed with hum-
mingbird tongues."

Tommy winced. "Do you have anything that doesn't involve tongues?"

"Don't sit down, Suzie," I said. "We're not staying for
dinner."

"You might not be," said Suzie. She'd already snatched
a breaded drumstick from a nearby diner and was chewing
it with a thoughtful look on her face. The diner sensibly decided not to make a fuss.

"We're looking for the sorcerer Merlin," I said to the
Steward. "Merlin Satanspawn. He is a Member here,
isn't he?"

"Only because nobody dared blackball him," said the
Steward, his lip curling. "But even so, he doesn't dare show
his face here any more. Not since the King and most of his
knights fell in battle, in the last great contest against the
bastard Mordred's forces; and all because Merlin wasn't
there to support his King. The pretender died, too, his
forces scattered, but still the age of Logres is over. Camelot
is simply a castle now, with an empty Throne and a broken
Table, and the ideals of the Court are already falling apart.
The end of an age; and all because one man wasn't where
he should have been. You want Merlin Satanspawn? Try a
tavern. Any tavern."

There was just enough bitterness in his voice to make
him convincing. I gathered Suzie and Tommy up with my
eyes and led them back out of the dining room. And as I
left I raised my gift, found the spell that held the iron collars around the slaves' throats, and undid it. The collars
sprang open, and the magic that had kept the slaves docile
fell away in a moment. Some of the slaves attacked the diners, while others ran for their lives and their freedom. The
dining room quickly descended into chaos.

"You big softie," said Suzie.

"There's some shit I just will not put up with," I admitted.

We strolled back through the lobby, most of which was on fire. There was no sign of the witch anywhere, but a great crevice had opened up in the middle of the floor, belching out soot and cinders and smoke that smelled strongly of brimstone. *My work here is done,* I thought, a little smugly. We nodded cheerfully to the Doorman as we passed him, then stood together in the street wondering where we should try next. God alone knew how many taverns, inns, and hole-in-the-wall drinking dives there were in the sixth-century Nightside, and I really didn't feel like searching them all. On the other hand, I also didn't feel like using my gift again. I'd been using it far too often, almost casually, and that was dangerous. Flare up often enough in the dark, and my Enemies would be bound to notice me, no matter how far I was in the Past. From their future vantage point, I was always in the Past.

"Strangefellows," I said suddenly. "That's where Merlin will be. Or whatever the oldest bar in the world is currently called. I remember the Merlin of our time telling me that he often drank there, to get away from the overbearing niceness of Camelot. That's probably why he chose to be buried in the bar's cellars, after he was killed. Yes. That's where we'll find him." I looked at Suzie. "You're frowning. Why are you frowning, Suzie?"

"Lilith brought us here, right?" said Suzie. "Had to be a reason. Could be because she wanted us to meet with Merlin. He is the leading major player in this Nightside. And if that's so, do we want to do what she wants us to do?"

"I'm past caring," I said. "All this guessing and double-guessing. I want to get this over with and get out of here. I want to witness the creation of the Nightside, so I can get my answers, so I can finally be rid of Lilith's influence in my life. I want this to be over!"

"Easy, John, easy," said Tommy, and it was only then that I realised my voice had risen to a shout.

"It'll never be over, John," said Suzie, as kindly as she could. "You know that."

"I can't believe that," I said. "I can't afford to believe that."

There was a long pause, then Tommy said, "If we can't find Merlin here in the Nightside . . . could we please try Camelot? I've always dreamed of visiting that legendary Castle, seeing the famous Round Table, and—"

"You heard the Steward," I said, perhaps a little roughly. "It's a mess there right now. All the heroes are dead, and the dream's over. We'll find Merlin in Strangefellows. Where else could such a disgraced man go to drown his sorrows in peace?"

"All right," said Tommy, resignedly. "Fire up your gift and point us in the right direction."

"There's an easier way," I said. I looked back at the Doorman. "The oldest bar in the world. What's it called, and where is it?"

He gave me a withering look. "Give me one good reason why I should assist you?"

"Because," I said, "if you don't, my companions and I will hang around here for hours and hours, acting cranky and lowering the tone."

"The bar you're looking for is called Avalon," said the Doorman. And he provided us with very clear and distinct directions, just to be sure we wouldn't have to come back and ask him again.

EIGHT

Sacrifices for the Greater Good

Not all that surprisingly, the Avalon bar turned out to be situated in a really sleazy area, even for the Nightside. The lighting was bad, the streets were filthy, and so were the people. There were bodies lying everywhere, dead or drunk or demonically possessed, with a fight on every street corner and couples humping in doorways. The sixth century was a particularly unselfconscious age, when it came to sin. I saw one preacher getting a blow job, even as he pontificated on the evils of the Gnostic heresies. No-one bothered us, though. It seemed word of our exploits and notoriously short tempers had got around. Whatever century you're in, nothing travels faster in the Nightside than gossip and bad news.

I still couldn't get used to having to step over lepers, though. Even if they were always very polite about it.

Avalon itself turned out to be a large and chunky tower constructed entirely of stained and discoloured bones, held together by some unseen but not entirely unfelt force. Just looking at the tower put a chill in my heart, and in my bones. Not least because I'd seen it once before, when it manifested briefly in Strangefellows, during my previous case. Just before everything went to hell, and the future Suzie turned up to kill me. I couldn't stop myself from glancing at her, and she caught my gaze.

"What's wrong, John?" she said quietly. "You've been looking at me strangely ever since we started this case. Do you know something I don't?"

"Always," I said, forcing a smile. "But nothing you need to worry about."

We headed for the base of the bone tower. It stood out against the night sky like the tomb of a dead god, unnatural and ill-omened. Approaching it felt like stepping down into an open grave. The door was a simple dark opening, with nothing beyond but silence and an impenetrable darkness. Anywhen else I would probably have been worried, but I was more concerned with Suzie. She knew I was hiding something from her, but how could I tell her? What good could it do? And I couldn't escape the feeling that simply by talking about it aloud, by accepting it, I might make that future more possible, more probable. I strode straight into the dark opening, while guilt twisted in my gut like a living thing, and Suzie and Tommy followed right after me.

The darkness quickly gave way to a friendly amber glow, the bar itself just a sprawling, smoke-filled room, roughly the same size as the bar back in my time. There were no windows, and the oil-lamps and torches filled the hot sweaty air with a thick, defusing smoke, but the general effect was not unpleasant. Once I was inside, it was clear the bone tower exterior was a glamour, designed to scare off unwanted visitors. I wandered unhurriedly between the packed long wooden tables, and everyone else ostentatiously minded their own business. Just as in my time, this was not a bar where you went for company and good fellowship.

Over in one corner, a number of musical instruments were playing themselves, providing basic but pleasant background music.

The customers were the usual unusual suspects, the men and women wearing a collection of clothing from all kinds of cultures and backgrounds. Anywhere else they would have been fighting each other to the death over religion or customs or plain foreignness, but not in Avalon. Humans stuck together in the face of so many other alternate threats. Three witches in embroidered saris sat huddled together, giggling like nasty children as they animated a number of stick figures and made them dance madly on the tabletop before them. Two seriously ugly Redcap goblins were knife-fighting, while a circle of onlookers cheered them on and laid bets on the outcome. Two lepers were playing knucklebones with their own fingers. Two heretical priests were arm-wrestling each other over the true nature of the Holy Ghost, and spitting obscenities at each other through clenched teeth. And in the middle of the bar-room floor, two smoke ghosts were dancing together sadly and elegantly, their smoke bodies blown apart by every passing breeze, but always re-forming.

And sitting very much alone in a corner, with his back to two walls, that mighty and renowned sorcerer, Merlin Satanspawn. The greatest magus of this or any other age. Who was born to be the Antichrist but declined the honour. You couldn't miss him. His sheer presence dominated the whole bar, even sitting there quietly, staring into his drink. Having him around was like sharing the room with a bloody street accident, or a man slowly hanging himself.

He didn't look much like the Merlin I knew, the dead man with a ragged hole in his chest where his heart used to be. Who had been buried for centuries in the cellars under

Strangefellows but occasionally deigned to manifest through his unhappy descendant, Alex Morrisey. This man was whole and hale and bloody scary with it. He was a big man in an age of small men, easily six feet tall and broad-shouldered, wrapped in a long scarlet robe with golden collar trimmings. Under a thick and tangled mane of bright red hair, stiffened here and there with clay, his face was heavy-boned and almost aggressively ugly. Two fires burned brightly in his eye sockets, leaping crimson flames that licked up past his heavy eyebrows. *They say he has his fa-ther's eyes* . . . Most of his face and bare hands were covered with curling Druidic tattoos in dark blue hues. His long, thick fingernails looked a whole lot like claws. And I re-alised that the Merlin I'd known before had only been a pale shadow of the real thing, this huge and vital man crackling with power and awful presence.

I'd meant to walk up to him, introduce myself, and de-mand his help; but suddenly I didn't feel at all like doing that. I felt much more like slinking away before he noticed me, and maybe hiding under a table for a while until I got my confidence back. The man was dangerous. You only had to look at him to know he could blast the soul right out of your body with a single Word. A quick glance at Suzie and Tommy showed they were having serious second thoughts, too, and that immediately put some backbone back into me. Gods or sorcerers or Things from Elsewhere, you couldn't show fear in front of them or they'd walk right over you. You had to find their weak spot . . .

"Let's buy the man a drink," I said.

"Couldn't hurt," said Suzie.

"Let's buy him lots of drinks," said Tommy. "And I think I could force down a few myself."

We made our way to the bar at the back of the room. It was the exact same long wooden bar from our time, though the assortment of drinks set out behind it looked to be far more limited. And the nearest thing they had to bar snacks were rats impaled on sticks. A few of them were still twitching, even though they'd been doused in melted cheese. Serving behind the bar was a sweet dreamy girl in a faded Roman-style dress. She had long dark hair, huge eyes, and a winning smile.

"That's a really first-class glamour you're wearing," she said cheerfully. "Would probably have fooled anybody else, but I've been touched by divinity. Frequently. Not from around here, are you, dears?"

"No," I said. "We've travellers, from the future."

"Gosh," said the barmaid. "How exciting! What's it like?"

"Noisy," I said. "And a bit faster paced, but otherwise pretty much the same."

"Well there's a relief," said the barmaid. "Why not have a whole bunch of drinks? Don't worry if you're supposed to be in disguise; I only saw through your glamour because I'm sort of godly. I'm Hebe. I used to be cup-bearer to the old Roman gods, until their faith base declined along with the Empire, and they decided to move on to pastures new. Didn't offer to take me with them, the ungrateful bastards. I decided I was too young to retire from the booze-slinging business, so I took over this place, and now I dispense good cheer to one and all. Go on, dears, get a little bit that way. Good booze is good for the soul. Trust me; I know these things."

I glanced around and confirmed that all three of us were willing enough to experiment in that direction, but unfortunately it turned out that the bar's stock consisted almost entirely of various forms of wine and mead. We sampled a fair selection of both, in the spirit of scientific enquiry, but the wines were all thin and bitter, and the meads were all thick and sweet. Often with bits floating in them. We pulled various faces and made thoughtful noises, but Hebe wasn't fooled.

"Booze is better in the future?"

"Let's say . . . more extreme. Is this really all you have?"

"Well," said Hebe, "I do stock a few special items, for the discerning customer with an educated palate and more money than sense. Winter Wine, Bacchus's Old Peculier, and Angel's Tears. Merlin's really fond of that one."

"The very stuff," I said. "One bottle of Angel's Tears, if you please."

It was only when she started rummaging for a bottle under the bar that it suddenly occurred to me to wonder how I was going to pay for it, along with all the other drinks we'd already consumed. Whatever they used for currency in the sixth century, I sure as hell hadn't brought any with me. I stuck my hands in my coat pockets, out of habit, and to my surprise discovered a heavy bag of coins I certainly hadn't put there. I pulled out the leather bag and opened the drawstrings, and blinked stupidly at a whole mess of gold and silver coins.

"Now that's impressive," said Suzie. "What did you do, pick someone's pocket at the Londinium Club?"

"Didn't think of that," I said. "But luckily, it seems Old Father Time thinks of everything."

I offered Hebe one of the larger gold coins, and she bit it expertly between her back teeth before accepting it with a smile. In return I received a slender glass phial of a pale blue liquor and absolutely no change. Bright sparks of light sputtered on and off in the slowly stirring liquor.

"Angel's Tears," said Hebe, wrinkling her adorably pert nose. "Awful stuff. It's only drinkable for a short period, then it goes off, and we have to bury it in consecrated ground."

"I want to try some of that," said Suzie.

"No you don't," I said very firmly. "This is for Merlin." I looked at Hebe. "What's his current state of mind?"

"Dangerous," said Hebe. "I don't think he's said half a dozen words to anyone since the King died. He's been here drinking for three solid weeks now. Doesn't eat, doesn't sleep. No-one bothers him, because if they do, he turns them into . . . things."

"What kind of things?" Tommy said warily.

"I'm not sure if they have a name or designation, as such," Hebe said judiciously. "But whatever they are, they don't look at all happy about being it. If I had to describe them, I'd say . . . ambulatory snot creatures."

"Maybe you'd better talk to Merlin alone, Taylor," said Tommy, and Suzie nodded solemnly.

"I wouldn't recommend talking to him at all," said Hebe. "The witch Nimue is the only one who can do anything with him these days."

I looked quickly at Suzie and Tommy. We all knew that name. The legendary traitorous witch Nimue, who captivated Merlin's heart, then stole it, ripping it literally out of his chest. The witch who seduced and betrayed Merlin while his defences were down and condemned him to death.

"Let's go and talk to the drunken dangerous sorcerer," I said. "Before things get even more complicated."

"Would you like to leave any message for your next of kin?" said Hebe.

"Don't worry about us," said Suzie. "We can be pretty dangerous, too, when we put our minds to it."

We turned and looked at Merlin Satanspawn, and it was like looking at a wild animal that had eaten its keeper and burst out of its cage.

"After you," said Tommy.

We headed towards Merlin's table in the corner. The bar got very quiet as they realised what was happening.

I raised my gift almost but not quite to the point of manifesting, just in case, and I could feel Tommy doing the same. Suzie already had a grenade in one hand, with one finger slipped casually through the ring-pull. And then Merlin turned suddenly and looked at us, and it was like walking into a brick wall. All three of us slammed to a halt, held where we were, transfixed by the flames leaping in his eye-sockets. Everyone in the whole bar held their breath. And then I slowly held up the phial of Angel's Tears, so Merlin could see it clearly, and his mouth twitched briefly in something like a smile. I took a deep breath and moved forward again, but Suzie and Tommy remained where they were, unmoving. I stopped short of the table and gave Merlin my best hard stare. Never let the bastards see you're intimidated.

"Let my friends go, Merlin. They're part of what I have to say to you."

Merlin actually raised an eyebrow. "I've killed men for speaking to me in that tone of voice, just to watch them die. Why should I indulge you, boy?"

"Because I'm Lilith's only son. And we half-breeds should stick together."

He nodded slowly, though whether he was impressed by my brass nerves or my mother's name was hard to tell. I grabbed a chair and sat down opposite him. Suzie and Tommy moved cautiously forward and chose to stand behind me. I was grateful for their presence. I've bluffed some powerful Beings with an empty hand before, but this was Merlin Satanspawn, dammit. I was glad I was sitting down, so he couldn't see my legs shaking under the table. I offered him the phial of Angel's Tears, and he wrapped a huge hand around it and hefted it thoughtfully. He pulled the cork out with his large, blocky teeth and poured the heavy blue liquor into the silver goblet before him. The stuff smelled awful. Merlin noticed my reaction and smiled unpleasantly.

"It's an acquired taste. Much like angel flesh. Talk to me, Lilith's son. What do you want with me?"

I introduced myself and my companions, and gave him the quick expurgated version. He nodded now and again, seeming more interested in his drink. The rest of the bar was still watching us, but the general chatter had begun again, now it was clear there weren't going to be any sudden and unfortunate transformations in the immediate future. I finished my tale, and Merlin nodded slowly.

"Interesting story," he said. "If I cared, I'd be impressed. But I don't care about anything, any more. Not since . . . he died. He was the best of us all. He gave me my faith in Humanity. He made me a better person, just by believing I was; and I would rather have died than disappoint him. Now he's gone, because I failed him, when he needed me most. The dream I dreamed is over; his dream of Reason and Respect for all, of Might for Right. A brief light, in a dark age."

He was still brooding over that when King Arthur appeared out of nowhere. I knew it was he. It couldn't have been anyone else. Arthur, the Great Bear of Briton, standing suddenly before our table, a huge blocky man in well-polished armour, under heavy bearskins and leather strappings. The sword at his side shone with supernatural brilliance. He had a strong, kind, somewhat sad face, but there was something about him . . . a natural majesty, a solid and uncompromising honour, a simple goodness, strong and true . . . I would have followed him to the gates of Hell and back. All across the bar, people knelt to him. Human and inhuman, they bent the knee and bowed the head to the one and only man they all worshipped and feared and adored. King Arthur of the Britons.

I slipped off my chair and knelt and bowed, too, along with Suzie and Tommy. It never occurred to me to do anything else.

Even though he wasn't really there. We could all tell he wasn't really, physically, present in Avalon. His image was only intermittently solid and complete, wavering from unfelt breezes, and sometimes you could see right through him. But he wasn't a ghost; there was a definite vitality to the man. He burned with life, with purpose, and with majesty. No, this was a sending, a mental projection of his image, his self, from some other place. He seemed distracted, unfocussed, looking vaguely about him, though his gaze always returned to Merlin, sitting at his table.

"Merlin," said Arthur, and his voice came from far and far away, like a whisper in a church gallery. "Old friend, old mentor. I have come a long way to find you. I sent word to every place I thought you might be, but you were at none of them. You've gone after her, haven't you? Even though I told you not to. It is the night before my greatest battle, and I have taken to my tent alone, that I go dream walking, in search of you." He smiled, kindly, sadly. "You tried so hard to teach me magic, but I never had the gift for it. So I had to settle for being a soldier, and a King. I always wondered if perhaps I disappointed you, in that."

"No," said Merlin. "You never disappointed me, Arthur. Never."

"But time is short, and my need is desperate, so I turn back to old, half-remembered lessons, of sendings and dream walkings. And here I am, and here you are. Wherever this is. I can't see anything clearly but you, old friend. I need your help, for the battle tomorrow. My son Mordred has raised a great force against me. Perhaps the largest army this land has ever seen. I have called together all my knights and all my soldiers, and all good men and true; and still I fear it will not be enough. My son . . . and I know you never accepted him as my son, but a man knows his own blood . . . My son Mordred has summoned up creatures ancient, vile, and powerful to stand with him. I need you, Merlin. I need your magic, your power. Why aren't you here?"

"Because I was busy," said Merlin. "Busy indulging myself in my greatest failing; my hunger for revenge."

"I can see you, but I can't hear you," said Arthur. "Merlin! Merlin!"

"You got the time-co-ordinates mixed up again," said

Merlin. "You never were any good at mathematics, boy. You've come to me too late. Too late."

"You should have warned me, Merlin," said Arthur. "Of the price I'd have to pay, for being King. For Camelot, and the Round Table and the Great Dream. A wife who loved another. A son who never loved me. Justice for everyone, but never for me. Why didn't you warn me, Merlin?"

"I never promised you justice," said Merlin. "Just a chance to be a legend. My poor Arthur . . ."

"I can't stay," said Arthur. "The winds between the worlds are pulling at me, drawing me back. My men are waiting. At first light, we go out to battle. And to victory, God willing. No doubt you have a good reason for being wherever you are. We'll talk about this later, after the battle. It was always my greatest regret that we never had the time to talk properly, after I became King."

He said something else, but it was lost as his image faded slowly away, like a ghost at the dawn, until he was gone. Slowly, everyone in the bar got up off their knees and went about their business again. None of them even looked at Merlin. I got back onto my chair. Merlin was staring into his drink again.

"I should have been there," he said. "But I was so angry, all I could think of was revenge. On that traitorous bitch, Mordred's mother. Morgan La Fae. Arthur took them in, gave them everything, and together they destroyed everything Arthur and I had built. It took me years to find proof against them, then they ran, like rats. Mordred to his secretly prepared forces. Morgan to the old woods and ancient places, and the Powers she worshipped there. I couldn't bear the thought of her escaping, of her getting away with it. So I left Arthur to raise his army, while I went after Morgan. I was so sure I'd be back in time. But Morgan led me a merry chase, and killing the bitch took so much more out of me than I'd expected. By the time I got back, it was all over. The battle field was soaked in blood, and there were bodies piled up, for as far as the eye could see. The few surviving knights looked at me like it was all my fault, and maybe it was. They called me traitor and false friend, coward, abomination. They wouldn't even let me see his body. I could have killed them all, with a look or a word, made them suffer as I suffered, but I didn't. Because Arthur wouldn't have wanted that.

"I couldn't even cry for him. My eyes aren't made that way. But if I could weep, I would. For my King, my friend. My son, in every way that mattered."

I was still trying to work out what I could say to that, to a loss so great, to a grief and a guilt so deep, when a bright young voice called out Merlin's name. We all looked round as a bright and bubbly young thing came tripping through the bar, smiling and waving in all directions, but heading remorselessly for our table. She was small, blonde, and busty, wide-eyed and wide-mouthed, clothed in shimmering silk that looked very out of place in these rough surroundings. She bounced along like she was full of all the energy in the world, blazing with fresh young sexuality. She couldn't have been much more than sixteen. She was pretty, in an obvious sort of way, with a third eye tattooed in blue on her forehead. More Celtic and Druidic designs curled up and down her bare arms. She strode straight up to our table, threw herself into Merlin's lap, laughing into his glowering face and tugging playfully at his long beard.

"Oh, sweetie, look at that long face! Who's been upsetting you this time? Honestly, darling, I can't leave you alone for a minute. It's a good thing your little Nimue is here, to take care of you!" She kissed him artlessly, took a sip of his drink, pulled a face, and squeaked a few baby swear words, then kissed him again and called him a *Silly old bear*. Merlin slowly smiled, then laughed and played with her breasts while she giggled happily. I was trying hard to keep my mouth from dropping open. This was the legendary witch Nimue?

"This is Nimue," said Merlin, after a while, looking back at me. "My only comfort. Nimue, this is John Taylor."

She pouted childishly at me. "Are you the one that's been upsetting my sweetie? Shame on you! Go on, Merlin; show me how to turn him into something squelchy."

"Hush, child," said Merlin. "He's come a long way to beg my help. I'm still considering whether to do anything about it."

"This is the witch Nimue?" I said, somehow keeping the disbelief out of my voice.

"Indeed," said Merlin, removing one hand from inside her dress to scratch at his great beak of a nose. "A renegade Druidic priestess, and now my student in the magical arts. Of all my various roles, I have always enjoyed that of teacher the most."

"That's not all you enjoy, you randy old goat," said Nimue, snuggling contentedly up against the sorcerer. "Running away from the Druids was the best thing I ever did." She looked plaintively at me with her huge dark eyes. "My parents sold me to them when I was only a child, but I never really fitted in. I was quite keen on the nature worship, and running around the forest with no clothes on, and having lots of sex to ensure the fertility of the crops, but I found all the human sacrifices and *Nail his guts to the old oak tree* very icky. So I grabbed a bit of everything valuable that wasn't actually nailed down, and left." She pouted suddenly, and playfully boxed Merlin's ear. "And you promised you'd teach me magic. Real magic. When are you going to teach me some real magic, sweetie?"

"All in good time," said Merlin, taking one of her earlobes playfully between his teeth.

"That's all very well, honey," said Nimue, pushing him away and sitting up straight on his lap. "But in the meantime, I have various tradespeople who insist on being paid. A girl has to live, darling . . ."

There was a lot more of this. Nimue chattered away,

while Merlin smiled on her indulgently, and the two of them cuddled like teenagers. I didn't know what to say. This was Nimue? The powerful and crafty witch who stole Merlin's heart and ran off with it? This cute and harmless little gold-digger? I turned round in my chair to look at Suzie and Tommy, but they were clearly as thrown as I, so I got up, excused myself to Merlin and Nimue, who barely nodded in return, and the three of us retired to another table to think things over. It was clear Merlin wouldn't be paying us any attention for a while anyway.

"She seems like a sweet young thing," said Tommy. "Though I can't help thinking he's a bit old for her."

"She's not nearly as helpless as she makes out," said Suzie. "I've seen her sort before, taking some old fool for everything he's got."

"The man's domestic arrangements are none of our business," I said firmly. "What matters is that for all his drunken self-pity, that man is clearly still a powerful sorcerer. If anyone in this period can send us further back in Time, it's him."

"But you heard him," said Tommy. "He doesn't care about us, or our problems."

"Don't care was made to care," I said.

Suzie looked at me for a long moment. "That's pretty hard-core, even for you, Taylor. I mean, this is *Merlin* we're talking about. The Devil's only begotten son. We don't have a hope in Hell of compelling him to do anything he doesn't want to."

"I've been thinking about that," I said. "And it occurred to me that since this witch Nimue is obviously quite incapable of stealing Merlin's heart . . . maybe we could do it instead. And with the heart in our hands, Merlin would have to do whatever we told him to."

They both looked at me like I was crazy.

"You're crazy!" said Tommy. "I mean, full-blown out of your head crazy! We're actually supposed to rip the living heart out of his chest? Merlin? The most powerful sorcerer of this or any other age? *You're crazy!*"

"Don't hold back, Tommy," I said. "Tell me what you really think."

"Even if we could incapacitate Merlin," said Suzie, "it would be pretty messy . . . I've removed a few hearts in my time, but I never had to worry about them being in good enough shape to put them back again."

"Don't encourage him," said Tommy. "We'll all end up as snot creatures."

"It's not as impractical as it sounds," I said patiently. "A lot of sorcerers would remove their hearts and hide them elsewhere, behind powerful magical protections, for safe-keeping. That way, no matter what happened, they couldn't be killed as long as the heart was still safe. Using the correct rites, Merlin's heart can be removed without killing him, and once we have it, we'll be in control. Look—we know someone's going to steal the heart, at some stage. Why not us? We'll do less damage with it than most."

"I don't like this," Tommy said flatly. "I really don't like this. In fact, I straight out hate it."

"He's got a point," said Suzie. "If we interfere in the Past . . ."

"Who's interfering?" I said. "We *know* someone took Merlin's heart. We've all seen the hole in his chest. You could say by doing this, we're helping to reinforce the Present we came from."

"I don't care," Tommy said stubbornly. "This isn't right. We're using the man, maybe even killing him, just to get what we want."

"What we need," I said. "We have to stop Lilith, by whatever means, to save the Nightside, and probably the world as well."

"But . . . what about this, as another alternative," said Tommy, leaning eagerly forward across the table. "Remember the knights in armour we saw in Old Father

Time's Waiting Room? The ones from a future where Camelot and its dream still held sway? What if we are here . . . to bring about that future? We have a chance to change *everything*. Camelot doesn't have to fall, here and now. If Merlin never lost his heart, and most of his power . . . maybe we could bring him back to sanity and pride. Give him a reason to live again. We could tell him what's coming, warn him of the Dark Ages that will last for almost a thousand years, if he doesn't act to prevent it. Advised by us, he could rise to power and influence again, and backed by him, Camelot could rebuild itself. King Arthur's legacy could continue!"

"Advised by us," I said. "Don't you mean, advised by you, Tommy? You're the one who's always been fascinated by Arthur, and this time."

"All right, why not?" Tommy said defiantly. "I've always loved the legends of Camelot. It was a better world under Arthur, and a brighter world, than we have ever known before or since! Think of what fifteen centuries of progress under Arthur's legacy could bring about . . . Maybe we wouldn't even need a Nightside any more."

"You're reaching now," I said. "We have to stick with what we know. We know Lilith is planning to destroy the Nightside, and most likely the rest of the world with it. I've seen that future, Tommy, and I'm ready to do anything at all to prevent it. That world is every nightmare you've ever had, Tommy. If you'd seen it . . ."

"But I haven't," said Tommy. "No-one has, but you. And we only have your word."

"Don't go there, Tommy," said Suzie, her voice cold and hard.

"Lilith's plans threaten all the Nightsides," I said. "Remember what Old Father Time said, about all the possible futures narrowing down, till we end up with the one, inevitable future? That's why we have to do this, Tommy. And I can't do it without your help. Merlin's bound to have set up incredibly powerful defences, to protect him while he's drunk or otherwise incapable. I can use my gift to find them, but I don't have anywhere near enough power to push them aside or shut them off. But you . . . can use your gift to confuse the defences long enough for us to slip past them and do what we have to do."

Tommy stared at me for a long time, and I couldn't read his face at all. He'd stopped using his effete voice. "I never knew you to be this . . . brutal," he said finally.

"Only because I have to be," I said. "The future depends on me; and needs must when the devil drives."

"Or the Devil's son," he said, and I had to wonder whether he meant Merlin or me. He slowly sat back in his chair again. "What are we going to do with the heart, afterwards?"

"Well, we can't just hand it back," I said. "Merlin would find some way to kill us all, no matter what we'd agreed. No, I think we hide it somewhere safe, then tell Nimue where we put it, after we've safely disappeared into the Past."

"We're bringing the witch into this?" said Suzie. "That simpering little airhead?"

"We need her," I said. "There's no way Merlin will ever relax while we're around, but he'll never see it coming from Nimue."

"Why should she help us?" said Tommy, frowning.

I smiled. "The day I can't outmanoeuvre a gold-digger like her is the day I'll retire. You aren't the only one who can talk people into things, Tommy."

"True," said Suzie. "You may be existential, Tommy, but Taylor is a crafty bastard."

"Thank you, Suzie," I said. "I think. All we have to do is convince the witch to slip a little something into Merlin's drink so he passes out sooner rather than later. That sound like a plan to everyone?"

"Sounds like a sneaky and underhanded plan to me," said Suzie. "I'm in. After we've taken his heart out . . . can I try shooting him, just to see what happens?"

"No," I said.

"You're no fun any more, Taylor."

I looked at Tommy. "Are you in, or not?"

"Reluctantly," he said at last. "And with grave reservations. But yes, I'm in. It seems dreams have no place in the real world."

"Stick to being existential," I said kindly. "You're much better off, not being sure about things."

So we sat, and watched Merlin drink. Hours passed, and he was still putting it away, with Nimue's enthusiastic help and bubbly company. But finally the sorcerer reached a point where he stopped raising his goblet to his lips and simply sat staring at nothing. Even Nimue couldn't get a response out of him. Interestingly enough, once she was sure he was out of it, she turned off the charm and leaned back in her chair, kicking her heels sulkily; and then she jumped up out of her chair and flounced off to the bar for a refill. Where I happened to be waiting, ready to buy her a drink of something expensive. I smiled at her and complimented her, and she giggled like a teenager on a first date. After a while, I invited her to join our table, and after a quick glance at Merlin to make sure he was still nodding, she trotted over to join us. Her face was flushed from so much drinking, and her hair was a mess, but her speech was still clear. She was enchanted to meet Tommy, but pretty much ignored Suzie. I got a few more drinks into her, then laid out our plan. Nimue didn't take much convincing. She had the morals of a cat and the brains of a puppy.

"We need Merlin's help," I said, putting it as simply as I could. "But he's too wrapped up in his own problems to listen. But if we take his heart, he'll have to listen. And when we have the heart outside his body, and therefore outside his defences, you'll be able to put a spell on it, so he'll forget all his worries and care about nothing but you. When you're finished, you can put the heart back, and everyone will get what they want. What could be simpler, or fairer?"

Nimue frowned over her drink, trying to concentrate. "The heart could make me powerful . . . with real magic . . . But really, I only want my old bear back the way he used to be. You should have seen him in his prime, at Camelot. At the King's side, where he belonged. They all bowed to him, then. I was never there myself, of course. I was just another dumb little priestess, back then, gathering mistletoe and worshipping the Hecate, the three in one . . . But I was always good at Seeing from Afar, and Camelot fascinated me. Merlin fascinated me. I watched him at Court, and even then I knew he needed looking after. Needed someone who cared about him. Everyone else put up with him, so they could call on his magic to bail them out when they messed up. When muscular clods in armour weren't enough to save the day."

Her voice was getting blurred as she got more emotional. "Even the King, bless him . . . even he never really cared about Merlin. Not like I do. Silly little priestess, silly little hedge witch, that's what they say . . . but I'm the only one who can reach his heart now . . . And when I'm powerful, I'll make them all pay . . ."

Her lower lip was trembling by then, and big fat tears ran down her cheeks. I didn't look round at the others. I already felt guilty enough about taking advantage of an oversized child like Nimue. But it had to be done . . .

"So you will help us?" I said. "It's for the best. Really."

"If you say so," said Nimue. "I've always needed other people to tell me what's for the best."

Something in her voice told me that would always be the case. Tommy heard it, too, and glared at me, but I concentrated on the witch.

"Have you got something you could slip into his drink, Nimue? Something to make him sleep?"

"Oh sure," Nimue said off-handedly. "Druids know everything there is to know about potions. I often drug his drink. It's the only way he can sleep these days. Poor sweetie."

And that was it. We waited till the customers had thinned out, and then I bribed Hebe to shut down the bar for a while. It took most of the coins in my purse, particularly when Hebe realised we wanted her to go home early as well, but money talks in the Nightside, as it always had. A few customers didn't want to go, but Suzie obliged them with a short but instructive example of how a shotgun works, and they couldn't get out of the bar fast enough. The two smoke ghosts looked at me reproachfully, then faded slowly away, still dancing. The bar seemed so much larger with everyone else gone, and the quiet was actually eerie. Merlin sat slumped and finally sleeping in his chair, while Nimue sat cross-legged in a hastily chalked circle, working a glamour so that no-one outside would be able to tell there was anything unusual going on in the bar. There were an awful lot of people, and others, who would jump at the chance to kill Merlin if they even suspected his defences were down. Suzie guarded the door anyway, while Tommy and I considered the unconscious sorcerer.

"So," said Tommy. "How do we do it?"

"Very carefully," I said. "If this looks like it's going wrong, I shall be heading for the nearest horizon, at speed. Try and keep up."

"This is a really bad idea," Tommy said miserably.

I raised my gift, opening up my third eye, my private eye, and right away I could See all of Merlin's defences. They lurked around his sleeping form like so many snarling attack dogs, layer upon layer of protective spells and curses, ready to lash out at anything that disturbed them. They stirred uneasily, just from being Seen. I grabbed Tommy by the hand, and at once he could See them, too. He cried out in shock and horror, and tried to pull away, but I wouldn't let him go.

"Shut up," I whispered fiercely. "Do you want them to hear you? Now use your gift. Do it!"

His mouth twisted, like that of a child being punished,

but I could feel his gift manifesting. And slowly, one by one, the defences became uncertain about why they were there, and what they were there for, until finally they disappeared back whence they'd come, to have a collective discussion, leaving Merlin sleeping and entirely unprotected. I moved forward quickly. I didn't know how long the effect would last. I could hear Tommy breathing harshly behind me, concentrating on maintaining his gift so the defences wouldn't return, while I checked out the sorcerer's condition.

His eyes were closed, the leaping flames damped down for the moment. His breathing was steady, though he stirred occasionally in his sleep, as though bothered by bad dreams. I pulled open his scarlet robe, revealing a shaved chest covered in thick, intertwining Druidic tattoos. I hissed for Suzie to come over and join me, and she reluctantly left her post at the door.

"How do we do this?" I said.

"Your guess is as good as mine, Taylor. I've taken a few hearts, for bounties, but that wasn't exactly surgery." She produced a long knife from the top of her knee-length boot, and hefted it thoughtfully. "I'm guessing brute force and improvisation isn't going to be good enough, this time."

"Give me the knife," I said resignedly. "And go back to guarding the door. Tommy, get over here and help."

"I've never done anything like this before," said Tommy, moving reluctantly forward.

"I should hope not," I said. "So, roll up your sleeves, follow my lead, try to help without getting in my way, and if you must puke, try not to get any in the chest cavity."

"Oh God," said Tommy.

I cut Merlin open from chest to groin, making sure I had a hole big enough to get both hands in. This was no time for keyhole surgery, and anyway, I was betting Merlin would be able to make all necessary repairs once he had his heart back. There was a lot of blood, and sometimes I had to jump back to avoid a sudden jetting gusher. I washed most of it out of the hole with wine, so I could at least see what I was doing. In the end, I had to cut and tear the heart free from its position under the sternum, tugging and pulling with both hands, while blood soaked both my hands up to the elbow, and Tommy said *Oh God, Oh God,* while he held the other organs back out of my way.

Finally, I held Merlin's heart in my hands, a great scarlet lump of muscle. It was bigger than I'd expected, and still beating, gouting thick dark blood. I took it to the next table, and wrapped it carefully in a cloth covered in protective symbols, which Nimue had put together. She was still sitting in her circle, mumbling spells with her eyes closed, so she wouldn't have to see what was happening. I went back to stand beside Tommy, who was looking at the great bloody hole we'd made and trembling violently. This really wasn't his kind of case. I clapped him on the shoulder, but he didn't even look round. Merlin was still breathing steadily, still sleeping, still living. I tried to push the sides of the wound together, over the mess I'd made, but the hole was too big. In the end, I closed his robes over it.

"Is it done?" said Suzie, from the doorway. "Have you finished?"

"Oh yes," I said. "I don't think I could do any more damage if I tried."

"Don't worry," she said. "It gets easier, the more you do it."

I looked across at her sharply and decided not to ask. I didn't want to know. I pulled Tommy away from the sorcerer, and we cleaned off our hands and arms as best we could with more wine. We couldn't do anything about our blood-spattered clothes. We didn't have anything to change into. Hopefully Old Father Time's glamour would hide the gore from others' eyes. Tommy looked at me accusingly.

"Is there anything you won't do, Taylor? Anyone whose

life you won't ruin, to get revenge on your mother for running off and abandoning you as a child?"

"That isn't what this is about!"

"Isn't it?"

"No! Everything I've done here, and everything I will do, is all about saving the Nightside, and the world! If you'd seen what I've seen . . ."

"But we haven't. And you won't tell us about it. Why is that, Taylor? What are you keeping from us? Are we supposed to take your word and trust you?"

"Yes," I said, holding his angry gaze with mine.

"And why the hell should I do that?" said Tommy.

"Because he is John Taylor," said Suzie, coming over from the door, with her shotgun in her hands. "And he has earned the right to be trusted."

"Of course you'd support him," Tommy said bitterly. "You're his woman."

Suzie stopped, then laughed briefly. "Oh, Tommy, you don't know anything, do you?"

And that was when the door slammed open behind her, and a huge blocky man in chain mail stormed into the bar. He had that functional compact musculature that comes from constant hard use and testing, rather than working out, and his ragged chain mail and the leather armour under it had the signs of long use and hard wear. He had a square, blocky, almost brutal face, marked with scars that had healed crookedly. His mouth was a flat line, his eyes cold and determined. In one hand he carried a huge mace with a vicious spiked head. I'd never seen a more dangerous-looking man in my life.

He came striding straight across the bar towards us, kicking tables and chairs effortlessly out of his way. Suzie turned her shotgun on him, and Tommy and I moved quickly to stand on either side of her, but the newcomer didn't stop until he could see past us to Merlin. He took in the blood soaking the front of Merlin's robes and actually

started to smile, only to stop as he realised the sorcerer was
still breathing.

"He's not dead," he said, and his voice was like stone
grating against stone.

"He's not dead," I agreed. "Who might you be?"

"I am Kae," he said. "Arthur's brother. Stepbrother only
by blood, but he always called me brother. We fought great
battles, shoulder to shoulder and back to back. Struck
down evil wherever we found it. Bled for each other and
saved each other's lives a dozen times. He was King, and
carried the responsibilities of the whole land on his shoulders, but he always had time for me, and I knew there
wasn't a day that passed where he didn't think of me.

"I never trusted Merlin. Never trusted magic. I tried to
warn Arthur, but he was always blind to the sorcerer's
faults. And when Arthur needed him most, where was Merlin? Gone. Nowhere to be found. I saw the bravest knights
in the land fall, brought down by jackals. I saw good men
dragged down by overwhelming forces. We fought for
hours, stamping back and forth through the blood-soaked
mud, and in the end . . . nobody won. Arthur and the bastard Mordred died, at each other's hands. The proud
knights of Camelot are fallen or scattered. The land is torn
apart by civil war as scavengers fight over the spoils, and
Merlin . . . still lives. How can that be right? How can there
be any justice, while the traitor still lives? I am Kae,
Arthur's brother, and I will avenge his death."

"Because Mordred is dead," I said. "And you don't have
anyone else."

"Stand aside," said Kae.

"Not one step closer," said Suzie, aiming the shotgun at
his face.

Kae sneered at her. "I am protected against all magics,
and unnatural weapons," he said coldly. "The charm that
brought me here will protect me from anything that might
keep me from my rightful prey."

"Thought you didn't believe in magic," I said, trying to buy some time while I thought what to do.

Kae smiled briefly. "Needs must, when the devil drives. I will damn my soul, if that's what it takes to buy me justice. Now stand aside or die with him."

He stalked forward, raising his spiked mace, and Suzie gave him both barrels right in the face. Or at least, she tried to. The shotgun wouldn't work. She tried again, uselessly, and threw the gun aside as Kae loomed up before her. She whipped a long knife from her other boot top, and slashed at his bare throat. Kae flinched back instinctively, and I hit him from the side with my shoulder, hoping my speed and impact would knock him off balance. Instead, he hardly moved an inch, and threw me aside with one sweep of his mailed arm. I crashed into a bunch of chairs and hit the ground hard. The impact knocked all the breath out of me and hurt my head. I fought to get back onto my knees, while Suzie and Kae went head to head with knife and mace, grunting and snarling at each other. He was bigger, but she was faster.

Tommy had grabbed up the cloth-wrapped heart, and was clutching it protectively to his chest, watching the fight with wide, shocked eyes. The witch Nimue had left her chalk circle and was bending over Merlin.

"Something's wrong!" she shouted. "Whatever charm Kae brought into this room, it's interfering with the magic keeping him alive! You have to get Kae out of here, or Merlin will die!"

"I'm doing my best," Suzie snarled.

She bobbed and weaved as Kae swung his mace. The weapon must have weighed a ton, but Kae wielded it like a toy, the wind whistling through the vicious spikes on its head. Suzie ducked and jabbed at him with her long knife, but mostly the blade jarred harmlessly off his chain mail. Kae had spent most of his life on one battlefield or another, and it showed in his every economical, murderous move.

But Suzie Shooter was a child of the Nightside, and her rage was every bit a match for his. She went for his face and his throat, his elbows and his groin, but always his mace was there just in time to block her. Suzie was a bounty hunter, a fighter, and a practised killer; but Kae was one of Arthur's knights, bloodied in a thousand wars and border skirmishes. He pressed her back, step by step, his arm rising and falling with terrible force, remorseless as a machine.

Somehow I got back onto my feet again and staggered over to Merlin's table. Suzie could look after herself. I had to see what was happening with Merlin. His breathing was ragged, and his colour wasn't good. I'd hit my head on something, and it ached unmercifully. Blood was running thickly down my face. I couldn't seem to think straight. Tommy was hovering helplessly at Nimue's side as she chanted spells over Merlin. From the growing despair on her face, I gathered they weren't helping much. Tommy grabbed my arm to get my attention, then realised the state I was in and helped hold me up. Nimue looked round frantically.

"You've got to do something! Merlin's dying! I'm having to use my own life force to keep him going!"

Tommy pushed his face close to mine, to make sure I heard him. "We have to put Merlin's defences back into place!"

"Right," I said. "Of course. Just jam the heart back in, and his own magics should heal him. Right. Come on, give me the heart. He's no use to me dead."

"It wouldn't work," said Nimue. She'd given up on chanting and waving her hands, and was crouching beside Merlin, holding one of his hands in both of hers. "Kae's charm will prevent his defences returning . . . You have to get him out of here. I'm giving Merlin . . . everything I've got; but I don't think it's going to enough. I'm only human . . . and he isn't."

"We have to think of something, Taylor!" said Tommy, glaring into my face. "Taylor! John! Can you hear me?"

His words came to me, but from far away, as though we were both underwater. I put a hand to my aching head, and it came away slick with blood. Whatever had hit me in that crash, it had really done a job on me. I gazed stupidly at my bloody hand for a moment, then looked back at Suzie and Kae.

Kae swung his mace around in a viciously fast sweep, but Suzie ducked under it and slammed her knife deep into his side, the blade punching right through the chain mail and the leather armour beneath. Kae roared with rage as much as pain, and his mace came sweeping back round impossibly fast. The spiked steel head slammed into Suzie's face and ripped half of it away. She screamed, and fell backwards onto the floor. Kae grunted once, like a satisfied animal, and turned to look at Merlin, ignoring the knife hilt protruding from his side.

I moved forward to block his way. Tommy wasn't a fighter, and Nimue was busy. It had to be me. I forced the pain and confusion out of my head for a moment, through sheer force of will, and tried to raise my gift. If I could only find the charm Kae had brought with him . . . but my head hurt too bad. I couldn't concentrate, couldn't See. Kae was still coming, headed straight for me. I jammed my hands into my coat pockets, searching for something I could use against him.

And then Suzie reared up from the floor, with a terrible cry. Half her face was a mask of blood, with only an empty socket where her left eye had been, but still she came roaring up off that bloody floor like the fighter she was. She ripped the knife out of Kae's side, and he stopped in his tracks, halted for a moment by the sudden blaze of pain. And while he hesitated, Suzie jammed her long knife all the way into his unprotected groin. Her triumphant laughter drowned out his cry of pain. She yanked the knife out, and thick dark blood coursed down both his legs. He staggered, and almost fell. She lashed out with the knife, and almost effortlessly cut open the wrist of the hand holding the mace. It fell to the floor as the feeling left his fingers, and he looked stupidly after it for a moment.

Suzie rose up onto her feet to give him the last, killing blow, and he roared like a bear and grabbed her to him, crushing her against his chain-mail breast with huge, muscular arms. She cried out as her ribs cracked audibly, then savagely head-butted Kae in the face. He roared again and dropped her. Suzie grinned fiercely at him through the bloody mask of her face, and went for him with her knife. And Kae grabbed a flaring torch from its iron wall holder and thrust it right into her ravaged face.

There was smoke, and spitting fat, and the stench of burning meat, but she didn't scream. She fell, but she didn't scream.

I screamed. And while they were both distracted, I surged forward, grabbed up the steel mace from the floor, and hit Kae across the head with all the strength I had. The force of the blow whipped his head round, and blood flew across the air, but he didn't fall. I hit him again, and again, and again, putting all my rage and horror and guilt into every blow, and finally he fell, measuring his length on the bloody floor like a slaughtered sacrificial beast. I dropped the mace, and went over to kneel beside Suzie, and take her in my arms.

She clung to me like she was drowning, burying her ruined bloody face in my shoulder. I held on to her, and all I could say was *I'm sorry, I'm so sorry,* over and over again. After a while she pushed me away, and I let go of her immediately. It was hard for Suzie to let anyone touch her, even a friend. Even then. Poor little broken bird. I made myself look at what remained of her face. The whole left side was gone, a ragged torn-up mess only held together by charred and blackened flesh. And then, as I watched, the terrible wounds began to heal. The torn flesh crawled together, slowly closing over and drawing itself together into old scar tissue. Even the empty eye-socket closed, the lids sealed together. Until at the end it was the awful, familiar, disfigured face I'd seen once before—on the Suzie Shooter from the future.

I had brought Suzie here, to this place and time, and made that face, that Suzie possible.

She smiled at me, but only half her mouth moved. She gingerly touched at the scarred half of her face with her fingertips, then took her hand away again. "Don't look so shocked, Taylor. You put werewolf blood into me to save my life, remember, back during the angel war? The blood wasn't strong enough or pure enough to make me into a were, but it did give me one hell of a healing factor. Very useful, in the bounty-hunting business. My face . . . will never be the same again, I know that. My healing factor has very definite limits. But I can live with this. It's not like I ever cared about looking pretty . . . John? What's the matter, John?"

I couldn't tell her. I lurched to my feet and looked around for the mace I'd discarded. Kae . . . It was all Kae's fault. He had barged in and ruined everything . . . everything. Suzie knew me well enough to see which way my thoughts were going, and she hauled herself to her feet to stand before me.

"No, John. You can't kill him."

"Watch me."

"You can't, John. Because Arthur wouldn't want you to. And because you're not a killer. Like me."

And because in the end I still hoped she was right about that, I turned away from Kae's unconscious body, and together Suzie and I moved slowly and carefully back across the bar to Merlin's table. Tommy was still there, holding the witch Nimue in his arms, his face set and cold. It was obvious Nimue wasn't breathing. Dead, her face looked more like a child's than ever.

"She died keeping Merlin alive with her own life energy," said Tommy. He looked only at me, his gaze openly accusing. "She gave her life for him, her present and all her future; and it still wasn't enough. He's dead, too, if you care. And all because of us."

"We never meant for any of this to happen," said Suzie.

Tommy looked at her briefly, taking in her scarred face, but his cold gaze returned almost immediately to me. "And that makes it all right, does it?"

"No," I said. "But what's done, is done. We can't help them, but we can still help ourselves. We don't need Merlin; we still have his heart." I leaned over the wrapped bundle on the table and pulled back the cloth to show that the heart was still slowly beating, even though there was no blood left in it. "Merlin put enough of his power into his heart that it still continues, still holds a large portion of his magic. We can tap into that magic and use it to send us further back into the Past."

Tommy put Nimue to one side, arranging her tenderly in a chair like a sleeping child, then he stood up to face me. "Did you know this all along, Taylor? Did you plan for this?"

"No," I said. "I Saw it with my gift, when I studied his defences."

"Why should I believe you?" said Tommy, and Suzie stirred at my side, picking up on the anger burning in the man.

"I've never lied to you, Tommy," I said carefully. "I'm sorry about Nimue, and even about Merlin, but I came into the Past to stop Lilith, and that's what I'm going to do."

"Whatever it takes? No matter who gets hurt?"

"I don't know," I said. "Maybe."

"If we take the heart with us, further back into the Past,

no wonder no-one could ever find it," said Suzie. "They were always looking in the wrong place, the wrong time."

"We'll take Nimue's body along with us," I said. "Dump it somewhere in the Past. So that when Merlin returns from the dead, he'll never have to know that Nimue died trying to save him."

"You pick the strangest ways to be thoughtful, Taylor," said Suzie.

"If you were to put the heart back," Tommy said slowly, "there's a real chance the magic stored in the heart would be enough to bring him back."

"We don't know that," I said. "And we need the magic in the heart . . ."

"We can't let him die!" Tommy said fiercely. "Not if there's even the smallest chance of saving him! Otherwise, we're as good as killing him ourselves."

"Think it through," I said. "If it doesn't work, we waste the magic, and we're stranded here. And if Merlin should wake up, and discover what we persuaded Nimue to do, and that she died as a result of it . . . he'd kill us all. Slowly and hideously painfully. This is Merlin Satanspawn we're talking about."

"So we do nothing?" said Tommy. There was a dangerous cold light in his eyes.

"Yes," I said. "He dies here, without his heart, as we know he did, and he'll be buried in the cellars under the bar. That's a part of our Past, our Present, our time-line. We just helped to bring about what we know happened anyway."

"You cold-hearted son of a bitch." Tommy was so angry his face had lost all its colour, and his hands were clenched into fists at his sides. "Just how far will you go, to get your precious revenge?"

I didn't look at Suzie. At her familiar, disfigured face. "I only do what I have to do," I said, keeping my voice as calm and reasonable as I could. "Let's get out of here, before Kae wakes up. I don't think you can stop a warrior like that for long just by hitting him over the head."

"No," said Tommy, still looking at me, and his eyes were cold, so cold. I don't think I'd ever seen him so angry. "This stops here, Taylor. You've done enough damage on your insane quest. Suzie's face. Nimue's death. Merlin . . . all for your petty, vindictive vendetta. To hell with Lilith, and to hell with you, too, you lying sack of shit. You'd sacrifice anyone and anything, just to get back at your mother. I don't see why . . . After all, you've made yourself into just as vicious and cold-hearted a monster as her. You're every inch your mother's son."

"Don't," I said. "Don't say that, Tommy."

"It's not true," said Suzie. "Don't do this, Tommy. Taylor knows what he's doing. He always knows what he's doing."

It was like a hand clenched around my heart then, squeezing it painfully, to hear her trust and faith in me, even after . . . everything that had happened. I wasn't worthy of trust like that. I would have said something, but I couldn't get my breath.

"Oh yes," said Tommy. "I think he knows what he's doing, all right. I simply don't trust his motives any more."

"I never meant for anyone to get hurt," I said finally. "I don't want anyone to get hurt. I've seen the future that's coming, if Lilith isn't stopped. I still have nightmares . . . And I am ready to die, to prevent it. But . . . I don't have the right to ask that of anyone else. What do you think we should do, Tommy?"

"I say we put Merlin's heart back," Tommy said stubbornly. "It could work. We save his life, and I'll use my gift to talk him out of killing us. You know how persuasive I can be. With his heart back and his power restored, he'll be able to repair Suzie's face and bring Nimue back from the dead. Don't look at me like that! This is Merlin; he could do it! I know he could. And then, with the right guidance and advice, he will restore the glory that is Camelot and make a better world, a better future!"

"Oh Jesus, are we back to that?" said Suzie. "Tommy, we've been through this. We daren't change the Past, because of what it could do to our Present. And there's no telling what kind of a future you and a half-mad Merlin might bring about anyway."

"Lilith still has to be stopped," I said.

"Why?" said Tommy. "Because of what she might do? Don't worry; Merlin will handle her."

"Merlin Satanspawn?" I said. "The Devil's only begotten son? For all we know, he'd help her."

"I can use my gift . . ."

"Against Merlin?"

"You're Lilith's only son," said Tommy. "You'd let the dream of Camelot die, just to further your own ambitions. I see right through you, Taylor. And I'll see you die first!"

He raised his gift, but I was already raising mine, and the whole bar shook as our powers manifested and clashed head-on. I used my gift to try and find his weaknesses, and he used his to try and reinforce a reality where I never reached the sixth century. My gift dealt with certainties, his with probabilities, and neither was really strong enough to overcome the other. We both put all our strength into this clash of wills, and reality itself became hazy and uncertain around us, until it seemed the whole bar might unravel, leaving us the only fixed and real things in the world.

There was no telling where that insane and dangerous struggle might have gone if Suzie hadn't put a stop to it by simply hitting Tommy round the back of the head with the butt of her shotgun. He cried out and fell to his knees, his gift snapping off as the pain in his head kept him from concentrating. He still tried to come up off his knees fighting, and Suzie calmly and dispassionately beat the shit out of him. He finally collapsed into unconsciousness, and I used my gift to find Old Father Time's touch on him and remove it. Tommy disappeared immediately, swept back to our Present.

(And that was when I finally remembered when I'd seen Tommy Oblivion before. He'd appeared out of nowhere in Strangefellows, during the Nightingale case, some months previously. He'd been badly beaten, and yelled threats at me before he was thrown out. Now I knew why. He'd obviously arrived back in the Nightside before he left. Still, it did beg the question of why, if Tommy knew what was going to happen on this trip, he didn't search out his younger self, and inform him . . . Unless something happened to the older Tommy to prevent it . . . That's why I hate Time travel. Just thinking about it makes your head hurt.)

I sat down in a chair while Suzie checked my head wound, then cleaned the blood off my face. I sat looking at Merlin's heart on the table before me, planning what I was going to do next. Even after everything that had happened, I was still determined to press on. I had to succeed in my mission to justify all the suffering and damage I'd caused.

"If nothing else," said Suzie, "we have discovered the answer to one of the great mysteries of the Nightside—who stole Merlin's heart? We did. Who would have thought it . . . Can it really take us further back into the Past?"

She was speaking calmly and professionally, so I did the same. "I don't see why not. The power's definitely there; I have to tap into it and guide it."

"And you're not worried about your Enemies locating you here?"

"I think they would have by now if they were going to," I said.

I took the heart in my hand and made myself look at Suzie's ruined face without flinching. I'd done that to her. I had to stop Lilith, or all Suzie's pain had been for nothing. I looked slowly round the bar, taking in all the damage I'd done, without meaning to. I had to wonder if perhaps it was my own implacable stubbornness that was forging the very series of causal links that would bring about the dead future.

Who caused this? I asked the future Razor Eddie, as he lay dying in my arms. *You did,* he said. *How do I stop it?* I asked him. *Kill yourself,* he said.

I'd promised him I would die rather than let that future happen. I'd promised Suzie back during the angel war that I would never let her be hurt again. I'd failed her. She didn't blame me, but I did. She would forgive me, but I never would. Perhaps . . . the only way to stop the awful future was to kill myself, now, before it was too late . . .

No. I could still stop Lilith. I was the only one who could stop her.

So I nodded to Suzie to pick up Nimue's body, while I raised my gift and tapped the power of Merlin's heart, and we went hurtling back through Time again.

NINE

When in Rome

We arrived. I looked around. I looked at Suzie. "Hold me back, Suzie, or I am going to kill absolutely everything that moves."

"Hold yourself back," Suzie said calmly. "You know very well I don't do the restraint thing. It's bad for my reputation."

"I don't believe this!" I said, actually stamping my foot in frustration. "We're still only part of the way back!"

"At least it doesn't smell so bad this time," said Suzie, judiciously. "I find a little horse shit in the street goes a hell of a long way."

"I could spit soot," I said.

We'd reappeared in the middle of a large open square, under the star-speckled sky and huge full moon of the Nightside. The buildings enclosing the square were low and squat, stone and marble, with the unmistakable classic touches of Roman architecture. Men in wraparound togas looked at us curiously, then went on their way, as though strange people appearing suddenly out of nowhere happened all the time. Maybe it did, in this Nightside.

"First or second century," said Suzie, showing off her knowledge again. "The Romans built Londinium over the River Thames, and were the first human society to colonize the already existing Nightside. Outside, Rome rules Britain, after Julius Caesar led a successful invasion in 55 B.C. It was actually his third attempt; the extremely savage Britons threw his armies back into the sea twice. And the defensive tactics used by the Druidic priests shocked even the hardened Roman Legionnaires. So Rome now rules, with an iron fist. They brought law, roads, slavery, and crucifixion. You're not into history, are you, Taylor? Taylor?"

My teeth were clenched so tight my jaws ached. I'd tried to play it light, but my heart wasn't in it. I couldn't believe we'd fallen short again. We were still at least a hundred years short of the Nightside's creation, maybe more, and with no means of going any further. Everything I'd done, all the hard and ruthless things I'd done, all the hurt and death I'd caused . . . had all been for nothing. I looked down at Merlin's heart, in my hand. It no longer beat or pulsed. It was just a dark red lump of muscle, all its magic used up. Which meant we were stranded. I threw the heart onto the ground, and stamped on it, but it was already too hard and leathery to crush properly. I sighed. I didn't have the energy left to throw a proper tantrum. Too tired to be angry, too bitter to be mad. Suzie sensed the pain in me and comforted me in the only way she could, by standing close beside me and reassuring me with her cold, calm presence. I could remember a time when it used to be the other way round. We'd both come a long way from who we used to be, Suzie and I.

"Hey, you!" said a loud, harsh, and not at all friendly

voice. "Stand right where you are, and don't even think about going for a weapon!"

"Oh good," I said. "A distraction."

"I pity the fools," said Suzie.

We looked around. The people in the square were scattering, in a dignified and civilised way, as a group of Roman Legionnaires headed straight for us. They wore the armoured outfits familiar from film and television, though these outfits looked rough and dirty and hard-used, much like the men who wore them. They were short and stocky, with brutal faces and eyes that had seen everything before. Typical city cops. They stamped towards us, short-swords in their hands, and quickly fanned out to form a semicircle facing and containing us. Suzie already had her shotgun out, held lazily in her hands. She glanced at me, and I shook my head slightly. Best not to start any trouble we didn't have to, until we had a better grasp on local conditions. Suzie had been carrying Nimue's body draped over one shoulder, but at the Legionnaires' approach she dumped it on the ground, to be free for any necessary action. The Legionnaires looked at the body, then at us.

"Tall, aren't they?" said a quiet voice from among them.

"When I want your opinion, Marcus, I'll beat it out of you," growled the leader. He gave us his best intimidating stare, not at all bothered that he had to incline his head right back to do it. "I'm Tavius, leader of the Watch. Are you a Citizen?"

"Almost certainly not," I said. "We're only passing through. Hopefully. I'm John Taylor, and this is Suzie Shooter. Don't upset her."

"You speak Latin like a Citizen," said Tavius. "I suppose it's possible you have legitimate business here. Who's the stiff?"

"No-one you'd know," I said.

"Identity papers!"

I checked my coat pockets, in case Old Father Time

might have supplied some, but apparently there were limits to his help. I shrugged, and smiled easily at the head of the Watch.

"Sorry. No papers. Would a bribe do?"

"Well . . ."

"Shut up, Marcus!" said Tavius. He gave me his full attention, turning his glare up another notch. "We have been given the task of maintaining order in this unnatural shithole, and we only accept tributes from legitimate Citizens. Now, I see a dead body, and I see blood all over the pair of you. I'm sure you're about to tell me there's a perfectly reasonable explanation for all this . . ."

"Actually, no," I said. "I've got an unnatural explanation, but frankly, life's too short. Why don't you take our word for it that this lady and I are very powerful, very dangerous, and extremely pissed off by recent events; so unless you want this lady and me to turn the whole lot of you into dog food . . ."

"Oh hell," said Tavius. "You're magical?"

"Told you we should have paid the extra insurance, for full godly cover."

"I won't tell you again, Marcus! Now bring me the bloody list."

The smallest of the Legionnaires hurried forward, handed his leader a rolled scroll, gave me a quick shifty smile, and dropped a wink to Suzie. Then he retreated swiftly back into the ranks. Tavius opened the scroll and studied it carefully.

"So, are you gods, walking in disguise?"

"Definitely not," I said. "And don't believe anyone who tells you otherwise. They're just guessing."

Tavius considered that for a moment, and then moved on to the next question on his checklist. "Are you a Power, a Force, or a Being?"

"Not as such," I said.

"Are you a magician, sorcerer, raiser of spirits, or soothsayer?"

"There's a lot of debate about that," I said, "but I prefer not to comment. However, it would be fair to say that this lady and I are dangerous in a whole bunch of unnatural and unpleasant ways."

"I can set light to my farts," Suzie volunteered.

"Don't go there," I said quickly to Tavius.

He blinked a few times, then looked back at his checklist. "We've already established you're not Citizens, so . . . which gods protect you?"

"Absolutely none, as far as I can tell," said Suzie.

"And I think we can safely assume I'm not going to find your barbarian names on the approved list," said Tavius, rolling up his scroll with a certain satisfaction. "Which means you're fair game. All right, boys, arrest them. We'll sort out some charges later."

"They said they were dangerous. Powerful and dangerous."

"Gods, you're a wimp, Marcus. How you ever got into the Legion is a mystery to me."

"They're tall enough to be dangerous."

"Look, if they had any magic worth the mentioning, they would have used it by now, wouldn't they? Now arrest them, or there'll be no honey with your dinner tonight."

"What the hell," I said. "I've been having a really rotten time, and I could use someone to take out my feelings on."

And I punched Tavius right between his beady little eyes. His head snapped back, and he staggered backwards two or three paces, but he didn't go down. Either they built them really tough in the Legion, or I was losing my touch. Tavius raised his short-sword and started towards me. I caught his gaze with mine, and he stopped short as though he'd run into a brick wall. I kept the stare going, and his face went blank, the short-sword slipping from his hand as the fingers slowly opened. I hit him again, and this time he went down and stayed down. Which was just as well. It felt like I'd broken every bone in my hand.

The rest of the Legionnaires were already advancing on us, hoping to overwhelm us with numbers. Suzie shot four of them in swift succession, working the pump on her shotgun with practised speed. The loud noise, the flying blood, and the terrible wounds scattered the Legionnaires like startled birds, and I thought they might run, but their training quickly reasserted itself. You don't choose the faint-hearted to act as the Watch in the Nightside. They spread out to make harder targets, then advanced on Suzie and me, sandalled feet stamping in perfect unison. I fell back on my standard response, which was to use the taking-bullets-out-of-guns trick. I wasn't actually sure what effect it would have, and so was pleasantly surprised when all the Legionnaires' weapons, armour, and clothing disappeared, leaving them utterly unarmed, and stark bollock naked. They looked down at themselves, then at us, and they turned as one and ran. There were limits to what even trained soldiers were prepared to face. Suzie started to raise her shotgun, but I shook my head, and she lowered it again. She looked at the departing bare arses and shook her head.

"Getting mean, Taylor."

"Everything I know, I learned from you," I said generously.

She considered me thoughtfully for a moment. "I'm never sure what you can or can't do."

I grinned. "That's the point."

We watched the departing Legionnaires leave the square at speed, probably on the way to tell on us to their superiors. Some of the people had wandered back into the square. They looked at Suzie, then at me, very disapprovingly. I glared right back at them, and they all remembered they had urgent appointments somewhere else.

"Feeling better?" said Suzie.

"You have no idea," I said.

I took a good look at our surroundings. The stone buildings were basic and blocky, prettied up with columns, porticoes, and bas-reliefs. Most of the latter featured gods, monsters, and people doing naughty things with each other. The centre of the square was taken up with a whole bunch of oversized statues, featuring either the local gods and goddesses or idealised men and women, most of them naked, all of them very brightly painted. I expressed some surprise at this, and Suzie immediately went into lecture mode again. I could remember when she hardly said a dozen words at a time. A little education is a terrible thing.

"All classical statues were painted, and repainted regularly. The Romans adopted the practice from the ancient Greeks, along with everything else that wasn't nailed down. Even their gods, though they at least had the grace to rename them. We're used to seeing the statues in museums, old and cracked and bare stone and marble, because that's all that survived." She stopped abruptly. "Taylor, you're looking at me strangely again."

"I'm impressed," I said. "Honest."

"Look, I got the History Channel for free, okay? I subscribed to the Guns & Ammo Channel, and History was part of the package."

"Cable television has a lot to answer for."

I went back to looking at the buildings, and I slowly realised they were all temples of one kind or another. Most were dedicated to the local Roman gods, of which there were quite a few, including Julius Caesar and Augustus Caesar, complete with idealised busts showing off their noble features.

"After Julius, all the Roman Emperors were declared gods when they died," said Suzie. "And sometimes even during their lifetimes. Good way to keep the colonized nations in line, by telling them their Emperor was a god."

"Actually, I knew that," I said. "I watched *I, Claudius*.

And the Penthouse *Caligula*. But only because Helen Mirren was in it."

Other temples were dedicated to Dagon, the Serpent, the Serpent's Son, Cthulhu, several of the old Greek gods, half a dozen names I vaguely remembered from the Street of the Gods, and a whole bunch I'd never even heard of. And, one temple dedicated to Lilith. I considered that for a while, but it seemed no more or less important than any of the others.

"There aren't any Christian temples," I said suddenly.

"Too early yet," said Suzie. "Though there are probably some underground, unofficial places."

I turned my attention to the people, and others, passing through the square. Less than half were in any way human. There were elves, moving silently together with mathematical precision, holding strange groupings and patterns as intricate as a snowflake, and as alien. Lizardly humanoids slid quickly through the darker parts of the square, unnaturally graceful, their scaled skin gleaming bottle-green under the occasional lamplight. Large squat creatures, composed entirely of heaving, multi-coloured gasses, progressed slowly and jerkily, their shapes changing and convulsing from moment to moment. Liquid forms as tall as houses splashed across the square, leaving sticky trails behind them. Earthy shapes crumbled as they stamped along, and living flames flashed and flickered, come and gone too quickly for the human eye to follow. In these early days of the Nightside, humanity was the minority, and forms and forces long since lost and banished to the Street of the Gods walked openly.

Two burly giants, great heaving monstrosities draped in flapping furs, lurched forward from opposite sides of the square. So tall they towered over the biggest of the temples, the ground shook under the impact of their every footstep. They cried out to each other in voices like the thunder, or the crash of rock on rock, and there was nothing human in the sound. They slammed together in the middle of the square, kicking aside the statues of gods and heroes, and had at each other with massive sledge-hammers.

There were humans in the square; but they mostly kept to the sides, out of the way, and gave all the others plenty of room. There were rough Celtic types, squat vicious men in wolf furs, with blue woad on their faces and clay packed in their hair. They carried swords and axes, and growled at anyone who came too close. There were Romans and Greeks and Persians, all of them moving in armed groups, for safety's sake. Some had the look of sorcerers, and some were quite clearly mad. And finally, a heavy stone golem came striding purposefully through the crowds, the word *Emeth* glowing fiercely on its forehead, above the rudimentary carved features.

This early Nightside was a strange, whimsical, dangerous place. And I felt right at home.

"So," said Suzie, her voice remarkably casual under the circumstances, "did Lilith want us here, or did Merlin's heart simply run out of power too soon?"

"Beats me," I said. "But it wouldn't surprise me at all if Mother dear was still interfering, for her own inscrutable reasons. Either she's still trying to keep us away from witnessing the Nightside's true beginnings, or there's something here she wants me to see. A situation further complicated by the fact that Lilith is probably actually here, somewhere. Her earlier self, that is. She might not have been banished yet. We're going to have to watch ourselves, Suzie. We can't afford to attract her attention."

"Why not?" said Suzie. "This Lilith wouldn't know who you are."

"I think . . . she'd only have to look at me, to know," I said. "And then she'd ask questions . . . If she were to find out about her being banished to Limbo, you can bet she'd take steps to stop it, and our Present really would be screwed."

"What do we do with the witch's body?" said Suzie. When in doubt she always retreated to the immediate practical problems.

I looked around and spotted what looked like a municipal dump in one corner of the square. It was a large dump, piled high, and surrounded by flies and dogs and other things. I pointed it out to Suzie, and she nodded. She bent down and slung Nimue's body casually over one shoulder again, and I retrieved Merlin's heart from where I'd thrown it. The dark muscle was already decaying into mush. We dumped both the heart and the body on the pile of accumulated refuse. Thick clouds of flies sprang up around us, buzzing angrily at being disturbed. Up close the smell was almost overpowering. In and among the city's piled-up garbage there were quite a few other bodies, in varying stages of decay. Some were human, some very definitely weren't, and there were a surprisingly large number of dead dogs and wolves. Small furry and scuttling things moved over and through the pile, feasting on the tastiest bits.

"No-one will notice one more body," said Suzie, satisfied. "I guess only Citizens get buried in this age."

I nodded, staring at Nimue. The crooked arms, the bent-back head, the staring empty eyes. "She died because of me," I said. "Just a kid, with a bit of ambition and an eye to the main chance. Who really did love her old sugar daddy, at the end. Dead and gone now, because I talked her into helping us."

"You can't save them all," said Suzie.

"I didn't even try," I said. "I was too wrapped up in my own concerns. I used her . . . to get what I wanted. I don't think I much like the man I'm becoming, Suzie."

Suzie sniffed. She'd never had much time for sentiment, with good reason. "What do we do now?" she said briskly.

"We need information," I said, glad of an excuse to push aside my conscience and concentrate on the here and now.

"There must be someone, or more probably Something, in this Nightside with enough power to send us further back in Time, to where and when we need to be. There must be."

Suzie shrugged. "Can't say I know of any, off-hand. Most of the Powers we know haven't even been born or created yet." She looked around at the various temples. "I suppose we could always pray to the gods. The Roman gods were quite keen in interfering in human affairs."

"I don't think I want to attract their attention either," I said. "They'd be bound to ask questions, and the answers would only upset them."

"We have to go to the Londinium Club," Suzie said abruptly.

"Why?" I said.

"Because the Doorman in the sixth century remembered that we did. So whatever it is we do, when we meet him, it must make one hell of a first impression."

I scowled. "I hate that kind of circular thinking. I say we break the circle, so that nothing is certain any more. I don't have to go to the Club, if I don't want to. I say we go straight to the oldest bar in the world, whatever it's called in this period, and make our enquiries there."

"We could do that," said Suzie. "Only, how are we going to find it, when we don't know its name, or where it's located? I take it you don't feel like using your gift . . ."

"No, I bloody don't. The Lilith of this time would almost certainly notice . . ." I stood and thought for a time, while Suzie waited patiently. She's always had great faith in my ability to think my way out of any problem. "We need directions," I finally decided.

"Sounds like a plan," said Suzie. "Want me to start grabbing people at random, and stick my shotgun up their noses?"

"There's an easier way," I said. I knelt beside the unconscious Roman Legionnaire I'd decked earlier and brought him back to consciousness by only somewhat brutal methods. I helped him sit up, while he groaned and cursed, then smiled at him encouragingly. "We need directions, Tavius. You tell us how to find the oldest bar in the world, and we'll go away and leave you, and you'll never have to see us again. Won't that be nice?"

"The oldest bar?" the Legionnaire said sullenly. "Which one? I can think of several that could make that claim. Don't you have a name for it?"

I sighed, and looked at Suzie. "I suppose it hasn't been around long enough to establish its reputation yet."

"Then we go to the Londinium Club?"

"Looks like it. You do know where that is, right, Legionnaire?"

"Of course. But it's only for Citizens. Strictly Members only, and protected by the whole Roman pantheon. There's no way the likes of you will ever get to see the insides of it."

I punched him out again, and then spent a while walking round in small circles, nursing my wounded hand and swearing a lot. There's a reason why I try to avoid brawls, which is that I'm really crap at them. Suzie very wisely had nothing to say.

We set off through the Nightside, following Tavius's directions. The first thing I noticed was that the air was cleaner and clearer in Roman times. I could see the Nightside sky clearly, without a hint of smoke or smog. And then something really big flew across the face of the oversized moon, actually blocking it out completely for a moment. I stopped and watched, genuinely impressed. Every now and again I needed reminding that this wasn't the Nightside I knew. They did things differently here. Even more than the sixth century, this was a dangerous time, where Powers and Forces walked freely and unopposed, and humanity was a barely tolerated newcomer.

The only light came from torches and oil-lamps, firmly bolted to every suitable structure, but there still wasn't enough of it. The shadows were very deep and very dark, and many things seemed to prefer them. Crowds of people and others bustled back and forth through the narrow streets and alleyways, intent on their own business, and there was hardly any distinction between the street traffic and the pedestrians. The traffic itself was slow and stately; some wagons, some horses (with slaves following along behind to clean up after them), and what were clearly upper-class people, being carried around on reclining couches by what I thought at first were slaves, but from their dead faces and staring eyes were quite definitely zombies.

"You're the expert," I said to Suzie. "What are those couch things called?"

"Palanquins," she said immediately. "I thought you said you watched *I, Claudius*?"

"I watched it, but I didn't take notes. Did you spot the zombies?"

"Of course. They're called liches, in this period. Maybe there's a shortage of good slaves, or maybe the slaves got too uppity. You don't get back talk from the dead."

Tavius's directions had been extremely explicit, so much so I'd had to write them down. (Tavius had been really impressed by my ballpoint pen.) They did seem to involve an awful lot of going back and forth and around and around, often for no obvious point or reason. In fact, it was taking us ages to get anywhere, and I was getting really fed up with having to plough through the unrespecting crowds. So when I saw the opportunity for an obvious short cut, I took it. I strode down a perfectly ordinary-looking street, got almost to the end, then was suddenly right back where I'd started from. I stopped and looked around me. Suzie looked at me patiently, while I considered the matter. She wasn't above saying *I told you so,* preferring to save it for those really irritating moments, but I don't think she trusted my mood, right then.

"I get the feeling," I said finally, "that space in this new Nightside hasn't properly settled down yet. Directions can be arbitrary, and space can actually fold back upon itself. I've heard old stories about that, but it hasn't happened in our Nightside for ages. The Authorities tend to keep such things constant because it's good for business. So . . . I guess we'd better stick to Tavius's directions exactly, from now on."

"I would," said Suzie.

"You're dying to say *I told you so,* aren't you?"

"I wouldn't dare."

We pressed on, following the directions exactly, but we hadn't been walking for ten minutes before we walked right into a trap. We were strolling through a suspiciously deserted square when it suddenly disappeared, and we were Somewhere else. The change hit us like a blow. The air was viciously hot and sticky, and smelled of spoiled meat. The light was dark purple, and when I looked up, I saw a big red sun in a sickly pink sky. And all around us was a jungle made of flesh and blood. It stretched away for miles, trees and bush and hanging lianas, and all of it made of meat. All of it moving, slowly, as it reacted to our sudden presence. Suzie already had her shotgun out and was looking for a target.

"Is it a Timeslip?" she said, her voice calm and controlled as always.

"Could be," I said, trying for the same tone. "Some extreme alternative time-line, past or future or . . . that bloody Tavius! He deliberately didn't tell us, hoping we'd walk right into it!"

"Ugly bloody place," said Suzie, and I had to agree.

We were standing in a small clearing, in a jungle made

of meat. The huge trees were red and purple, and the large
leathery leaves had bones in them. Some of the trees were
clearly pregnant, with bulging, distended boles, patterned
with dark veins. All the plants were flesh and blood, their
pink skins sweating in the furnace heat. The stench of decaying flesh came to me from every direction, carried on
the shifting breezes, thick and nasty, leaving an indescrib-
able taste in my mouth. There were flowers, too, great
pulpy growths like Technicolor cancers, and here and there
roses red as blood stood tall on thorny spines, the crimson
petals surrounding mouths stuffed with needle teeth. The
roses all turned their heads in our direction, orientating on
Suzie and me, and harsh, hissing noises emanated from the
roses' mouths. They were talking to each other.

And beyond and underneath the heavy layers of jungle
growth, I could barely make out the blurred forms of ancient, ruined buildings. Old, very old structures, long aban-
doned by whoever or whatever built them. This was a
world where evolution had taken a very different turn. Nature, red in tooth and claw, replaced by nature red in vine
and thorn.

It was an alien landscape, like a different planet, and
Suzie and I didn't belong there. I felt . . . horribly alone.
Already some of the meat plants were turning slowly in our
direction, and the roses were hissing angrily at each other.
Plants like lumps of spoiled liver tore their pink roots out
of the dark ground and lurched towards us. Thorned ten-
drils opened out around them, like some vicious grasping
umbrella. Sticky mouths opened in the dark-veined plants.
Suzie opened up with her shotgun, fanning it back and
forth, and the plants before and around us exploded in gobbets of bloody flesh. A high, keening rose on the air, inhumanly grating, as though the whole jungle was crying out
in pain and outrage. A quick glance around showed the jungle pressing in from every direction. Even the great trees

were leaning towards and over us. Suzie kept up a steady rate of fire, the noise deafening at close range, but she wasn't even slowing the advance down. The fleshy plants soaked up the punishment and kept coming. Suzie realised she was only wasting ammunition and grabbed for one of the grenades on her belt.

I decided it was time to step in, before things really got out of hand. I grabbed the nearest rose and yanked it out of the dark ground. It squealed like a pig pulled away from its trough, thrashing its thorny spine about and trying to twist it around my wrist and arm. I held the rose firmly below the flower, took my monogrammed silver lighter out of my coat pocket, and flicked on the flame. The other roses cried out in unison, and the jungle grew very still. I held the flame close to the rose, and the petals shrank away from it.

"All right," I said. "Back off, or the rose gets it."

There was a pause, then the whole of the meat jungle fell back perceptibly. They might not understand my words, but they knew what I meant. I looked at Suzie and jerked my head backwards. She checked that the way behind us was clear and nodded. And slowly, step by step, we moved back along the path that had brought us into this awful world. The jungle watched us go, the fleshy leaves quivering with rage. The rose writhed violently in my grasp, fighting to break free, snapping at me with its nasty teeth. And then, suddenly, the purple glare snapped off, replaced by the soothing gloom of the Nightside. We'd retreated back across the border of the Timeslip. The rose let out a howl of anguish, until I slapped it round the petals and shut it up. I stuffed the rose into my coat pocket, and it grew still. I wasn't worried about the rose trying to escape; my coat can look after itself. I took several deep breaths, trying to clear the stench of spoiled meat out of my head.

"Really ugly place," said Suzie, calm and unruffled as always. She put away her shotgun and looked at me. "How did you figure out the roses were so important?"

"Easy," I said. "They were the only ones that had a language."

"Let's go to the Londinium Club," said Suzie. "And face dangers I can understand."

We followed Tavius's directions exactly, suspicious all the time for further pitfalls, but soon enough we came safely to the Londinium Club. The exterior looked the same as always, only much cleaner. The stone exterior was spotless, gleaming brightly under many lanterns, and the erotic bas-reliefs showed off details so powerful they practically leapt off the wall and mugged you. And there, standing at the stop of the steps and guarding the entrance, was the Doorman. He really was as old as everyone said he was. This time, he wore a simple white tunic, his muscular arms folded firmly across his broad chest. He took one look at Suzie and me, in our battered and blood-stained clothes, and actually came all the way down the steps to block our way more thoroughly. Since reason and kind words were clearly not an option, I reached into my coat pocket, pulled out the rose, and presented it to the Doorman. He accepted it automatically, then cried out in shock and revulsion as the thorny spine wrapped itself around his arm, and the flower went for his face, the teeth snapping at his eyes. He had to use both hands to hold it back. And while he was preoccupied, Suzie and I walked right past him, through the door, and into the lobby, our noses in the air like we belonged there.

This time, the lobby was all gleaming white tiles, with a huge coloured mosaic covering the entire floor; all of it gleaming new and fresh and shining clean. There were oil-lamps burning everywhere, filling the lobby with a golden light, so that not a single shadow should spoil the effect. The mosaic on the floor showed the entire pantheon of Roman gods and goddesses doing something so erotic and entangled I was hard-pushed to make sense of it, but it was the mosaic on the ceiling that caught my attention. It was a stylized portrait of a woman's face. My mother's face.

"I don't care if they are gods," said Suzie. "Some of those proportions can't be correct."

I drew her attention away from the floor and indicated the face on the ceiling. "That's Lilith," I said. "That's Mommie Dearest. They say she slept with demons and gave birth to monsters."

Suzie sniffed, conspicuously unimpressed. "Yeah, she looks the type. I'm more concerned with what's going on here on the floor. I mean, look at that guy on the end. You could club a baby seal to death with that."

"You don't get it," I said. "Why would the Londinium Club put Lilith's face on their lobby ceiling?"

Suzie shrugged. "Maybe she was a founding Member. That could explain its longevity . . ."

I shook my head, unconvinced. "There's got to be more to it than that. This means something . . ."

"Everything means something."

Perhaps fortunately, we were interrupted by the Club Steward walking across the lobby to join us. I knew he had to be the Steward; they all have that same arrogant poise, the same disdainful gaze. Somehow I knew we weren't going to get on. He stopped a respectful distance away from us, bowed slightly, and presented us with his best long-suffering smile.

"Your reputation proceeds you, sir and lady. The Legionnaires you ran off are still being treated for shock, and so far you are the only people ever to venture into the carnivorous jungle and come out again in one piece. You are also the first people ever to get past our Doorman. There is some talk of presenting you with a medal or striking you down with a lightning bolt. Either way, it's clear that though you are not Citizens or Members, or ever likely to be, it's got to be less trouble for all concerned if I welcome you to the Club and ask how best we can serve you. On the grounds that the sooner we can get rid of you, the better."

I looked at Suzie. "Why can't everyone be that reasonable?"

"Where would be the fun in that?" said Suzie.

"May I enquire why you have come here, sir and lady?" said the Steward.

I gave him the short version, and he nodded slowly. "Well, there are any number of gods and beings and sorcerers who are currently Club Members in good standing, who might be able to help you; and quite a few of them are in residence here today. Go through those doors, and you'll find most of them taking their ease in the steam-baths. I'm sure you'll find someone or something that can assist you. Feel free to help yourselves to the Club oils and lineaments, but don't steal the towels. We're running short again."

"Oh, I don't think we need to disturb them at their bath," I said quickly. "The dining area will do fine."

The Steward raised a shocked eyebrow. "The dining area and vomitorium are beyond the baths, sir. It is expected that all Members cleanse themselves thoroughly, before being allowed through to dine. You could not possibly be admitted in your . . . present condition. We have standards to maintain. If you will remove all your garments . . ."

"All of them?" said Suzie, a little ominously.

"Well, of course," said the Steward. "You don't take a bath with your clothes on, do you? I mean, you're obviously barbarians, but there really are limits to the kind of behaviour we're prepared to tolerate here. This is a civilised Club for civilised people. Clean civilised people. If you expect to meet with our most distinguished Members, we can't allow . . ."

"Can't?" said Suzie, her hand dropping to one of the grenades at her belt.

The Steward might not have known what a grenade was, but he knew a threat when he saw it. He drew himself up to his full height. "This Club is under the protection of the entire pantheon of Roman gods and goddesses. Start any trouble here, and you'll be leaving this lobby in several buckets."

Suzie sniffed loudly, but took her hand away from the grenade. "I don't think he's bluffing, Taylor. There's no-one more strict and unyielding about its rules and traditions than a newly formed exclusive Club. And the Roman gods were famous for their hands-on approach to smiting unbelievers."

I looked at the Steward, and he actually fell back a pace. "They couldn't keep us out."

"Maybe not," said Suzie. "But if we were to force our way in, you can bet no-one would talk to us. The kind of beings who could help us are not going to be the kind we can hope to bribe or intimidate. Hell, Taylor, what's it coming to when I'm being the voice of reason? What's the matter, you forget to put on clean underwear?"

"You don't have to do this, Suzie," I said. "You can stay here, while I go in."

"Hell with that. You need someone to watch your bare back. Especially in a place like this."

"I'm trying to protect you, Suzie. After . . . what happened to you . . ."

"I don't need protecting." She looked at me levelly. "I don't care about this, John. Really. You're being very . . . sweet, but don't worry yourself on my account."

I glared at the Steward. "This had better be worth it. Do you have any real Powers present tonight?"

"Oh yes, sir. All sorts. We even have an actual deity in residence. Poseidonis, god of the seas, has graced us with his noble presence. Be tactful with him, he's been drinking. He's also the god of horses, though no-one seems to know how that came about. Don't bring it up, you'll only upset him, and it takes ages to get all the seaweed out of the pool afterwards. If you'll follow me . . ."

He led us through the doors at the far end of the lobby and into a pleasant little changing room, with long wooden benches. Beyond the next set of doors, I could hear voices and splashing sounds. The air was perfumed and pleasantly warm. The Steward coughed meaningfully.

"If you'll let me have your . . . garments, sir and lady, I'll have them thoroughly cleaned before you leave. It won't take a moment . . ."

"Watch out for the coat," I said. "It has serious protections built in."

"I wouldn't doubt it for a moment, sir."

"And don't mess about with my weapons," growled Suzie. "Or they'll be scraping your people off the walls with a trowel."

She shrugged off her shotgun in its long holster, then took off her bandoliers of bullets and her belt of grenades. The Steward accepted them, suitably gingerly. Suzie didn't look at me as she shrugged off her leather jacket, and nothing moved in her face, nothing at all. I took off my trench coat. It felt like removing a suit of armour. Suzie took off her shirt and stepped out of her leather trousers. Underneath, she was wearing basic, functional bra and panties. It made sense. No-one else was ever expected to see them. I took off my shirt and trousers, glad I had remembered to put on a clean pair of jockeys that morning. I've never liked boxers. I like to be sure of where everything is. Suzie took off her underwear, and so did I. The Steward gathered everything up, going out of his way to make it clear our nakedness meant nothing to him. He sorted everything out into one manageable pile and lifted it up, almost disappearing behind it.

"Your clothes will be cleaned, and your weapons guarded, until you are ready to leave, sir and lady. Enjoy the baths, stay as long as you like, and please remember to get out of the pool to take a piss."

He backed out, and the doors swung shut behind him, leaving Suzie and me alone together. For a long moment we stood and looked at each other. For all the things we'd done and been through together, we'd never seen each other naked before. I'd thought I'd feel awkward, but mostly I still felt protective. I kept my gaze on her face at first, trying to be polite, but Suzie didn't bother with any of that. She looked me over with frank curiosity. So I did the same. She had so many scars, so many old hurts, tracking across her body like the map of her troubled life.

"And those are only the ones that show," said Suzie. She smiled, as our eyes met. "Not bad, Taylor. I always wondered what you'd look like, without the trench coat."

"You look great," I said. "I always thought you'd have tattoos, somewhere."

"Nah," she said dismissively. "I could never make my mind up. I just knew I'd end up hating it in the morning."

"Just as well," I said. "It would have been like scribbling graffiti across a masterpiece."

"Oh please, Taylor. I have no illusions about how I look. Even before my new face."

"You look fine," I said firmly. "Trust me."

"You smooth-talking devil, Taylor."

We couldn't maintain the light tone any more, so we stopped talking. She had a good body, with large friendly breasts and a pleasantly padded stomach. But the scars were everywhere; knife wounds, bullet wounds, the marks of tooth and claw. You don't get to be the best and most feared bounty hunter in the Nightside without being willing to fight up close and personal.

"You have scars, too," Suzie said finally. "Life has left its mark on us, John."

She reached out a hand, and slowly, cautiously, she traced some of my scars with her fingertip. Only the very tip of her forefinger, a touch gentle as a breeze, wandering across my body. I stood very still. Suzie had been sexually abused repeatedly as a child, by her own brother. She killed him for it, eventually. But ever since she'd never been able to touch or be touched, by anyone. Not even the briefest touch, the gentlest caress. Not by lovers, or friends, or even me. She stepped a little closer, and I held myself very still, not wanting to frighten her off. God alone knew how much strength it took, for her to do this small thing. I could see her breasts rising and falling as she breathed deeply. Her face was calm, thoughtful. I wanted so much to reach out to her . . . but in the end, her hand dropped to her side, and she turned her face away.

"I can't," she said. "I can't . . . Not even with you, John."

"It's all right," I said.

"No it isn't. It'll never be all right."

"You've come such a long way, Suzie."

She shook her head, still not looking at me. "What's done can't be undone. I've always known that. I can't . . . care for you, John. I don't think I have it in me any more."

"Of course you do," I said. "Five years ago, you shot me in the back to stop me leaving, remember?"

She nodded, and looked at me again. "It was a cry for attention."

I moved in close, trying hard to seem supportive without crowding her. "There was a time . . . you wouldn't even have been able to do this much, Suzie. You're changing. So am I. And we monsters must stick together."

She looked at me, and though she didn't smile, she didn't look away. Slowly, and very cautiously, I raised my hand, and with the very tips of my fingers I touched the ridged mass of scar and burn tissue that now made up the right side of her face. The hard skin felt cold and dead. Suzie looked into my eyes, hardly blinking, but she didn't flinch.

"You do know," I said. "That I will never let you be hurt like this again. I will bleed and hurt and die before I let this happen again."

But that was a step too far. The warmth went out of her eye, and I quickly took my hand away from her face. She looked at me for a long moment, her expression calm and cold and utterly controlled.

"I can look after myself, Taylor. But thanks for the thought. Shall we go and take a look at the baths?"

"Why not?" I said. The moment of intimacy had passed, and I knew there was nothing I could do to retrieve it. "But if anyone points at me and laughs, I am going to slam his head against the wall until his eyes change colour. Even if he is a god."

"Men," said Suzie. She flexed her hands unhappily. "I feel naked without my shotgun."

"You are naked."

We pushed open the changing room doors and stepped out into a large steam-filled chamber, most of it taken up with a grandiose pool. The air was immediately hot and sweaty, the steam thick as fog. Half a dozen slaves were kept busy heaping up coals on an iron brazier and pouring large jugs of water over them. Suzie and I moved forward, and the steam thinned out some as we approached the pool. Reclining at their ease on padded couches were any number of naked men and women, and a whole bunch of other forms whose nakedness made it clear they weren't even slightly human. The pool itself held several mermaids, all saucy smiles and bobbing breasts and long, forked fish tails. Half a dozen dolphins frisked up and down in the water, showing off their virtuosity with big toothy grins. There were undines and sirens and some more of the lizardly types; and sitting at the far end of the pool, thirty feet tall if he was an inch, the god of the sea, Poseidonis himself. His head brushed against the ceiling, and his legs took up the whole end of the pool. His huge body was thick with hair, and his bearded face was almost impossibly handsome. His dimensions were still human, apart from a really impressive set of equipment. I looked away. I couldn't afford to feel intimidated before I even started negotiating. In and around the pool, men and women and

others looked curiously at Suzie and me. I couldn't help
feeling that a lot of the people would have looked better
clothed.

"Hey," said Suzie. "Have you noticed about
Poseidonis . . ."

"I'm trying not to."

"Lift your eyes, Taylor. I meant, he hasn't got a navel."

I looked. He hadn't. "Of course," I said. "He was believed into being, not born."

By this time we'd reached the edge of the pool. Conver-
sation had stopped as we moved cautiously between the
Members reclining on their couches. Apparently our reputation had proceeded us here, too. Unfortunately, it didn't
stop one poor fool from reaching out and lazily caressing
Suzie's arse. She kicked him right off his couch and into
the pool. There was general laughter, and even some ap-
plause, and I relaxed a little.

"Bravely done, my dear," said Poseidonis, his great
voice rumbling through the steamy air. "Come forward,
mortals, and tell me what boon you wish of me."

We walked forward along the edge of the pool and
stopped at the end, looking up at the god. Up close, his face
was big and broad and smiling, and for all the god's size and
overwhelming presence, my first thought was *He doesn't
look too bright.* I suppose when you're a god, with a god's
power, you don't have to be.

"You're not from this Time, are you?" he said easily.
"You have the smell of Chronos about you."

"Wasn't he a Greek god?" said Suzie.

Poseidonis shrugged. "We kept a few from the old order, for completeness."

"We're travellers," I said. "From the future."

"Oh, tourists," said Poseidonis. He sounded disappointed.

"You've seen other travellers, like us?" said Suzie.

"Oh, yes." Poseidonis scratched lazily at the curly hair
on his bulging stomach. "There's always a few, passing

through, always terribly keen to tell us all about the futures they've come from. Like I care. Futures are like arseholes; everyone's got one. After all, no matter what societies men come up with, they'll always need their gods. Nothing like being immortal and powerful beyond reason, to give you job security." He frowned suddenly. "And far too many of them will insist on talking about this new god, the Christ. Can't say I know the chap. Is he popular, in your time? Has he joined our pantheon?"

"Not exactly," I said. "Where we come from, no-one believes in your pantheon any more."

His face clouded, then darkened dangerously. I knew the words were a mistake, even as I heard them coming out of my mouth, but there's something about being naked in front of a naked man five times your size that keeps you from concentrating. Poseidonis stood up abruptly and banged his head on the ceiling. Tiles cracked and shattered, broken pieces falling into the pool, while Poseidonis clutched at his head and bellowed with pain. No-one laughed, and most of the creatures in the pool retreated to the far end. The god glared around him, then he lifted his hands and lightning cracked down out of nowhere. Vivid bolts stabbed down all through the bath house, and the various Members jumped up off their couches and ran for their lives. I got the sense they'd had to do this before. The creatures in the pool vanished, disappearing back to wherever they'd come from. I grabbed a couch and overturned it, and Suzie and I hid behind it as the lightning storm continued.

"Nice one, Taylor," said Suzie.

"For a god powerful beyond all reason, he has really lousy aim," I said.

The lightning broke off abruptly and the couch was plucked away from us. Poseidonis threw it the length of the pool, and then leaned over to glare at Suzie and me. His face was bright red with rage, and very ugly. Suzie and I scrabbled backwards, then ran like hell to the other end of the bath house as his long arms stretched after us. Poseidonis was standing bent over in the pool, his hunched back pressed against the ceiling. He was growing bigger by the minute, actually filling his end of the bath house. He roared like a maddened bull, and the sound was deafening as it echoed back from the tiled walls.

"So," said Suzie, a little breathlessly. "We're naked and unarmed, facing a really pissed off god. What's your next bright idea?"

"I'm thinking!"

"Well, think faster!"

Poseidonis was still growing, the bath's ceiling cracking apart as his back and shoulders heaved up against it. He reached for Suzie and me with his huge hands, and we scattered in different directions. The god paused for a moment, torn between two conflicting decisions, and while he wrestled with the problem, I happened to notice that the great pool was almost completely drained of water. Poseidonis was the god of the sea, and he'd sucked all the water out of the pool to make up his new bulk. But this was also a steam bath . . . I grabbed one of the couches, used it as a lever, and overturned the iron brazier full of coals right into the pool. There was a great rushing up of steam, as the coals hit what was left of the water, and in a moment everything disappeared behind a thick fog. Poseidonis cried out angrily, but his voice didn't sound nearly as loud.

The steam slowly thinned away, to reveal an almost human-sized god, standing confusedly by the side of the pool. The extreme heat had boiled the excess water right out of him. Suzie ran forward and was upon him in a moment, a length of jagged wood from a dismembered couch in her hand. She grabbed a handful of the god's curly hair, jerked back his head, and set the sharp wooden edges at his throat.

"All right, all right!" yelled Poseidonis. "Mortal, call your woman off!"

"Maybe," I said, strolling down the pool to join them. "Are you feeling in a more cooperative mood, now?"

"Yes, yes! You've got to let me get out of here, before the heat evaporates me completely! I hate it when that happens."

"We need a favour," I said firmly.

Poseidonis scowled petulantly. "Anything, to get rid of you."

"My associate and I need to go further back in Time," I said.

"Two hundred years should do it," said Suzie.

"To the very beginnings of the Nightside," I concluded.

"Ah," said the god. "Now that's a problem. Gods! Ease off with that wood, woman! Just because my godly person can repair any damage, eventually, it doesn't mean I'm not sensitive to pain! Look, I don't do Time travel. That's Chronos's province. I'm only the god of the sea, and horses, because of a book-keeping error, and I have no power over Time. We gods are really very strict when it comes to demarcation. And no, I can't introduce you to Chronos; no-one's seen him in years. I'm sorry, but I really can't help you!"

"Then who could?" said Suzie.

"I don't know . . . I don't! Honestly I don't! Oh gods, I'm going to end up with splinters, I know it . . . Look; there's this really awful bar not far from here, supposed to be the oldest bar in the Nightside. That's the place to ask."

Suzie glared at me. "Don't you even think of saying *I told you so,* Taylor."

"I wouldn't dare," I assured her. I looked at Poseidonis. "What's the bar called?"

"Dies Irae. Which only goes to show that someone there has a classical and very warped sense of humour. Would you like me to transport you right there?"

"You can do that?" I said.

"Only with your consent, in my current weakened state,

or I'd have transported you both to the moon, by now . . . Ow! That hurt, woman!"

"Send us to the bar," I said. "Straight there, with no detours, and with all our clothing and weapons. And don't even think about coming after us."

"Believe me," said the god, "I never want to see either of you, ever again, for the whole of my immortal lifetime."

TEN

To Die for

When Suzie Shooter and I arrived at the oldest bar in the world, we were wearing each other's clothes. Now, whether this was one last act of spite from an extremely pissed off god, or simply another example of his not being terribly bright, the result was that Suzie and I arrived seeming both surprised and vulnerable. Which is always dangerous in the oldest bar in the world, whatever period you're in. A great hulking figure wrapped in an entire bearskin lurched up to Suzie, grinning nastily. Suzie kicked him square in the nuts, with such force and enthusiasm that people sitting ten feet away made pained noises in sympathy, and I rabbit-punched the guy on the way down, just to make my feelings on the matter plain, too. Several of the bear man's friends decided to get involved and got to their feet, drawing various weapons and making various threatening noises. I drew Suzie's shotgun from the holster hanging down my back and tossed it to her, and shortly there were blood and brains all over the nearest bare stone wall. And after that, everyone left us strictly alone.

People at the surrounding tables and long wooden benches carefully paid no attention as Suzie and I stripped off and exchanged outfits. Modesty be damned; there was no way in hell I was going to fight my way through the Nightside wearing Suzie's bra and pants. And judging by the speed with which Suzie disrobed, she had clearly had similar thoughts. We reclaimed our own clothes, dressed quickly, and spent some time checking that all our weapons and devices were where they should be. We didn't want to have to go back to the Londinium Club and register a complaint. Suddenly and violently and all over the place. But everything was where it should be, and it had to be said, the Club had done an excellent job of cleaning our clothes. There wasn't a blood-stain to be seen anywhere, and my white trench coat hadn't looked so dazzlingly clean since I bought it. They'd even polished the metal studs on Suzie's leather jacket and buffed up all the bullets in her bandoliers. Having thus re-established our dignity, Suzie and I glared around us and strode through the packed tables and benches to the long wooden bar at the rear of the room.

The place was a dump: overcrowded, filthy dirty, and it smelled really bad. There were no windows, no obvious ventilation, and greasy smoke hung on the air like floating vomit. Torches in holders and oil-lamps set in niches in the bare stone walls only just pushed back the general gloom. There was something sticky on the floor, and I didn't even want to think about what it might be. There weren't any rats, but that was probably only because the current clientele had eaten them. For once, the bar's customers seemed mostly human. Rough and nasty, and the dregs of the Earth, most of them looked like being thugs and scumbags would be a definite step up the social ladder. They wore simple filthy tunics and furs that looked as though they'd still been attached to their donor animals as recently as that morning. Everyone was heavily armed and looked ready to use their weapons at a moment's provocation.

The bar was a raucous place, with half a dozen fights going on and an awful lot of really bad community singing. Someone who'd been dipped in woad from head to toe was tattooing a complicated Druidic design on a barbarian's back, with a bone needle, a pot of woad, and a small hammer; and the barbarian was being a real wimp about it, to the amusement of his companions. Two unconscious drunks were being very thoroughly rolled by half a dozen whores who looked more scary than sexy. One of them winked at me as I passed, and I had to fight not to flinch. There were a dozen or so hairy types I was pretty sure were werewolves, at least one vampire, and one bunch of particularly brutal types that I wouldn't have accepted as human without a detailed family tree and a gene test.

"You take me to the nicest places, Taylor," said Suzie. "I hope all my shots are up to date."

"I guess this place hasn't had time to establish its reputation yet," I said.

"It has nowhere to go but up. I feel like shooting everyone here on general principles."

"You always do, Suzie."

"True."

People actually drew back as we approached the long wooden bar, giving us plenty of room. In a dive like this, that was a real compliment. I slammed the flat of my hand on the bar, to get the bar staff's attention, and something small, dark, and scuttling ran over the back of my hand. I didn't scream, but it was a near thing. Someone further down the bar caught the small, dark, scuttling thing, and ate it. A man and a woman were serving behind the bar, handing out wine in cheap pewter mugs and cups. The man was tall for this age, being a good five-foot-seven or -eight, and wore a rough tunic so filthy it was impossible to tell what colour it might have been originally. He had a long pale face, with jet-black hair and a bushy beard, separated by scowling eyes, an aquiline nose with flaring nostrils, and a sulky mouth. The woman with him was barely five feet tall but made up for it with a constant glare of concentrated malevolence that she bestowed on one and all. She had sculpted her dark blonde hair into two jutting horns with liberal use of clay, and she had a face like a bulldog's arse. Her filthy tunic successfully hid any other feminine charms she might have possessed. Between them, these two poured drinks, handed them out, snatched up the money, and loudly refused to give any change. Every now and again they hit people with large wooden clubs they kept under the bar. It wasn't always clear why they did so, but in a place like this I had no doubt the victims deserved it, and probably a whole lot more. The man and the woman stubbornly ignored my attempts to get their attention, until Suzie fired her shotgun into the bottles stacked behind the bar; an action that has always been one of her favourite attention-getters. The customers around us moved even further away, some of them remarking loudly on the lateness of the hour and how they really had to be getting home. The man and woman behind the bar slouched reluctantly over to join us. He looked even more sulky; she looked even more venomous.

"I don't suppose there's any chance of getting you to pay for the damage?" said the man.

"Not a hope in hell," I said cheerfully.

He sniffed lugubriously, as though he hadn't expected anything else. "I'm Marcellus. This is the wife, Livia. We run this place, for our sins. Who are you, and what do you want?"

"I'm John Taylor, and this is Suzie Shooter . . ."

"Oh, we've heard about you," snapped Livia. "Trouble-makers. Outsiders. Barbarians with no respect for the proper ways of doing things." She sniffed loudly, very much like her husband. "Unfortunately, it seems you are also very powerful and dangerous with it, in nasty and un-expected ways, so we are forced to be polite to you. See, I smile upon you. This is my polite smile."

It looked more like a rat caught in a trap. I looked at Marcellus. His smile wasn't much more successful. I got the feeling he didn't get a lot of practice, with a wife like Livia.

"You should be honoured," he said gloomily. "She doesn't smile for just anyone, you know."

"Shut up, Marcellus, I'm talking."

"Yes, dear."

"I suppose you expect a drink on the house?" said Livia, in the tone of voice normally associated with accusing someone of doing rude things with corpses. "Marcellus, two cups of the good stuff."

"Yes, dear."

He carefully poured out two quite small measures of red wine, into pewter cups that looked like they'd been beaten into shape by someone who was already drunk. Or at least in a really bad mood. Suzie and I tried the wine, then we both pulled back our lips in the same disgusted expression. I must have tasted worse in my life, but I'd be hard-pressed to say when. It was like vinegar that had been pissed in, only not as pleasant.

"This is the good stuff?" said Suzie.

"Of course," said Livia. "This is what we drink our-selves."

That explains a lot, I thought, but for once had the sense not to say it out loud. "You run this bar?" I said.

"Sort of," said Marcellus. "Some old witch owns the place; we only run it for her. We're slaves, bound to this bar by law and magic for the rest of our lives. We do a good job because the geas compels us to, but in our few free moments we dream of escape and revenge."

"And making others suffer, as we have been made to," said Livia.

"Well yes, that, too, naturally."

"We weren't always slaves, you know," said Livia, with well-rehearsed bitterness. "Oh no! We were respectable people, I'll have you know. Roman Citizens, in good standing. Wouldn't have been seen dead in a place like this . . . But then *he* got into business troubles . . ."

She turned the full force of her glare on her husband, who drooped a little more under the pressure of her gaze. "They were strictly transitory difficulties," he said sullenly. "Cash flow problems. That sort of thing. If I'd been allowed a little more time, I'm sure I could have sorted things out to everyone's satisfaction . . ."

"But you couldn't," Livia said flatly. "So our creditors had our business shut down and sold us both off as slaves at public auction, to cover our debts." She actually sniffled a moment, overcome by the memory. "The humiliation of it! All our friends and neighbours were there, watching. People who'd eaten at our table and made free with our money and influence! Some of them laughed. Some of them even bid!"

"We were lucky to be sold as a set, my dear," said Marcellus. "As husband and wife. We might have been parted forever."

"Yes," said Livia. "There is that. We have never been parted, and never will be."

"Never," said Marcellus. They held hands, and while neither of them actually stopped scowling, there was a definite togetherness about them. With anyone else, it might have even been touching.

"Anyway," said Marcellus, "because we had some experience of running a drinking establishment, from earlier in our lives, we were bought by the owner of this appalling place, who needed staff in a hurry. We were bought by a factor; we've never seen the owner in person. If we'd known who it was, and what the bar was, we'd probably have volunteered for the salt mines. This place goes through staff faster than a slave galley. The last husband and wife were killed, cooked, and eaten, on a somewhat rowdy Saturday night. No-one even knows what happened to the pair before that."

"No-one has ever lasted as long as us," said Livia, with a certain amount of pride. "Mainly because we don't take any crap from anyone. You have to be firm, but fair. Firm, and occasionally downright vicious. My husband may not look like much, but he's a real terror when he's roused."

"Ah, but no-one could be more dangerous than you, my dear," Marcellus said generously. He smiled fondly as he patted her hand. "No-one can slip a purgative or a poison into a wine cup better than you."

"And no-one cuts a throat more neatly than you, dear Marcellus. He's like a surgeon, he really is. It's a joy to watch him work."

"Who actually owns this bar?" I said, feeling a distinct need to change the subject.

"Some powerful sorceress, of old times," said Marcellus. "Been around for ages, supposedly. Her name is Lilith."

"Of course," I said heavily. "It would have to be."

"We've never met her," said Livia. "Don't know anyone who has. A real absentee landlady."

Suzie looked at me. "Why would Lilith want to own a bar?"

"I'll ask her," I said. "After I've asked all the other questions on my list."

"So," said Marcellus. "What unfortunate but necessary business brings you to this appalling place? What help and or advice can we offer you, so that you'll go away and stop bothering us?"

"We're looking for a Being of Power," I said. "Someone or something with enough magic to send us both back in Time, at least a couple of hundred years. Can you recommend anyone?"

Marcellus and Livia looked at each other. "Well," Livia said finally, "if that's what you want . . . Your best bet would be the Roman gods and goddesses. They've all got more power than they know what to do with, and every single one of them is open to prayer, flattery, and bribes."

"Not really an option," I said. "We upset Poseidonis really badly."

Marcellus sniffed loudly. "Don't let that worry you; the gods don't like each other much anyway. One big dysfunctional family, with incest and patricide always on the menu. I can name you half a dozen off-hand who'd help you out just to spite Poseidonis."

"He's supposed to call himself Neptune these days," said Livia. "But he's so dim he keeps forgetting."

I considered the suggestion. "Can you trust these gods?" I said finally.

"Of course not," said Marcellus. "They're gods."

"Suggest someone else," said Suzie.

"Well, there is supposed to be this small town somewhere out in the South-West, where you can meet the Earth Mother in person, and petition her for help," Marcellus said thoughtfully. "But that's at least a month's travel, through dangerous territory."

"Then there's the Druidic gods," said Livia. "Technically, it's death to have any dealings with them, under Roman law, but this is the Nightside, so . . . How much money have you got?"

"Enough," I said, hoping it was true.

"The Druid shamans are powerful magic-users," said Marcellus. "Especially outside the cities, but they're a vicious bunch, and treacherous with it."

"We can look after ourselves," said Suzie.

"What would they want for helping us?" I said.

"An arm and a leg," said Marcellus. "Possibly literally. Very keen on live sacrifice, when it comes to granting boons, your Druidic gods. Can you think of anyone you wouldn't much mind handing over to the Druids, for ritual torture and sacrifice?"

"Not yet," said Suzie.

Livia shrugged. "Most of the gods or beings will want payment in blood or suffering, your soul, or someone else's."

"I suppose . . . there's always Herne the Hunter," Marcellus said doubtfully.

"Yes!" I said, slamming my hand down on the bar again, and then wished I hadn't, as something sticky clung to it as I pulled my hand back again. "Of course, Herne the Hunter! I'd forgotten he was here, in this time."

"Herne?" said Suzie. "That scruffy godling who hangs around Rats' Alley with the rest of the homeless?"

"He's a Power, here and now," I said. "A Major Power, drawing his strength from the wild forests of old England, and all the creatures that live in it. He was, or more properly will be, Merlin's teacher. Oh yes . . . He's got more than enough power to help us out."

"If you can convince him," said Livia.

"I can convince anyone," said Suzie.

"Where can we find Herne the Hunter?" I said.

"He lives out in the wild woods, far and far from the cities and civilisation of Man," said Marcellus. "No-one finds him unless he wants to be found, and those that do mostly regret it. But my wife and I have had dealings with Herne and his Court in the past. We can take you right to him."

"We could," Livia said quickly. "But what's in it for us? What will you give us to take you right to Herne the Hunter?"

Suzie and I looked at each other. "What do you want?" I said resignedly.

"Our freedom," said Marcellus. "Freedom from this awful place, our awful lives, our undeserved slavery."

"We will do anything, to be free again," said Livia. "And then we shall have our revenges on all those who scorned and mocked us!"

"Free us from our chains," said Marcellus. "And we will do anything for you."

"Anything," said Livia.

"All right," I said. "You've got a deal. Take us to Herne, and I'll break you free from whatever geas holds you here."

Livia sneered at me. "It's not that simple. The old witch Lilith is powerful; can you stop her sending agents after us, to reclaim her property?"

"She'll listen to me," I said. "She's my mother."

Marcellus and Livia looked at me blankly for a moment, then they both backed away from me, the same way you'd back away from a snake you'd just realised was poisonous. There was shock in their faces, and fear, and then . . . something else, but they turned away to mutter urgently to each other before I could figure out what it was. Suzie looked at me thoughtfully.

"I thought we'd agreed it would be a bad idea for this period's Lilith to find out you were here?"

"Give me a break," I said quietly. "I'm thinking on my feet here. I can find a way to break their geas; that's what I do, remember? But I don't think I trust either of this pair further than I could throw a wet camel, certainly not enough to let them in on all my little secrets, okay?"

Marcellus and Livia approached us again. Their faces were carefully blank, but their body language was decidedly wary.

"We'll take you to Herne," said Marcellus. "We've decided that if anyone can get us our freedom and our revenge, it's you. But know this: Herne the Hunter is not the easiest of gods to deal with. He cares nothing for mortal men and women. He has been known to use them as prey in his hunts. And he hates everything that comes from the cities."

"Don't worry," I said. "We have something we can use to buy his help."

"We do?" said Suzie.

"Knowledge of what the future holds for him," I said. "If he listens, it's possible he could change what fate currently holds in store for him. But he probably won't; gods always think it can't happen to them. But . . . I never met a Being yet who could resist knowing the future."

"Can I point out that Poseidonis didn't handle this knowledge at all well?"

"Well, yes; but Poseidonis is a dick."

"And a big one, too," Suzie said solemnly.

"If you two have quite finished muttering together," Livia said severely, "may I point out that my husband and I are prevented from leaving this bar until either our replacement shift arrives, or the bar is empty?"

"No problem," I said. "Suzie?"

And several shotgun blasts and one shrapnel grenade later, the bar was completely empty.

"What do you mean, we have to ride horses?" said Suzie, scowling ominously.

"Herne the Hunter holds his Court in the wild woods," Marcellus explained patiently. "He never enters the city. So, we have to go to him. And since that involves a lengthy journey, we need horses."

I looked at the four horses Marcellus wanted me to buy. The horse-trader kept bowing and smiling and saying complimentary things about my obvious good judgement, but I faded him out. Marcellus and Livia had chosen these four horses out of the many available, and I wasn't about to show myself up by saying something inappropriate. All I knew about horses was that they had a leg at each corner and which end to offer the sugar lumps to. The horses looked back at me with slow insolence, and the nearest one casually tried to step on my foot. I glared at Marcellus.

"How do I know the trader isn't cheating me over the price?"

"Of course he's cheating you," said Marcellus. "This is the Nightside. But because Livia and I have done business with him before, he's prepared to let us have these horses at a special, only mildly extortionate price. If you think you can do any better, you are, of course, free to haggle for yourself."

"We don't do haggling," Suzie said haughtily. "We tend more to intimidation."

"We noticed," said Livia. "But since we really don't want to attract attention, pay the man and let's get going."

Reluctantly, I handed over more coins from Old Father Time's seemingly bottomless purse. The trader retired, bowing and grinning and scraping all the way, and I knew I'd paid tourist prices. The four of us approached our new mounts. I'd never ridden a horse in my life. It was a big beast, and a lot taller at the shoulder than I'd expected. Suzie glared right into her horse's face, and it actually looked away bashfully. Mine showed me its huge blocky teeth and rolled its eyes meaningfully. Matters became even more complicated when I discovered that in Roman times, horse-riding didn't involve saddles, stirrups, or even bridles. Just a blanket over the horse's back and some very flimsy-looking reins.

"I can ride a motor-bike," said Suzie. "How much harder can this be?"

"I have a horrible suspicion we're about to find out," I said.

Marcellus boosted Livia onto her mount, and then vaulted onto his horse's back like he'd been doing it all his

life. Suzie and I looked at each other. Several false starts
and one really embarrassing tumble later, the horse-trader
provided us with special mounting ladders (for an extra
payment), and Suzie and I were up and onto our horses,
trying to hold our reins like we looked like we knew what
to do with them. It seemed a very long way off the ground.
And then suddenly Old Father Time's protective magic
kicked in again, and immediately I knew all there was to
know about how to ride a horse. I sat up straighter and took
up the slack in the reins. The horse settled down, as it realised I wasn't a complete idiot after all, and a quick glance
at Suzie showed she was in control, too. I nodded curtly to
Marcellus and Livia, and we set off.

It took quite a while to get to the boundary of the city.
The Nightside was a big place, even in its early days, and
just as before we had to go the long way round, to avoid
Timeslips and places where directions were often a matter
of opinion. But finally we rounded a corner, and all the
buildings stopped abruptly. Ahead of us there were only
vast rolling grassy flatlands, stretching away like a great
green ocean, with the dark mass of the forest standing out
in spiky silhouette on the far horizon, standing proudly
against the night sky. Occasional strange lights would
move within that dark mass, fleeting and unnatural. The air
was still and cold, but pleasantly fresh after the thick
smells of the city.

Suzie and I followed Marcellus and Livia as they set out
across the grasslands. They set a brisk, steady pace, but
though we soon left the city behind, the grassy plain
seemed to stretch away forever, untouched and unspoiled
in this new young land that wasn't even called England yet.
The night was strangely quiet, and there was no sign anywhere of another living thing, but still I couldn't shake the
feeling of being observed by unseen, unfriendly eyes. Now
and again we'd pass a long burial cairn, standing out
among the tall grasses. Piled-up stones marking the resting

place of some once-important person, now long forgotten, even their names lost to history. It suddenly occurred to me to look up, and there in the night sky were only ordinary stars and a normal full moon. We had left the Nightside behind with the city.

The dark forest grew steadily larger, spreading across the horizon until it filled our whole view. The horses stirred uneasily as we drew near, and by the time we reached the edge of the forest they were snorting loudly and trying to toss their heads, and we actually had to force them across the forest boundary. They were smarter than we were. The moment we entered the wild woods, I knew we'd come to an alien place, where mortal men did not belong. The trees were bigger and taller than any I had ever seen before, huge and vast from centuries of growth. This was the old forest of old Britain, an ancient primal place, dark and threatening. Moving slowly between the towering trees was like being a small child again, lost in an adult-sized world. A single beaten path led between closely packed trees, often blocked by low-hanging branches we had to brush aside. "No swords, no cutting," Livia whispered. "We don't want to wake the trees."

It was still impossibly quiet, like the bottom of the ocean. No animal sounds, no birds or even insects. The air was heavy with a sharp, musky scent, of earth and vegetation and growing things. And now and again a gusting breeze would bring us the impossibly rich scent of some night-blooming flower. Shafts of shimmering moonlight fell between the trees, or illuminated some natural clearing, somehow always supplying just enough light for us to follow the rough path.

"Do any people live here?" Suzie quietly asked.

"They wouldn't dare," said Livia, just as quietly. "This is a wild place. This is what we build cities against."

"Then who's watching us?" said Suzie.

"The woods," said Marcellus. "And Herne's people, of

course. They've been aware of us ever since we crossed the boundary. The only reason they haven't attacked is because they remember me and Livia; and they're curious. They can tell there's something different about you two."

And suddenly, without any warning, there were things moving in between the trees. Moving silently and gracefully, in and out of the moonlight, at the edge of our vision. Things that moved along with us, darting ahead or dropping behind, but always keeping pace. Now and again something would pause in a pool of light, showing itself off, tantalizing us with glimpses. There were bears and giant boars, both long since vanished from the few tame woods remaining in modern England. Huge stags, with massive branching antlers, and grey wolves, long and lean and stark. Animals moved all around us, padding along in unearthly silence, slowly closing in on us, until suddenly I noticed that we'd left the beaten path and were being herded in some new direction. I looked quickly at Marcellus and Livia, but they didn't seem at all disturbed, or even surprised. Suzie had her shotgun out. I gestured for her to remain calm, but she kept the gun balanced across her lap, glaring suspiciously about her.

Sparkling lights appeared in the darkness up ahead, bright and scintillating glows that danced in patterns too intricate for human eyes; will-o'-the-wisps, with no body or substance, only living moments of gossamer light, all mischief and malice and merry madness. They sang sweetly in no human language, beckoning us on. Birds began to sing and hoot and howl, but again it was no form of bird-song that I had ever heard before. It was a light, mocking, dangerous sound, a clear warning that we were in enemy territory. And once, in a ragged clearing lit eerily bright, I saw a group of elves dancing in silent harmony, moving elegantly through strict patterns that made no sense at all; or perhaps so much sense that mere human minds could not comprehend or contain their true significance. A procession of badgers crossed our path, then stopped to watch us pass by with wise, knowing eyes. I could feel the wild woods coming alive all around us, showing us the shapes of all the life we had passed by and through, unknowing. Life that had hidden itself from us, until then—when it was too late for us to turn back, or escape.

The great trees fell suddenly back and away to both sides, and the horses came to a sudden halt. Their heads hung down listlessly, as though they'd been drugged, or ensorcelled. Ahead of us lay a huge clearing, lit bright as day. Will-o'-the-wisps spun in mad circles, and there were other, stranger shapes also made of nothing but light. They drifted back and forth overhead, huge and graceful, flowing like fluorescent manta rays. And straight ahead of us, on the far side of the clearing, sat the old god Herne the Hunter, and all the monstrous creatures of his wild Court.

Marcellus and Livia swung down from their horses and looked at me expectantly. I looked at Suzie, and we both dismounted. Suzie carried her shotgun casually, but somehow it was always aimed right at Herne. The four of us slowly walked forward across that great open space, Marcellus and Livia leading the way as easily and calmly as though they were going to church. And perhaps they were. With every step I took, I could feel the pressure of watching eyes. We were surrounded. I could feel it. And more than that, I knew that none of us were welcome here, in this ancient, primordial place.

We finally stood before Herne the Hunter, and he looked nothing like the small, diminished thing I'd known in Rats' Alley. That Herne had been many centuries older, shrunken in upon himself, his power lost to the relentless encroachment of man and his civilisation, sweeping across the great green lands of England. This Herne was a Being and a Power, a nature god in his prime and in his element, and his wide, wolfish grin made it clear that we had only been allowed before him by his permission. We were at his mercy. He was still a squat and ugly figure, heavy-boned with an animal's graceful musculature, but his compact body burned with rude good health and godly power. Huge goat's horns curled up from his lowering brow, on his great leonine head, and his eyes held the hot, gleeful malice of every predator that ever was.

There was a force and a vitality in him that burned like a furnace, and simply looking at him you knew he could run all day and all night and never tire, and still tear his prey limb from limb with his bare hands at the end of the hunt. His dark copper skin was covered with hair so thick it was almost fur, and he had hooves instead of feet. He was Herne and Pan and the laughter in the woods. The piper at the gates of dawn, and the bloody-mouthed thing that squatted over endless kills. His unwavering smile showed sharp, heavy teeth, made for rending and tearing. He smelled of sweat and shit and animal musk, and even as we watched he pissed carelessly on the ground between his feet, the sharp acidic smell disturbing the animals around him. They stirred and stamped their feet uneasily. Their god was marking his territory.

This was not the Herne I had known, or expected, and I was afraid of him. His thick scent stirred old atavistic instincts in me. I wanted to fight him, or run from him, or bow down and worship him. I was far from home, in an alien place, and I knew in my blood and my bone and my water that I should never have come here. This was Herne, the spirit of the hunt and the thrill of the chase, the brute animal force that drives the raw red passion of savagery in nature, dripping red in tooth and claw. He was the wildness of the woods and the triumph of the strong over the weak. He was everything we left behind, when we went out of the woods to become civilised.

And I had thought to come here, to trick or intimidate him into granting me a favour? I must have been mad.

Herne the Hunter sat in mocking majesty on a great

scalloped Throne fashioned from old, discoloured bones. Furs and scalps hung from the arms of the Throne, some of them still dripping fresh blood. There were arrangements of teeth and claws, too, souvenirs and trophies of past hunts, too many to count. Suzie leaned suddenly in close to whisper in my ear, and I almost jumped out of my skin. Her expression was as cold and controlled as always, and her voice was reassuringly steady.

"Marcellus and Livia seemed to find their way here surprisingly easily," she murmured. "And none of this seems to come as any surprise or shock to them. A suspicious person might almost think they'd been here before. You know; it's still not too late for me to shoot and blow up anything that moves, while we beat a dignified but hasty retreat."

"I think we passed 'too late' when we entered the wood," I said, quietly. "So let's keep the murder and mayhem as a last resort. Besides, we're not going to win Herne's help by shooting up his Court."

"I'm not deaf, you know," snapped Livia. "As it happens, my husband and I have been here before, many times."

"Oh yes," said Marcellus. "Many times. We know the god Herne of old, and he knows us."

"You see, we weren't sold into slavery over business debts," said Livia, smiling a really unpleasant smile. "It was more to do with the nature of our business."

"We sold slaves to Herne," Marcellus said briskly. "Bought them quite legally, at market, then brought them here, into the wild wood, to be prey for the god's Wild Hunt. They do so love to chase human victims, you see. Partly for revenge, for cutting down the forests to build their towns and farms and cities, but mainly because nothing runs better or more desperately than a hunted human. And for a while, all was well. We supplied a demand, for a suitable price, the Court enjoyed their Hunts, and everyone was happy. Well, apart from the slaves, of course, but no-one

cares about slaves. That's the point. But one cold winter
there was a desperate shortage of slaves, and prices went
through the roof. So Livia and I took to abducting people
off the streets. No-one who would be noticed or missed—
only the weak and the stupid and the poor."

"Only they were missed," said Livia. "And someone
made a fuss, there's always some busybody sticking their
nose in where it isn't wanted, and the Legions got involved. And they caught us in the act."

"We'd made an awful lot of money," said Marcellus.
"And we spent most of it on lawyers, but it didn't do any
good. I gave what I considered a very spirited defence before the magistrates, but they wouldn't listen. I mean, it's
not as if we ever abducted a Citizen . . ."

"It was an election year," Livia said bitterly. "And so they
took everything from us and sold us into slavery. But thanks
to you, we now have a chance for freedom, and revenge."

"Revenge," said Marcellus. "On all our many enemies."
And they both laughed.

They turned abruptly away from us and bowed low to
the god Herne. I thought it diplomatic to bow, too, and even
Suzie had the sense to incline her head briefly. The monstrous creatures of Herne's Court were watching us avidly,
and I really didn't like the way they looked at us. Livia
noticed my interest, and took it upon herself to introduce
various members of the Court. Her voice was openly
mocking.

Hob In Chains was a huge and blocky humanish figure,
a good ten feet tall with huge slabs of muscle and a boar's
head. Great curling tusks protruded from his mouth, and
his deep-set eyes were fierce and red and mad. Long iron
chains fell about his naked malformed body from an iron
collar round his thick neck. Man had tried to chain him up
long ago, but it hadn't taken. His hands and forearms
looked as though they'd been dipped in blood, so fresh it
still dripped and steamed on the air. Half a dozen little men

with pig's heads squatted on their haunches about his cloven feet, grunting and squealing as they vied for position. They looked at Suzie and me with hungry, impatient eyes, and thick strings of slaver fell from their mouths. Some of them still wore rags and tatters, from the time when they used to be human, before Hob In Chains bent them to his will.

Tomias Squarefoot was quite clearly a Neanderthal. Barely five feet tall, he was nearly as wide, with a squat, hulking body and a face that was neither human nor ape. He had no chin, and his mouth was a wide, lipless gash, but his eyes were strangely kind. He studied Suzie and me thoughtfully, scratching unselfconsciously at his hairy, naked body.

A dozen oversized wolves were pointed out to me as werewolves, and I saw no reason to doubt Livia. Their eyes held a human intelligence, alongside an inhuman appetite. There were liches, so recently risen from their graves that dark earth still clung to their filthy vestments. They had dead white flesh and burning eyes, and hands like claws.

There were ogres and bogles and goblins, and other worse creatures whose very names and natures had been lost to human history. Herne's Court—wild and fierce and deadly. And backing them up, pressing in close from every side, all the wild animals of the forest, gathered together in the only place where they could know a kind of truce. They glared at Suzie and me like a jury, with Herne the hanging judge. The god leaned suddenly forward on his bone Throne, and will-o'-the-wisps circled madly above his horned head like a living halo.

"Marcellus and Livia," said Herne, in a voice warm as summer sun, rough as a goat's bray. "It has been some time since you graced our Court with your mercenary presence. We had heard that you had fallen from grace, in that damned city."

"So we had, wild lord," Marcellus said smoothly. "But

we have escaped those who would hold us slaves, and we come to you to restore our fortunes again. My wife and I bring you a gift—two travellers called John Taylor and Suzie Shooter. They think they are here to beg a boon from you."

"They're really not very bright," said Livia.

"Told you so," murmured Suzie. "Who do you want me to shoot first?"

"Hold off a while," I murmured back. "There's still a chance I can talk our way out of this."

"I can always use two more victims for my Hunt," Herne said lazily. "But it will take more than this to restore you to my goodwill."

"But the man is special," said Livia. "He is the son of that old witch Lilith."

And at that the whole monstrous Court rose up as one. Herne surged up out of his Throne, roaring like a great bear, but the savage sound was all but drowned out in the massed braying and howling of his Court. They swept forward, from all sides at once, with reaching hands and claws and fanged mouths, and the hatred in their raised voices beat on the air like a living thing. Suzie didn't even have time to bring her shotgun to bear on a single target before the creatures of the wild were all over her. They tore the shotgun out of her grasp and bore her to the ground, fighting and kicking all the way.

I didn't fare any better. Marcellus hit me expertly behind the ear with a leadweighted cosh even as his wife sold me out to Herne, and I was already on my knees and only half-conscious when the Court hit me from all sides. And for a long time there was only the impact of blows and kicks, and the pain of flesh torn by tooth and claw, and blood spilling thickly onto the dirty ground around me.

Eventually they tired of their sport, or Herne called them off, and the monstrous Court reluctantly drew back, resuming their previous positions around the perimeter of the clearing. They were panting and laughing, and all of them had some of my and Suzie's blood on them. We were hauled to our feet and held roughly in position before the Throne by the pig-headed men. Herne sat regally before us and regarded the damage his people had done with smiling satisfaction. There was blood on my face and in my mouth, and I hurt everywhere I could feel, but my head was already clearing. I'd been worked over by professionals, and this bunch of animals didn't even come close. Let me get my thoughts together, and I'd show this wood god a few tricks he'd never forget. I grinned savagely at Herne, ignoring the blood that spilled down my chin from split lips, and for a moment he looked uncertain. He had made a mistake in not letting his creatures kill me while they could; and I vowed I would make him and them regret such foolishness.

And then I looked across at Suzie, and forgot about everything but her. Her leathers were torn and bloody, and her head hung low. Only the pig-headed men kept her upright. Blood dripped steadily from her damaged face. They'd really done a job on her; because Suzie Shooter would never stop struggling as long as there was an ounce of fight left in her. And so she hung between the pig men like a bloody rag doll, and didn't answer me when I called her name. Marcellus and Livia laughed at me, and the Court laughed, too, in their various ways. I fought madly against the hands holding me; but there were too many of them, and my head hurt too much for me to concentrate enough to work my usual tricks. I couldn't even get my hands near my coat pockets.

They hit me some more, just because they could, and I tried not to cry out. But of course I did. After a while, I realised dully that they had stopped, and Herne was speaking to me. I raised my head and glared at him.

"Lilith's son," said Herne, in a thick gloating voice. "You have no idea how pleased we all are, to have you here. In our presence, in our power. There is no name more hated to us than that of Lilith, who created the city Nightside, in the name of absolute freedom, then banned us from it. Because we are wild, and like to break the things we play with. Because we would tear down the city, and stamp out the human civilisation she favours. There is the city and there is the wild, and only one can triumph. We have always known that. Lilith offered freedom for all, but only on her terms. And only we were wise enough to see the contradiction in that, so only we were banished. Lilith has made us the past, a thing to be passed by, to be superseded and forgotten, and we will have our revenge for that."

"This is all news to me," I said, as clearly as I could. "But then, Mother and I have never talked much. What do you want with me, Herne?"

"To hurt you, and thus by proxy hurt Lilith," said Herne. "You shall be the prey in our Wild Hunt, and we shall chase and harry you all through the wild woods, hurting and killing you by inches, driving you on till you can go no further. And while you grovel before us and beg for mercy, we will tear you apart. Only your head shall be left intact, that we might send it to your mother, as a sign of our regard for her."

"She won't know me," I said. "My death will mean nothing to her."

Herne laughed, and the monstrous creatures of his Court laughed with him.

"This is all about me," I said. "You don't need the woman for this. Let her go . . . and I promise you, I'll give you the best run you've ever seen."

"I think not," Herne said easily. "She is your woman, and so by hurting her we hurt you. So she runs first. And when you see the terrible things we have done to her, it will give you reason to run even faster."

"You know," said Suzie, lifting her beaten face, "I am getting really pissed off with everyone assuming I'm Taylor's woman."

Her elbow shot back into a pig man's stomach, and he fell backwards, squealing loudly. She broke free of the hands that held her and kicked a pig man square in the nuts, actually lifting him off the ground. He folded up and hit the ground without a sound. She grabbed another pig man by the head and twisted it all the way round till the neck snapped loudly. She threw the body aside, and headed for Herne on his Throne. The pig men swarmed around her, trying to drag her down by sheer force of numbers, but she was tall and proud and strong, and would not yield to them. Her burning gaze was fixed on Herne, and step by step she forced her way towards him. I struggled fiercely against the hands holding me, but I was never as strong as Suzie Shooter. And I'd never been as proud of her, as I watched her fight against such odds and refuse to fall. And then the giant Hob In Chains stepped forward, and one of his long iron chains snapped out to wrap itself around Suzie's throat. The cold links tightened cruelly, choking all the breath and strength right out of her, until finally she fell to her knees, and the pig men brought her under control again.

"We really should be leaving now, Lord Herne," said Marcellus, a little nervously. "We have brought you a great gift and beg only a single boon in gratitude."

"You find me in a giving mood," Herne said lazily. "What do you want?"

"Power," said Livia, her voice cold and flat and vicious. "Power to revenge ourselves upon our enemies, to spread fear and suffering against all those who brought us low. Make us into Beings of Power, Lord Herne, that we might join your Court, and prey on Man as you do."

"And is that the wish of both of you?" said Herne.

"It is," said Marcellus, his voice thick with anticipation. "Give us Power, that we might never be parted, and we shall see that all suffer as we have suffered."

"As you wish, so shall it be," said Herne, and the disdainful amusement in his voice really should have warned them. Certainly they sensed something, for all their stupid wide grins, and they moved protectively together. Herne smiled upon them. "You shall be a Power, together forever, my curse to unleash upon Man and his Nightside city."

He laughed, and again his whole monstrous Court laughed with him, a horrible hellish sound. Herne gestured abruptly, and Marcellus and Livia slammed together. They both cried out as their bodies pressed so tight their ribs cracked and broke. Their flesh stirred and became fluid, merging and mixing together. Their faces melted into each other. They were screaming by then, in a single awful voice. And all too soon there before the wood god stood a single joined creature, twice the size of a man, with protruding bones and too many joints, and a horrible mad gaze burning in its single set of eyes. The creature tried to speak with its single mouth, but shock had driven speech from it, for the moment, so it mewled and howled piteously. It fell forward onto all fours, unable to find the balance in its single form, shaking its malformed head again and again.

"Go forth, and be a plague in the Nightside city," said Herne. "All who suffer shall be drawn to you, and from their pain you will find the Power you crave. Hurt and horror and despair will make you strong, and the suffering you cause in turn shall be your vengeance on an unfeeling world. And by my gift, you shall never be parted again. That is what you wanted, after all."

He sat back on his Throne and gestured contemptuously, and the creatures of his Court drove the new-born Power out of the clearing. It scrabbled away on all fours, like an animal, howling and screeching like a mad thing, its long torment just begun. And of all of us there, only I knew that someday it would be called the Lamentation, the Saint of Suffering; and I would be the one to destroy it.

Time has a great fondness for circles.

Hob In Chains stepped forward suddenly, and all eyes went immediately to his great form. He jerked cruelly on his chain, and Suzie was pulled forward to kneel before Herne. All the fight had been beaten out of her, for the moment. Herne looked thoughtfully at the giant with the boar's head and nodded his permission to speak.

"We have this woman for the Hunt," said Hob In Chains. Its voice was grunts and squeals, only made clear to me by Old Father Time's magic, but still it was a harsh and ugly thing to hear; the sound of something that should never have learned to talk. "Let us give the son to Lilith. Trade him back to her. Who knows what she might grant us in return? To spare him torment and death."

There were barks and yells of agreement all around the Court, but most stayed silent, watching Herne for his response. And the wood god was already shaking his great shaggy head.

"Lilith is too proud to yield to anyone, even over her own flesh and blood. She would never give up an ounce of power, no matter what we threatened to do to her son. She'd probably kill him herself rather than have him used against her. No; all that is left to us is a chance to hurt her, by destroying something that belongs to her. To show our contempt for her city and her restraints. A chance to prove that whatever she can create, we can destroy, as we will one day tear down her damned city."

"I really wouldn't bank on her being that upset," I said, in my most reasonable voice. "I'm from the future. Many centuries from now. She doesn't even know I exist yet."

The Court stirred uneasily as they tried to make sense of that, and again they looked to Herne for guidance. They weren't really equipped for abstract thought. Herne rubbed slowly at his bearded chin.

"I hear the truth in your voice . . . but past or present or future, you are still her son. She will recognise that in you."

"All right," I said, thinking quickly on my feet. "How about this—since I'm from the future, I know what's going to happen to you, Herne. I know your future and your fate;

and you really need to know what's coming if you're to stand any chance of avoiding it."

Herne considered this, while his whole Court looked confusedly at each other, then he nodded to the pig men holding me, and they beat me savagely, driving me back down onto my knees, my arms wrapped around my head to protect it. Suzie cried out and tried to reach me, but the iron chain around her throat tightened again, until she had to stop, to breathe again. I retreated deep inside myself, away from the pain. Finally, the beating stopped, and I slowly raised my head to look at Herne. I tried to speak, but all I could do was drool fresh blood from my slack mouth. He laughed in my face.

"Nothing matters as much as the pain and horror you will suffer, at my hands and by my will. Revenge will be mine." He stood up from his Throne, and raised his hands above his horned head. "Let there be a Hunt! A Wild Hunt, of old standing and most ancient tradition!"

The whole Court roared and bayed their approval, stamping their feet and hooves and paws upon the ground, and raising their faces and snouts and muzzles to the full moon above the clearing. There was a new hunger and urgency on the air, hot and heady, pulsing like a giant heartbeat. The fever of the chase was in their blood and in their heads, and they could already taste the bloody slaughter that would end it. They looked at me with hot and happy eyes, and their musky stench was thick on the air.

"We shall start with the woman," said Herne, smiling almost fondly down on Suzie. "A lesser sport, of course, but still a sweet and savage run, to pique our appetite for the main event. Look your last upon your woman, Lilith's son. When you see her next, or what's left of her, you probably won't recognise her."

He laughed at me, savouring the thought of my horror and helplessness, and so did his Court. But I am John Taylor, and I am never helpless. I pushed the pain and weakness out of my head, thinking furiously. I couldn't let this happen. Couldn't let Suzie suffer and die on my behalf. I had sworn to bleed and suffer and die before I let that happen, and I meant every word of it.

"What's the matter, Herne?" I said loudly. "Haven't you got the guts for a real Hunt? Haven't you got the balls to go after Lilith's son, that you have to work up your courage by first hunting a woman?"

The laughter broke off abruptly. The whole Court looked at Herne. He strode forward, raising his hand to strike me, and I laughed right into his face. He paused, suddenly uncertain. I shouldn't have had any fight left in me. I should have been broken in body and spirit by now. But I was Lilith's son, after all . . . and for the first time Herne began to get a feeling for what that really meant. He looked round his Court, to see how they were taking this, and saw uncertainty building in their eyes, too. I had planted a seed in his mind and in theirs, that he was only proposing to hunt Suzie to put off the moment when he would have to raise his courage to hunt me. I'd challenged his pride and his daring, in front of everyone, and he knew he couldn't afford to seem weak in front of his people. In front of Lilith's son.

"Very well," he said finally, and he gestured to the pig men, to hold me on my knees so he could stick his face right into mine. I'd forgotten how short he was. "Forget the woman. She shall die here and now in front of you, and you shall come to envy her swift and easy death, as we drive you screaming and bleeding through the wild woods, ripping and tearing at your hide every foot of the way, drawing every last drop of blood and suffering and horror out of you, killing you by inches . . . until you can't run any more—and then we'll rip you open and eat your entrails as you watch."

"Hell with that," I said flatly. "If you kill her, I won't run. I'll just stand here and die, to spite you, and refuse you the pleasure of the Hunt. No. The deal is, you get me instead of her. You let her live, and I promise you a run like you've never seen before."

Herne scowled. "You think you can make a deal with me? You think you can enforce terms with Herne the Hunter?"

"Of course," I said. "I'm Lilith's son."

He laughed suddenly, and turned away from me to bark orders at his Court. Hob In Chains released his hold on Suzie, and the iron chain slithered back to him like a shining snake. There was much milling about and raised growling voices, as the various creatures argued over orders of precedence, and the proposed route of the Hunt, and other matters I was too tired and too hurting to follow. I concentrated all my strength and will into moving slowly across the clearing on my knees, to join Suzie. It seemed to take forever, but eventually we were kneeling side by side. We leaned against each other, shoulder to shoulder, holding each other up. The pig men watched us carefully, but noone had given them orders to do anything else. So Suzie and I sat together for a while, comforting each other with our presence, our blood-streaked faces close together.

"Not one of your better ideas, this, Taylor," she said finally.

"I'd have to agree," I said, testing my teeth with the tip of my tongue, to see which ones were loose. "Don't worry. I'll get us out of this. I always do."

"I'm in better shape than I look," Suzie said quietly. "Werewolf blood, remember? My strength's already coming back. All I need is for these swine to take their eyes off me for a moment, and . . ."

"They won't," I said. "They've done this before. And what could you do, anyway? Attack Herne, with one of those daggers you keep in your boots? You wouldn't get within ten feet of him before his creatures dragged you down. You could run; but they'd catch you, and kill you. Eventually."

"I wouldn't run, without you," said Suzie.

"If I work this right, you won't have to run," I said. "I've got a plan."

She smiled, briefly. "You always do, John."

I closed my eyes for a while. I'd never felt so tired, so beaten down. "God, I feel bad, Suzie. I'm sorry I got you into this."

"Stop it, John." She sounded worried, for the first time. "You give up here, and we're both dead."

"I'm all right," I said, forcing my eyes open.

She looked me over, her cold face controlled as ever as she took in the extent of my injuries. "You've looked better, Taylor. I don't think I like the odds on this one. You're in no shape to run before the Wild Hunt. Don't think you'd even necessarily make it out of the clearing. You'd better let me do it. Once the werewolf factor really kicks in, I can outrun anything they send after me."

"No you couldn't," I said. "Anyone else, maybe, but not Herne and his Court. They live for the hunt. You have to let me do this, Suzie. Trust me. I know what I'm doing."

She looked at me for a long while, her face cold as always. "You don't have to do this, John. Not for me."

"Yes, I do," I said.

I couldn't tell her why. I couldn't tell her I was ready to die, to save her from the future I'd seen for her. I couldn't tell her I needed to do this, to prove to myself that I wasn't just the ruthless bastard Tommy Oblivion had named me. To prove I was something more than my mother's son. So I would run, and maybe die, to save her life and my soul.

And besides, I had a plan.

I looked round sharply, as I realised the clearing had suddenly gone quiet. Every animal and creature in the Court had frozen where they were, all the beasts and Beings watching intently as Herne the Hunter and the Neanderthal known as Tomias Squarefoot squared off against each other, glaring unflinchingly into each other's face, neither prepared to give an inch. There was a new tension in the clearing, a clash of wills, and seniority. Herne was scowling fiercely, Squarefoot as calm as ever, but there was an ancient dignity and steadfastness in the Neanderthal that the wood god, for all his power, couldn't quite match.

"I am the oldest here," said Tomias Squarefoot, in a voice slow and steady as a flowing river. "I was here before you, Herne. I walked this land, this forest, long before there was a wood god, or any of the Forces you have gathered around you. I was here before the Nightside. I alone remember when the forest was truly alive, and the trees still talked, with slow, heavy voices. I remember the spirits of stone and water and earth. I have seen all my people die, and vanish, and the rise of Man. You came after Man, wood god, though you prefer not to remember that. I am the oldest here, and I say you have forgotten the way of the Wild Hunt."

"You are old," Herne acknowledged. "But age does not always bestow wisdom. I lead here, not you. I have made the Wild Hunt a thing to be feared, and spoken of in hushed whispers all through the land. And you dare to challenge my directing of the Hunt?"

"You gave the Wild Hunt new strength and power by imposing a stricter structure," Squarefoot said calmly. "You made up the rules that govern it, for the greater pleasure of all who participate in it. You cannot break those rules now, just because your pride has been challenged. For if the master of the Wild Hunt will not follow his own rules, why should anyone else? And then, where would be the point in playing?"

There was a growling murmur of agreement all across the Court. Herne heard it but did not dare acknowledge it.

"What rules have I broken?" he said. "What customs do I flout? I say this Hunt will be run as always, and all rules and customs shall be followed."

"Then the prey must know where he runs, and why,"

said Squarefoot. "And the prize he may yet win, if he is strong and fast and true. For the prey that runs without thought or hope makes poor prey indeed."

Herne's scowl deepened. "If you're thinking of interfering in this Hunt . . ."

"Of course not," the Neanderthal said calmly. "That would be against the rules. It is your Hunt, Herne. So name the conditions, and the destination, and the prize to be won."

Something like amusement moved through the Court, as the creatures saw how clearly Herne had been herded into a corner, but the sound died quickly away as Herne glared about him. He turned brusquely away from Squarefoot to face Suzie and me. He gestured sharply, and the pig men hauled us up onto our feet. I still felt like hell, but the brief respite had put some strength back into my legs. My head still pounded, but my thoughts were clear again. And my hands were very near my coat pockets. I grinned nastily at Herne. He really should have killed me while he had the chance.

Herne smiled back at me.

"Here are the rules of the Wild Hunt, Lilith's son. You will run, and we will chase you. You will run through the wild wood, in whatever direction you choose, along whatever paths you may find; and if by some miracle you find your way out of the wood, and back to the city, all you have to do is cross the boundary into the city, and you will live, safe from all pursuit. And to add spice to the game, you don't run for your own life but for your woman's life as well. She will be held at the city boundary, under guard. Reach her, and she will be set free. You both will live. But if you fail to reach her, then she will die as slowly and horribly as you. Think about that as you run." His smile widened. "I should perhaps point out that no-one in living memory has ever made it through the wild woods, let alone back to the city."

"But I'm not just anyone," I said, holding his gaze with mine. "I'm John Taylor. Lilith's son. And I'm smarter and craftier and nastier than you'll ever be."

He turned his back on me and stalked away. Suzie looked at me thoughtfully.

"That's your great plan? You run, and if you die I die, too? You look like shit, Taylor. You're in no condition to run any race."

"You heard the bastard," I said. "I have to run. At least now, I have a chance to save both of us. And he doesn't know about my gift, my little tricks, or even the contents of my coat pockets. I've outsmarted brighter things than him and his whole damned Court before this. Don't give them any trouble, Suzie. Let them take you back to the city. Your chances are better there. And then if you get a chance to escape, take it."

"I don't like any of this," said Suzie. "I thought you said you couldn't afford to use your gift in this Time."

"Hell with that," I said. "I'll worry about the consequences of using my gift if and when I survive the Hunt."

"If you die," Suzie said slowly, "I will avenge you, John. I'll kill them all. I will burn down the wild wood and everything in it, in your name."

"I know," I said.

Herne called my name, and I looked around. All the monstrous creatures of his Court had formed into two long lines, facing each other. They grinned and slavered and stomped their feet, showing me their teeth and claws. Some of them had clubs. Herne gestured grandly from his Throne, flanked by Hob In Chains and Tomias Squarefoot.

"And so the Hunt begins. Run the gauntlet, John Taylor, Lilith's son. Pass between your enemies. They won't kill you, not now, but they will shed enough blood for you to leave a clear trail when you run. When you finally get out of the gauntlet, you'll be facing in the direction of the Nightside. Our gift to you, to get you started."

I shuddered, despite myself. They'd tear me up bad, long before I could reach the other end. So . . .

"Some gift," I said. "I'll find my own way."

And I turned my back on the waiting gauntlet and ran in the opposite direction, out of the moonlit clearing and into the darkness of the waiting wood. Behind me, I heard outraged yells and howls, and I grinned. When you're playing a game and the rules are stacked against you, change the rules. I've always been a great believer in lateral thinking.

I plunged through the gloom between the tall trees, leaving the light of the clearing behind me. I'd worry about directions later; for the time being, I simply needed to put some distance between me and my pursuers. I ran steadily, keeping a good pace, careful to preserve what strength and breath I had. For now I was coasting on adrenaline, but I knew that wouldn't last. I hurt all over, but my head was clear. Behind me, I could hear the Hunt starting up, hear the rage and bloodlust in their raised voices. I grinned. Get your opponent angry, and you've already won half the fight. I hoped they wouldn't take their anger out on Suzie . . . No. I pushed the thought aside. Suzie could take care of herself. I had to concentrate on my own problems.

And so I ran, knowing they could run faster but trusting to my wits and my gift and my sheer bloody-minded stubbornness to see me through. I'd beaten worse than this and rubbed their noses in it. The forest air was cool and bracing, and I sucked in great lungfuls of it as I ran. My legs felt strong. My arms hurt, so I folded them across my chest. There was enough light to see where I was going, and the trees were so tightly packed the Hunt wouldn't be able to come at me en masse. I could hear them, drawing closer already. I tried to remember how far it was, back to the city, but the journey in had been on horseback. No. I couldn't afford to think about that. I had to concentrate on the here and now.

I unfolded my arms and scrabbled in my coat pockets,

coming up with a disposable flashlight. I turned it on, and light sprang out ahead of me, warm and yellow and comforting. And then I turned it off, because I didn't want to attract attention. My eyes were pretty well adjusted to the gloom. But it might come in handy later, and I was glad I had it. I put the flashlight away and let my fingers wander over other useful objects in my pockets. They really should have searched me thoroughly, but that was something men did, not animals. Or perhaps they didn't care, secure in their overwhelming numbers and savagery. Perhaps they didn't see me as any kind of threat. I grinned unpleasantly. I'd change that.

I slowed my pace, as my breath began to run short. I'd hoped my wind would last longer, but the beatings had really taken it out of me. I pushed on, ignoring the tightening pains in my sides. Huge trees loomed all around me, and I deliberately chose the narrowest ways, so that whatever came after me would have to do it single file. Break up the numbers, and you take away the advantage. Gnarled branches loomed out in front of me all the time, and I had to duck and weave to get past them. Thick roots bulged up out of the ground, always threatening to trip me, and they slowed me down, too. The tightly packed earth was hard and unyielding under my feet, and the impact of every step shuddered up through my legs.

A sudden cry went up behind me, harsh and strident in the night, and something heavy came crashing through the branches, not far behind me. The sounds grew louder, closer. Something had found my scent. Time to break the rules again, to use the advantages they didn't know I had. I fired up my gift. Let my Enemies find me; the Hunt would take care of whatever my Enemies might send after me. And Lilith, present or future . . . was a problem for another time.

It only took a moment for my gift to find me the direction of the city, and I changed course, immediately shutting down my gift again. It was too confusing, to See clearly in the wild wood. In the brief glimpse through my third eye, I had Seen ghosts and phantoms, running frantically along paths that were no longer there, and old vast Beings who had lived in the woods long and long ago, but had since moved on to other places, other worlds. I Saw things I didn't understand, and couldn't hope to, Forces and Powers still abroad in the night, ancient and awful, beyond human comprehension. I think some of them Saw me.

I ran on, slipping as quietly as I could between the great trees, curving around Herne's clearing and back towards the city. According to what I'd Seen with my gift, it was a long way off. I slowed to a jog, to preserve my breath. I grabbed moss and leaves from the trees I passed, and rubbed them over my coat and bare skin, to disguise my scent. I might be a city boy, but I'd been around. I knew a few tricks.

I could hear animals running on both sides of me now, running fast and freely. They weren't even panting hard, the bastards. I stopped abruptly, breathing through my nose to keep silent, and looked carefully around me. There were wolves, dodging in and out of the trees, grey fur shining in the sparse moonlight. Real wolves from their size rather than werewolves, but no less dangerous for that. They stumbled to a halt, as they realised I'd stopped running, and milled back and forth, before and around me. I crouched in the deepest shadows I could find. Grey snouts rose in the air, trying to catch my scent. I stayed very still. There wasn't a trace of wind on the chill night air. The wolves gathered on my left, muzzles to the ground, searching for tracks. I heard fresh sounds on my right and slowly turned my head. Half a dozen huge boars came snuffling loudly through the wood towards me, grunting and tossing their great heads, moonlight gleaming on their vicious curved tusks. So, enemies to my left and to my right. Perfect.

I ran straight forward, deliberately making as much

noise as possible. The wolves and the boars came charging forward, each keen to get to me first. I waited till the very last moment, then I slammed to a halt and dived to the ground. And while I lay there with my arms over my head, the wolves and the boars slammed right into each other. Confused by an unexpected attack, they tore blindly at each other. Howls and roars and squeals of pain filled the night air, as wolves and boars forgot all about me in their outrage over being attacked. They savaged each other in a great squabbling mess, while I rose carefully to my feet and slipped quietly away through the shadows.

I didn't even see the bear coming. It suddenly loomed out of the gloom right ahead of me, a huge dark shape against the night, big as a tree. One great clawed paw came sweeping through the air towards me, moonlight gleaming on the vicious claws, and then it slapped me to one side, as casually as that. It was like being hit by a battering ram. I flew through the air and hit the ground hard, before rolling on to slam up against a tree-trunk. The impact knocked all the breath right out of me. My shoulder was on fire, and it felt like half my ribs were cracked, maybe broken. I pulled myself up and set my back against the tree-trunk, fighting to get some air back into my lungs. The bear was already coming for me, snuffling and growling. It lashed out again, and I only dodged it by throwing myself to one side. The vicious claws tore a great chunk out of the tree. I scrambled to my feet and slipped round the other side of the tree. The bear paused, confused because it couldn't see me any more, and I was off and running again. I could feel fresh blood flowing down my left arm from my clawed shoulder, and my whole side was screaming with pain.

The wolves were after me again. They came flying through the shafts of moonlight, grey as ghosts, eyes gleaming brightly. Too many to count, running smoothly as the wind. They streamed ahead of me, then cut in to block my way. I grabbed a sachet of pepper from my coat pocket, tore it open, and threw the whole lot in their faces. They went mad as fire filled their sensitive noses and eyes, and they fell back, yipping and yelping, snapping at the air and at each other, unable to concentrate on anything but the horrid pain in their heads. I ran straight through them. Some snapped and tore at me reflexively, and I cried out despite myself as new pains cut through me, then I was past them and running on, into the night. I gritted my teeth against the hurt, breathing heavily.

I had to force myself on now, to maintain a good pace. I couldn't stop to rest, or see to my wounds. I was leaving a clear blood trail. I could hear the Hunt, crying out in many voices behind me. My breath was coming raggedly, and my whole chest hurt. Damn, I was out of shape. I'd got too used to fighting instead of running for my life. I plunged on, through shadows and moonlight, crashing through branches and sometimes slamming into trees I didn't see in time, following the direction my gift had given me.

And behind came the Wild Hunt.

I ran through a clearing, and a whole crowd of elves watched me pass, incuriously. They were moving slowly in strange patterns, leaving long blue ectoplasmic trails behind them, creating an intricate glowing web. I didn't call out to them for help. Elves have never given a damn for anyone but themselves.

It seemed like the whole wood was alive with howls and cries now, as though every living thing in the night was awake and on my trail. Long-buried instincts made my blood run cold and raised the hackles on the back of my neck. Old, atavistic instincts, from Humanity's distant past, when to be Man was to be hunted. I grinned fiercely. Things had changed since then, and I would show them how much. I'd show them all. I ran on, fighting for breath, ignoring the pain—hate and desperation and stubborn doggedness keeping me going long after exhaustion should have driven me to my knees.

In the next clearing I came to, Hob In Chains was waiting for me, surrounded by his pig men. He stood proud and tall in the shimmering milky light, his great boar's head looking straight at me as I stumbled to a halt on the edge of the clearing. Hob's iron chains rattled noisily as he swung a huge hammer back and forth before him. The thick wooden shaft was easily four feet long, and the head was a solid slab of iron, matted and crusted with old dried blood and hairs. I probably would have had trouble even lifting the thing, but he swung it lazily back and forth as though it was nothing. The giant smiled at me around his huge tusks and grunted loudly, a deep, satisfied sound. The pig men crowded round his legs grunted and squealed along with him, like hogs waiting for the swill to be poured into their trough, held back only by their master's will. They all looked at me hungrily, with nothing in their eyes of the men they'd once been. Hob In Chains moved forward, and they scattered to let him pass. I stood my ground. He knew I wouldn't run. The rest of the Hunt were too close behind me. I had to get through the clearing.

Even so, I think he was a bit shocked when I strode forward, heading straight for him. He hefted his great hammer, grunting greedily as he waited for me to come within range. I grinned at him, which I think unsettled him even more. He was only used to prey that screamed and sobbed and begged for mercy. He decided not to wait, and stamped towards me, raising his great hammer above his head with both hands. The pig men fell back to give him room, squealing hysterically. And I used my oldest trick, the one that takes bullets out of guns, to take all the air out of their lungs. The pig men collapsed as one, hitting the ground like so many hairy sacks. Hob In Chains staggered backwards, dropping his hammer as though it had suddenly become too heavy for him. Then he dropped to his knees, his great boar's head gaping stupidly. I walked right past him and didn't even look back as I heard him crash to the ground.

But the clattering of his iron chains gave me a new idea, and I stopped and looked round. The chains would make good weapons, and I could use every advantage I could steal. I went back to kneel beside Hob In Chains and tugged at one of the long iron chains, but it was firmly fixed to the collar round his throat. They all were. I could have wept with frustration. I lurched to my feet and kicked Hob In Chains in the ribs.

And Hob In Chains rose up. He lurched unsteadily to his feet, snorting and grunting, shaking his boar's head as he sucked air back into his great lungs. I hit him in the gut with all my strength, but all I did was hurt my hand. He reached out for his hammer, and I kicked him in the balls, putting all my strength behind it. The air shot out of Hob In Chains' lungs for a second time, and his beady eyes squeezed shut as he sank back down onto his knees again, forgetting all about his hammer. And I was off and running again.

The Hunt was close behind me still. Creatures and beasts came darting in, now from one side, then from another, to bite and claw and tear at me. Not even trying to bring me down, not yet. Just doing their bit to hurt and harry me, and enjoy the Hunt. Some of them I dodged, some I struck out at, but all of them left their mark on me. I didn't even try not to cry out any more, simply concentrated on keeping moving. I was deathly tired, stumbling and staggering as much as running, blood soaking my tattered trench coat. Blood and sweat mixed as they ran down my face, leaving the taste of copper and salt in my mouth. My left arm hung almost uselessly at my side, clawed open from shoulder to wrist by something I didn't even see coming. There was laughter in the woods, all around me. I hurt so bad it flared up every time my foot hit the hard ground, but my head stayed clear. Anywhen else, so much pain and accumulated damage would have brought me to my knees long ago, but I wasn't only running for myself. I was running for Suzie.

The Wild Hunt swarmed all around me, taking it in turns to dart in and hurt me some more, just enough to spur me on. And at the head of his Hunt, riding his glorious moon stallion ahead and to my left, Herne the Hunter. Laughing as he watched his prey suffer. His horse was made of pure moonlight, a glorious luminous creature that carried Herne effortlessly on. A pack of werewolves followed in his wake, howling with unnervingly human voices.

I had no idea how long I'd been running. How far I'd come, or how far I still had left to go. It felt like I'd always been running, like one of those nightmares where you flee forever and never get anywhere. I was staggering along now, gasping for breath, fighting to keep putting one foot in front of the other. Every breath hurt, in my chest and in my sides and in my back. I couldn't even feel my feet or my hands any more. I no longer lashed out at the beasts that attacked me, saving my strength.

I had a plan.

Herne the Hunter finally steered his moon stallion right in front of me, blocking my path, so I had to stop. I crashed to a halt, breathing so hard I couldn't hear anything else. I could still see him laughing, though. Hear the rest of the Hunt closing in around me. Herne leaned over his mount's shoulder to address me, and I ached to wipe the smile off his face. Dark shadows filled the woods around me, milling restlessly, impatient for the kill, held back only by Herne's will. He leaned right over, pushing his face close to mine, so I would be sure to hear his words.

"You ran well, for a mortal. Led us a merry chase, to our great entertainment. But now it's over. The Hunt ends as it always has and always will, in the slow, horrid death of the prey. Be sure to scream loudly, so perhaps your woman will hear you and know something of the fate that awaits her, too."

"She's not my woman," I mumbled through slack bloody

lips. "Suzie can take care of herself. And just maybe, she'll take care of you, too."

Herne laughed in my face. "Die now, Lilith's son, alone and in torment, and know that everything you've done and endured has been for nothing. Your woman will suffer and die, just like you. After we've had our fun with her."

He leaned right over to spit these last words directly into my face, and at last he was close enough for me to grab him with both bloody hands, and haul him right off his glowing moon stallion. Overbalanced, he toppled off easily, and I slammed him to the ground. I hit him once in the mouth, for my own satisfaction, then used the last of my strength to grab the moon stallion's enchanted bridle and pull myself up onto his back. The stallion reared up on its hind legs, pawing at the air and tossing its head, but I had the bridle in my hands, and when I pointed the stallion's head in the direction of the city, the creature had no choice but to carry me there. I drove it mercilessly on, faster and faster, and we sped through the wild wood like a dream of motion, swerving effortlessly between the trees, never slowing or stopping, while I hung on desperately with all that was left of my hoarded strength.

Behind me I could hear the cheated howls of the Wild Hunt, and Herne crying out in rage and shame, and I laughed breathlessly.

I urged the moon stallion on to even greater speeds as the Hunt pursued us, and we fled through the night, the pounding hooves hardly seeming to touch the ground. The whole of the Wild Hunt was on my trail, but they were a long way back. I slumped forward over the neck of the moon stallion, horribly tired, but my hands had closed around the controlling enchanted bridle in a grip that only death would loosen. I'd snatched a second chance from the very edge of defeat, and I was going home—to the city, and the Nightside, and Suzie Shooter.

The great trees flashed past me on either side, seemingly

as insubstantial as a dream, come and gone impossibly
fast. And still the Wild Hunt followed. Until suddenly the
tall trees fell away behind me, and the moon stallion was
racing across the open grasslands. I slowly raised my
aching head and saw the lights of the city burning up
ahead. I risked a look back over my shoulder. All the monstrous creatures of Herne's Court were pouring out of the
forest, so caught up in the bloodlust of the chase that they
would even leave the safety of the wild wood to come after
me. I couldn't see Herne. Perhaps he was having trouble
keeping up, on foot. I grinned, then I coughed, and fresh
blood spilled down my chin. Damn. Not a good sign. My
head was swimming madly, and I could barely feel the
moon stallion beneath me. For the first time, I wondered if
there was enough left in me to hang on until we reached the
city. But in the end I did, because I had to. Suzie Shooter
was waiting for me.

The moon stallion pounded on, flashing across the
grasslands like a streak of light, the city and its lights growing steadily before me. And almost before I knew it, we
had crossed the boundary into the city, into streets and
buildings, stone and plaster, and the moon stallion crashed
to a halt. It was of the wild wood and would go no further,
bridle or no. For a long moment, I sat there. I'd made it.
The thought repeated slowly in my head. I looked down at
my hands, slick with my own blood, but still gripping the
enchanted bridle so firmly the knuckles showed white. I
forced my fingers open, released the bridle, then slid off
the side of the stallion and fell to the ground. And the moon
stallion turned immediately and raced back across the city
boundary, across the grasslands and back to the wild wood,
where it belonged. I sat up slowly and watched it go, bright
and shining as a departing dawn. I sat there, my head nodding, my hands in my lap, broken and bloodied. The whole
of the front of my trench coat was a ragged bloody mess,
but I was too deathly tired to feel most of my hurts. I didn't

seem to have the strength to do anything, and that worried me vaguely, but I had made it back to the city; and that was all that mattered. I watched impassively as Herne the Hunter came running across the grasslands. He seemed so much smaller, so much less, outside the forest. The rest of his monstrous Court came after him, but they seemed to be hanging back. I smiled slowly. Let them come. Let them all come. I'd beaten him. Suzie was safe now.

I was cold, so cold. I started to shiver and couldn't stop. I wondered if I was dying.

Footsteps approached behind me, but I didn't have enough strength left to turn and look. And then Suzie Shooter was kneeling beside me, free and unguarded. I tried to smile for her. She looked me over, and made a low, shocked sound.

"Oh God, John. What have they done to you?"

"It's not as bad as it looks," I said, or thought I said. More blood spilled down my chin as my lips split open again. It was only a small hurt after so many worse ones, but it was the last straw, and I started to cry. Just from shock and weariness. I'd given all I had to give, and there was nothing left. My whole body was shaking and shuddering now, from simple exhaustion. And Suzie took me in her arms and held me to her. And bad as I felt, I knew how much it took for her to be able to do that. She rocked me slowly, my head resting against her leather-clad shoulder, while she made soothing, hushing noises.

"It's all right, John. It's all over. I'm free, and you're going to be fine. Find you a sorcerer, get you fixed up good."

"I thought you were under guard here," I said , slowly and distinctly.

She snorted loudly. "Beat the shit out of them the moment I was safely back in the city. There's no-one left here to hurt us."

"I knew you could look after yourself," I said. "But I couldn't take the risk . . . of being wrong."

Suzie sniffed. "Bloody pig men. You wouldn't believe how many times they felt me up on the way here. Smelled really bad, too. Couldn't kill them fast enough. Maybe we'll have a barbecue, later?"

"Sounds good," I said. "I'm cold, Suzie. So cold."

She held me tighter, but I could barely feel it. "Hang on, John. Hang on."

"Journeys end . . ."

"In lovers' meeting?" said Suzie, her cheek against my forehead.

"Maybe," I said. "If only we'd had more time . . ."

"There will be time for many things . . ."

"No. I don't think so. I'm dying, Suzie. I wish . . ."

She said something, but it couldn't hear it over the roaring in my head. I could see the blood running out of me, but everything was disappearing into darkness as the world slipped slowly away from me. I was ready to die; if it meant the future I'd seen for Suzie, and the Nightside, might not happen after all.

"I saved you," I said.

"I knew you would," she said. "I knew they'd never catch you."

That wasn't what I meant, but it didn't matter.

Then I felt her whole body tense as she looked up sharply. I pushed the darkness back through a sheer effort of will and lifted my head to look. And there before us was Herne the Hunter, standing on the other side of the city boundary, his face dark with rage. His Court was spread out behind him, keeping well back. Herne actually danced with rage in front of me, driven half out of his mind at losing.

"You cheated!" he screamed at me, spittle flying on the air with the force of his words. "You didn't run the gauntlet! You used tricks and magics! You stole my lovely moon stallion! Cheat! Cheat!"

I grinned at him even though it hurt. "Told you I was smarter than you. All that matters is I won. I got here. You and your whole damned Court couldn't stop me. I beat you, Herne, so go away and pick on someone smaller than yourself."

"You didn't beat me! No-one beats me! You cheated!" Herne was almost crying by then with the strength of his emotions, and his Court stirred uneasily behind him. He shook a gnarled fist at me. "No-one wins unless I say they win! You're dead, you hear me? I'll drag you out of there and back into the woods, and then, and then . . . I'll do such terrible things to you!"

Tomias Squarefoot stepped forward, and Herne turned viciously to glare at him. The Neanderthal stood calmly before the wood god, and his voice was cold and unmoved. "You cannot pursue them any further, Herne. They are in the city now, and beyond our reach. By the rules of your own Hunt, they are safe from you."

"I am the god of the wild places! Of the storm and the lightning! I am the glory of the hunt and the wolf who runs and the antlers on the rutting stag! I am the power of the wild wood, and I will not be denied!"

"He ran well and bravely," said Squarefoot, and some of the Court actually grunted and growled in agreement behind him. "He won, Herne. Let it go."

"Never!"

"If you do this," Squarefoot said slowly, "you do it alone."

"Alone then!" spat Herne, turning his back on them all, and he wouldn't even look round when Tomias Squarefoot went back to join the Court, and they all headed back across the grasslands, to the wild wood, where they belonged. Herne leaned slowly forward, as though testing the strength of some unseen, unfelt barrier, his curling goat's horns trembling with anticipation. His eyes were fierce and staring, and more than a little mad.

Suzie put me carefully to one side and stood up to place herself between Herne and me. They'd taken her shotgun, so she drew the two long knives from her boot tops. She stood tall and proud, and it looked like it would take the whole damn world to bring her down. Herne regarded her craftily, his shaggy head cocked slightly to one side, like a bird.

"You can't stop me. I'm a god."

"You wouldn't be the first god I've killed," said Suzie Shooter. "And you're on my territory now."

It might have been a bluff, or knowing Suzie, maybe not, but either way it did me good to hear her say it with such scorn and confidence. And I discovered I was damned if I'd sit there and let her face the threat alone. I forced myself up onto one knee, then onto my feet. I moved unsteadily forward to stand beside Suzie. I was swaying, but I was up. If I was going out, I was going to do it on my feet.

"Lilith's son," Herne whispered. "Child of the city and hated civilisation. You would wipe away all the woods and all of the wild. I'll see you dead even if it damns me for all time."

He stepped forward, and Suzie and I braced ourselves to meet the fury of the wood god. And that was when a dark-haired man in a long flowing robe, carrying a long wooden staff, appeared out of nowhere to stand between us and Herne. Suzie actually jumped a little, and I had to grab her arm to steady myself. Herne held his ground, snarling uncertainly at the newcomer, who slammed his staff into the ground before Herne. It stood there, alone and upright, quivering slightly.

"I am the Lord of Thorns," said the newcomer. "Newly appointed Overseer of the Nightside. And you should not be here, Herne the Hunter."

"Appointed by who?" snapped Herne. "By that new god, the Christ? You have his smell on you. I was here before him, and I shall hold sway in the woods long after he has been forgotten."

"No," said the Lord of Thorns. "He has come, and nothing

shall ever be the same again. I have been given power over all the Nightside, to see that agreements are enforced. You set up the rules of the Wild Hunt, and so are bound by them. You invested your own power in the Hunt, to make it the significant thing that it is, and so it has power over you. You cannot enter here."

"No! No! I will not be cheated out of my prey! I will have my revenge! I will feast on his heart, and yours!"

Herne grabbed at the Lord of Thorns' standing staff, to tear it out of the ground and perhaps use it as a weapon; but the moment he touched it, the ground shook, and bright light surged up, and the wood god cried out despairingly in pain and shock and horror. He fell writhing to the ground, curled up into a ball, and sobbed at the feet of the Lord of Thorns, who looked down on him sadly.

"You did this to yourself, Herne. You are of the city now, by your own act, cut off from the woods and the wild places, only a small fraction of what you once were, now and forever."

"I want to go home," said Herne, like a small child.

"You can't," said the Lord of Thorns. "You chose to come into the city, and now you belong here."

"But what am I to do?"

"Go forth and do penance. Until finally, perhaps, you can learn to make your peace with the civilisation that is coming."

Herne snarled up at the Lord of Thorns, with a touch of his old defiance, and then the broken god, smaller and much diminished, crept past the Lord of Thorns and disappeared into the streets of the city.

I was watching him go, when suddenly I found I was lying on the ground. I didn't remember falling. I was tired, and drifting, and everything seemed so very far away. I could hear Suzie calling my name, increasingly desperately, but I couldn't find the strength to answer her. She grabbed me by the shoulder to try and sit me up, but my body was so much dead weight, and I couldn't help her. I thought, *So this is dying. It doesn't seem so bad. Maybe I'll get some rest, at last.*

Then the Lord of Thorns knelt beside me. He had a kind, bearded face. He put his hand on my chest, and it was like my whole body got jump-started. Strength and vitality slammed through me like an electric charge, driving out the pain and weariness, and I sat bolt upright, crying out loud at the shock and joy of it. Suzie fell back on her haunches, squeaking loudly in surprise. I laughed suddenly, so glad to be alive. I scrambled up onto my feet, hauling Suzie up with me, and I hugged her to me. Her body started to tense up, so I let her go. Some miracles take longer to work out than others.

I checked myself over. My trench coat was a thing of rags and tatters, mostly held together by dried blood, but all my wounds were gone, healed, as though they had never been. I was whole again. I looked blankly at the Lord of Thorns, and he smiled and bowed slightly, like a stage magician acknowledging a clever trick.

"I am the Overseer, and it is my job and privilege to put things right, where a wrong has been committed. How do you feel?"

"Bloody marvellous! Like I could take on the whole damned world!" I looked down at my tattered coat. "I don't suppose . . ."

He shook his head firmly. "I'm the Overseer, not a tailor."

I turned and smiled at Suzie, and she smiled back. The scratches and bruises were gone from her face, though the scars remained. "You should smile more," I said. "It looks good on you."

"Nah," she said. "It's bad for my reputation."

We looked back at the Lord of Thorns, as he coughed meaningfully. "It is my understanding that you seek to travel further back in Time, to the very creation of the Nightside itself. Is that correct?"

"Yes," I said. "How did . . ."

"I know what I need to know. Comes with the job. I am here to help, after all. That's what the Church of the Christ is supposed to be about. Helping, and caring, and teaching others to take responsibility for their own actions."

"Even in a place like this?" said Suzie.

"Especially in a place like this," said the Lord of Thorns.

He slammed his long wooden staff against the ground once more, and the whole world flew away from us, as we dropped back into Time's river, sweeping back into Yesterday.

ELEVEN

Angels, Demons, and Mommie Dearest

This time it didn't feel like falling through Time but more like being flung from a catapult. A rainbow exploded around us, punctuated by exploding galaxies and the cries of stars being born, while from all around came the screaming and howling of Things from Outside, crying *Let us in! Let us in!* in languages older than the worlds. Suzie Shooter and I finally dropped out of the chronoflow and back into Time, slamming back into the world like a bullet from a gun. Breathing harshly like new-born children, we looked around us. We'd materialised standing among the trees at the edge of a great forest, looking out over a huge open clearing. The clear night sky was full of every-day stars, and the full moon was no bigger than it should be. Wherever or whenever we were, the Nightside hadn't happened yet.

Yet the clearing lying vacant and open before us, so vast its far side was practically on the horizon, was clearly no natural thing. Its edge was too sharp, too distinct, cutting through some of the surrounding tree-trunks like a razor's edge, leaving half trees with their insides laid bare, oozing clear sap like blood. The clearing itself held only dark earth, bare and featureless. Its making had definitely been unnatural; raw magics were still sparking and spitting and crackling on the air, the last discharging remnants of a mighty Working. Someone had made acres of forest disappear in a moment, and I had a pretty good idea who.

The forest around and behind us was dark and foreboding, with massive trees reaching up to form an interlaced canopy, like the intricate ceiling of some natural cathedral of the night. The air was cool and still, and thick with the heavy scents of slow growth. I could almost feel the great green power of the dreaming wood, which had stood for thousands of years and never known the touch of Man, or his cutting tools. This was old Britain, ancient Britain, the dark womb from which we all sprang.

And suddenly I was back running between the trees again, with Herne and his Wild Hunt howling triumphantly at my back. Terrible memories of pain and horror surged through me, and I swayed on my feet. I had to put a hand out to the nearest tree and lean on it to steady myself, as my knees threatened to buckle under me. I was shuddering all over, and I could feel my heart slamming painfully fast in my chest. No-one had ever hurt me so deeply, terrorized me so completely, as Herne and his monstrous Court. I'd won, but he had left his mark on me. Maybe forever. I made myself breathe slowly and deeply, refusing to give in. One of my greatest strengths has always been my refusal to be beaten by anyone or anything, even myself. My head slowly came up, my face dripping with sweat, and Suzie Shooter stepped in close beside me and put a comforting hand on my shoulder. The sheer unexpectedness of this pushed everything else out of my head, but I was careful not to react or even turn around too quickly. I didn't want to frighten her off. I looked round slowly, and our eyes met. Her face was as cold and controlled as ever, but we both knew what a big effort this was for her. She managed a small smile, then, seeing that I was myself again, she took her hand away and looked out into the clearing. The gesture was come and gone, but of such small steps are miracles made.

"How far back have we come, this time?" said Suzie, in her usual calm voice. "When is this?"

"I don't know," I said, still looking at her rather than the clearing. "But it felt a hell of a lot further than a few hundred years. If I had to guess, I'd say thousands . . . thousands of years. I think we're back before there were any cities, any towns, any gatherings . . ."

Suzie scowled. "Iron Age?"

"Further back even than that. I think we've arrived in a time before Man even appeared, as we would recognise him. Listen."

We stood close together, listening. The huge and mighty forest was full of the sounds of life—of birds and animals and other things, crying out in the night. The sound of hunters and their prey, up in the air and down on the ground, sometimes crashing through the undergrowth, snorting and grunting. Slowly we turned and looked back, and as our eyes adjusted to the gloom, we could see things moving cautiously in the shadows, observing us from a safe distance. Suzie drew a flare from inside her leather jacket, lit it, and threw it some distance into the trees ahead of us. The sharp crimson light was briefly dazzling, and all around us we could hear the beasts of the forest retreating into the safety of the dark. But there were other sounds now, new movements. Suzie drew her shotgun from its holster on her back.

The light from the flare was already dying down, but I

could just make out strange shapes moving on the very edge of the light, large and powerful things, drifting eerily between the trees. I could feel their presence more than see them. Their shapes were huge, alien, almost abstract; and yet still I knew they belonged in this place more than I did. They were Forces and Powers, old life in an old land, barely material as yet, life in its rawest forms.

"What the hell are they?" whispered Suzie. "I can barely make them out, as though they're only just there . . . Nothing that lives looks like that . . . It's as though they haven't decided what they are yet."

"They probably haven't," I said, just as quietly. I really didn't want to attract the attention of such wild, unfocussed Beings. "These are the first dreams and nightmares of the land, given shape and form. I think in time . . . these forms will eventually define themselves into elves and goblins and all the fantastic creatures of the wild wood. Some will become gods, like Herne. All this will come with the rise of Man, of course. I think maybe these things need the belief and imagination of Man to give them fixed shapes and natures. Man's fears and needs will distil these Beings and Powers into definite shapes; and soon they will forget they were ever anything else. And they will prey on Man and serve him, as he worships and destroys them . . ."

"All right, you're getting creepy now," said Suzie.

The last of the flare's light flickered and went out, and the old deep dark of the forest returned. I couldn't see or even sense the abstract Forces any more, and though I strained my ears, all I could hear was the natural course of bird and animal, going about their nightly business. Reluctantly, I turned and looked out at the clearing again. Suzie turned and looked, too, but she didn't put away her shotgun. Moonlight lit the vast clearing bright as day, but though the open space was still and quiet, there was a feeling of anticipation on the air, as though some curtain was about to rise on a brand-new show.

"Lilith did this," I said. "And from the feel of it, not long before we arrived. This is where she will create and place her Nightside. Not far from here is undoubtedly a river that will someday be called the Thames. And men will come here and build a city called London . . . I wonder what form Lilith's creation will take, before Man invades it and rebuilds it in his own image?"

"How many living things did Lilith destroy when she made this clearing?" said Suzie, unexpectedly. "How many animals, stamped out in a moment, how many ancient trees, blasted into nothing, to serve her purpose? I don't care much, but you can bet good money she cared even less."

"Yeah," I said. "That does sound like Mommie Dearest. She never cared who she hurt, to get her own way."

"Why didn't she create the Nightside immediately?" said Suzie, suspicious as always. "Why stop at the clearing? Is she waiting for something?"

I considered the point. "It could be . . . that she's waiting for an audience."

Suzie looked at me sharply. "For us?"

"Now that is a disturbing thought . . . No. How could she know we'd be here?"

Suzie shrugged. "She's your mother. She's Lilith. Who knows what she knows or how she knows it?" She scowled at me, as another thought struck her. "We only got here because the Lord of Thorns used his power to send us here. How are we supposed to get back to our own time, assuming we survive whatever appalling thing happens next?"

"Good question," I said. "Wish I had a good answer for you. Let's wait and see if we do survive, and worry about it then. We have more than enough to worry about as it is." Then it was my turn to look at her thoughtfully, as something new struck me. "Suzie . . . I think we need to talk. About us. Right now."

Suzie looked straight back at me, not giving me an inch. "We do?"

"Yes. The odds are that we're not going to survive whatever comes next. I've always known that. It's why I didn't want you along on this case. But, here we are, and things have changed between us. So, if we're ever going to say anything, anything that matters, we need to say it now. Because we may never get another chance."

"We're friends," said Suzie, in her cold, controlled voice. "Isn't that enough?"

"I don't know," I said. "Is it?"

"You've got closer to me . . . than anyone," Suzie said slowly. "I never thought I'd ever let anyone get that close. Never thought I'd want anyone to. You . . . matter to me, John. But, I still couldn't . . . be with you. In bed. Some scars go too deep, to ever heal."

"That isn't what we're talking about," I said gently. "What matters is you, and me. It's a miracle we've made it this far, really."

She considered me for a long moment, with her scarred face and her single cold blue eye and her unyielding mouth. I didn't think she even knew she was cradling her shotgun to her chest, like a child, or a lover. When she finally spoke, her voice was as cold as ever. "My new face doesn't bother you? I never cared about being pretty, but . . . I know what I must look like. The outside finally matches the inside."

"You said it yourself, Suzie," I said, as lightly as I could. "We monsters have to stick together."

I leaned forward, slowly and very carefully, and Suzie watched me like an animal of the wild, that might turn and run at any moment. When our faces were so close that I could feel her breath on my mouth, and she still hadn't moved, I kissed her gently on her scarred cheek. I kept my hands by my sides. The ridged scar tissue of her cheek was hard and unyielding. I pulled back, looked into her cold blue eye, then kissed her very gently on the mouth. Her lips barely moved under mine, but she didn't back away. And finally, slowly, she put her arms around me. She held me only lightly, as though she might pull away at any moment. I moved my mouth back from hers, pressed my cheek against her scarred face, and put my arms around her, just as lightly. She sighed, just a little. Her leather jacket creaked quietly under my arms. She held me for as long as she could stand it, then let go and stepped back. I let her go. I knew better than to try and go after her. I knew she still had her shotgun in one hand, even if she didn't. She looked at me with her cold eye and her cold expression, and nodded briefly.

"You know I love you, right?" I said.

"Oh sure," she said. "And I care for you, John. As much as I can."

And then we both looked round sharply. The whole forest had gone quiet, and there was a new feeling on the air. Just for a moment everything was so still I could hear the rasp of my own breathing, feel the beating of my heart. Suzie and I looked out into the clearing, our attention drawn to the open space like beasts in the wild sensing a coming storm. There was a sound. A sound on the air, but not of it, coming from everywhere and nowhere. It filled the whole world, filled my mind, and it was not a natural sound. It was the cry of something being born, of something dying, an emotion and an experience and an ecstasy beyond human knowledge or comprehension. The sound rose and rose, growing louder and more piercing and more inhuman, until Suzie and I had to clap our hands over our ears to try and keep it out, and still the sound rose and rose, louder and louder, until it became unbearable; and still it rose. Finally, mercifully, it rose beyond our ability to hear it, and Suzie and I were left shaking and shuddering, breathing harshly and shaking our heads as though trying to clear something out. I couldn't hear anything, even when Suzie spoke to me, and we both looked out into the clearing again. Something was going to happen. We could feel it. We could still feel the sound, feel it in our bones and in our souls.

And then Lilith was suddenly *there,* standing in front of the trees at the edge of the clearing, perhaps as little as twenty feet from where Suzie and I stood watching. The sound was gone. Lilith had made her entrance. She stood staring intently out at the clearing she'd made, her dark eyes fixed and unblinking. Suzie and I silently stepped further back into the dark of the forest, concealing ourselves in the deepest shadows. Just to see Lilith was to be scared of her. Of the power that burned in her, like all the stars in all the galaxies. She might have been created to be Adam's wife, but she'd come a long way since then.

She hadn't simply appeared. It was as though Lilith had stamped or imprinted herself directly onto reality, by sheer force of will. She was there now because she chose to be, and somehow she seemed *realer* than anything else in the material world. She looked . . . pretty much as I remembered her, from the last time I'd seen her. In Strangefellows bar, at the end of my last case. Just before everything went to hell.

She was too tall and almost supernaturally slender, the lines of her bare body so smooth they looked like they'd been streamlined, for greater efficiency. Her hair and her eyes and her lips were jet-black, and together with her pale, colourless skin, she looked very much like a black and white photograph. Her face was sharp and pointed, with a prominent bone structure and a hawk nose. Her dark mouth was thin-lipped and far too wide, and her eyes were full of a dark fire that could burn through anything. The expressions that came and went on her face were in no way human. She looked . . . wild, elemental, unfinished. She wore no clothes. She had no navel.

I remembered the man called Madman, who Saw the

world and everything in it more clearly than most, saying
that the Lilith we saw and experienced was only a limited
projection into our reality of something much greater and
more complex. We only saw what we could stand to see.
He also said that the human Lilith was really just a glori-
fied glove puppet that she manipulated from afar.

Lilith. Mother. Monster.

I said as much to Suzie, and she nodded. "It doesn't
matter. If she's real, I can kill her."

We both kept our voices low, but I don't think even a
thunderclap could have interrupted Lilith's concentration.
Whatever she saw in the clearing wasn't there yet. She
spoke a Word aloud, and it hit the air like a hammer. The
sound of it filled the world, its echoes reaching out to touch
everything. It was a word from no language I knew or
could ever hope to understand, even with the assistance of
Old Father Time's magic; it was an old word out of an old
language, perhaps the basic language from which all others
evolved. I could understand enough of its meaning to be
glad I didn't understand any more.

Summoned by that terrible Word, the world opened up
to birth monsters. Awful creatures came stomping and hop-
ping and slithering out of the trees behind Lilith. They towered over her and oozed past her feet, huge and dreadful
and utterly appalling, even by Nightside standards. In them
was found every forbidden combination of animal and
lizard and insect, vicious and ugly beyond belief. Bulging
muscles swelled like cancers under suppurating flesh. Dark
carapaced things scuttled on broken legs, with complicated
mouth parts working furiously under too many eyes. Tall
and spindly things lurched out of the trees on tripod legs,
flailing long tentacles like barbed whips. And still they
came, bursting up out of the dark earth of the clearing.
Great white worms with rows of human arms and hands,
rotting hulks large as whales, chattering heads with long

toothy spines. Bat-winged shapes dropped out of the night with a predator's grace, and terrible shapes swept across the sky, blocking out the stars and darting across the face of the full moon.

The air was full of the stench of blood and offal and brimstone. And Lilith looked upon them all, and smiled.

I suddenly realised Suzie was training her shotgun on the group and preparing to open fire. I quickly pushed the barrels down, then actually had to wrestle with her to keep the barrels pointing at the ground. I knew better than to try and take the gun away from her. She finally stopped fighting and glared at me, breathing hard.

"Let me shoot them! They need shooting, on general principles!"

"I feel the same way," I said, glaring right back at her. "But we can't afford to be noticed yet. And I'm pretty sure most of those things would shrug off a shotgun blast anyway."

She nodded reluctantly, and I cautiously let go of the gun. "I loaded up with cursed and blessed ammunition," she said, a little sulkily.

"Even so. I know what those creatures are, Suzie. After being thrown out of Eden, Lilith went down into Hell and lay down with all the demons there, and in time gave birth to all the monsters that have plagued Mankind. Those things out there . . . are her children."

"How can you be so sure of that?" said Suzie.

"I feel it," I said. "I know it like I know my own name. Those things will become the Powers and Dominations of our time, and their many descendants will become vampires and werewolves and ghouls and all the other predators of the Nightside."

"I've got some really powerful grenades . . ."

"No, Suzie."

She sniffed, then glared out at the monstrous creatures

rising and falling around Lilith. "So," she said finally. "Lilith's children. Your half-brothers and -sisters. They are the audience she was waiting for."

Lilith looked out across the writhing, pulsating crowd before her, and her wide smile was as cold and unreadable as the rest of her. She could have been thinking anything, anything at all. Finally, she gestured briefly, brutally, and the crowd split in two, falling back on both sides as Lilith frowned, concentrating, and spoke another Word. Even her monstrous children cringed back from the sound of it, and I could feel reality itself shake and shudder as Lilith enforced her awful will upon it. The whole of the dark forest stirred and groaned, a living thing in pain, then, all in one terrible moment, Lilith gave birth to the Nightside through a single effort of will and determination.

A great city suddenly filled the clearing from boundary to boundary, shining bright as the sun, massive and ornate, a singular creation of wonder and beauty. It was a vision of great sparkling towers and massive shimmering domes, delicate elemental walkways and insanely elegant palaces—a glorious ideal city, a thing of dreams made real in stone and wood, marble and metal. It was magnificent, like the cities we see in our minds when we dream of distant places. All its shapes were curved, smooth and rounded, almost organic, the buildings rising and falling like waves in an artificial sea, and none of them were in proportion to each other. The city Lilith had created was inhumanly beautiful, and flawed, just like her.

"That . . . is not at all what I expected," said Suzie. "It's stunning. A city of light, and splendour. How could something as marvellous as that become the corrupt city of our time?"

"Because that thing before us isn't a city," I said. "It's an ideal. No-one lives in it. No-one ever could. That's simply a construct, a sterile unchanging place, designed to be looked at and admired, not lived in; even if Lilith doesn't realise that yet. Most of it's out of proportion, none of it belongs together, and from the look of those towers they only stay up because Lilith believes they will. The streets probably don't go anywhere, and I doubt she's left any room for the practicalities of city life, like clear entrances and exits, sewers and throughways. No . . . this is a dead end, like a beautiful cemetery. Can't you feel the coldness of it? This is only Lilith's idea of a city, a fantasy impressed on reality. No wonder Mankind eventually knocks it all down and builds a new one."

"An ideal," Suzie said slowly. "Like the human body she's made for herself?"

"Good point," I said.

"But . . . what is this city based on?" said Suzie, scowling fiercely. "There aren't any human cities around yet to inspire her."

"Another good point. I didn't know you had it in you, Suzie. I suppose . . . this could be a material reflection of places she's known. Heaven, Hell, Eden. A wordly version of a spiritual ideal. The ur-city, which only exists in our imaginations, a glimpse of a better place waiting . . . You know, we are getting into some pretty deep philosophical waters here, Suzie."

"Yeah," said Suzie. "You could drown in waters like these."

"Look at the stars," I said suddenly. "And the moon, shining down on the new Nightside. They're still the same, the ordinary unaffected night sky we saw before Lilith even arrived. Nothing up there's changed. And that's not the stars and moon we're used to seeing over our Nightside."

"So?" said Suzie.

"So, I don't think our Nightside is necessarily where and when we always assumed it was."

I would have gone further with that thought, but Lilith turned suddenly and addressed her assembled offspring. Her voice rose on the unnatural quiet, strong and hard and vibrant, and only partly human. Or feminine. She spoke in that old, ancient, language that predated Humanity. And I understood every word of it.

"Denied the comfort of Eden, I have made myself a new home, here in the material world. A place where everyone can be free from the tyrannical authority of Heaven or Hell. My gift to you all, and to those who will come after you."

The monsters cried out in various unpleasant voices, praising her, and bowing and fawning before her. I smiled slowly. They hadn't been listening. The city had never been intended for them alone. And the more I thought about what she said, the more things finally became clear to me.

"You're scowling again," said Suzie. "Now what?"

"Freedom from Heaven and Hell," I said slowly. "Freedom from reward or punishment, or the consequences of your own actions. If there is no Good or Evil, then actions have no meaning. If you no longer have to choose between Good and Evil, if nothing you do matters, then what meaning or purpose can your life have?"

"You've lost me," said Suzie. "I don't think that much about Good and Evil."

"I had noticed," I said. "But even you make a distinction between friend and enemy. Those you approve of and those you don't. You understand that what you do has consequences. Look, think it through. Why is virtue its own reward? Because if it weren't, it wouldn't be virtue. If you only did the right thing because you *knew* you'd get to Heaven, or avoided doing the wrong thing because you *knew* you'd end up in Hell, then Good and Evil wouldn't exist any more. You have to do the right thing because you believe it's the right thing, not because you'll be rewarded or punished for doing it. That's why there's never been any concrete proof of the true nature of Heaven or Hell, even in the Nightside. We were given free will, so we could choose between Good and Evil. You have to choose which one to embrace, for your own reasons, to give your life meaning and purpose. Otherwise, it would all be for nothing. Existence would be meaningless."

"That's why Lilith will destroy the Nightside in the future," said Suzie, nodding slowly almost despite herself. "Because Good and Evil and consequences have a way of creeping in, whenever people get together. She will destroy what the Nightside has become because that's the only way she can restore the purity of her original vision. By removing or destroying all the living things that corrupted her city by inhabiting it."

"Yeah," I said. "That sounds like Mother."

Suzie looked thoughtfully at Lilith, standing tall and proud before her awful children. "Creating the Nightside is supposed to have weakened her," Suzie said, meaningfully. "If I could get close enough to stick both barrels up her nostrils . . ."

"She doesn't look that weakened," I said firmly.

Abruptly Lilith walked forward into the glorious city she'd made, to show it off to her children. They slumped and slithered and crashed after her, filling the night with a celebration of their terrible voices. Suzie and I watched them go, and were glad to see the back of them. Just the sight of them hurt our eyes and made our stomachs churn. Human eyes were never meant to deal with such spiritual ugliness.

And that was when the two angels suddenly appeared before us.

It was obvious they came from Above and Below. They were suddenly standing there before us, two tall idealised humanoid figures with massive wings spreading out behind their backs. One was composed entirely of light, the other of darkness. We couldn't see their faces. There was no question but they were angels. I could feel it in my soul. Part of me wanted to kneel and bow my head to them, but I didn't. I'm John Taylor. Suzie already had her shotgun trained on them. She's never been much of a one for bowing either. I had to smile. The angels looked at each other. We weren't what they'd expected.

"As if things aren't complicated enough," I said, "now Heaven and Hell are getting directly involved. Wonderful."

"Bloody angels," growled Suzie. "Bullyboys from the afterlife. I ought to rip your pin-feathers out. What do you want?"

"We want you," said the angel of light. Its words rang in my head like silver bells.

"We want you to stop Lilith. We can help you," said the dark angel. Its words stank in my head like burning flesh.

"I am Gabriel."

"I am Baphomet."

"This is not how we really are," said Gabriel. "We found these images in your heads."

"Comfortable fictions," said Baphomet.

"Designed to make you comfortable with our presence."

"But not too comfortable. We are the will of Heaven and Hell made flesh, and we have been given jurisdiction in this matter."

"You will obey us," said Gabriel.

"Want to bet?" said Suzie.

"We don't do the 'o' word," I said.

The angels looked at each other. Things were clearly not going as expected. "This new city was never intended," said Gabriel. "The material world is not prepared to deal with such a thing. It will . . . unbalance matters. It cannot be allowed to flourish."

"Lilith must be stopped," said Baphomet. "We are here to help you stop her."

"Why?" I said. "I really would love to hear the official line on this."

"We cannot tell you," said Gabriel. "We do not know. We only ever know what we need to know, when we are unleashed upon the material world. It is not for us to make decisions or have opinions. We only enforce the will of Heaven and Hell."

"We are here to do what must be done," said Baphomet. "And we will see it done, no matter what it takes."

I'd seen this kind of limited thinking before, back during the angel war. Angels of either House were always much diminished by being made material. They were still unutterably powerful, and their very nature made them unwavering in their purpose, but you couldn't argue or reason with them. Even when conditions had clearly changed so much that their original purpose was no longer relevant. Angels were spiritual storm-troopers. If a city had to be destroyed, or the first-born of a generation destroyed, send in the angels. Of course, that was still to come.

"You want Lilith taken out, why don't you get on with it?" said Suzie.

"We cannot simply walk into her city and destroy her," said Gabriel. "Lilith has designed her creation so that simply by entering it, all emissaries of Heaven and Hell would be terribly weakened."

"And then she would destroy us," said Baphomet. "She hates all emissaries of authority, whether from Above or Below."

"We do not fear destruction," said Gabriel. "Only the failure of our mission. You can help us."

"You must help us."

Neither angel had much of a personality, as such. Presumably that would come later, after centuries of interaction with Humanity. For the moment, they were more like machines set in motion, programmed to carry out a distasteful but necessary task. It occurred to me that both the light and the dark angel had more in common than they would probably care to admit.

"If you can't enter the city without being destroyed, what use are you?" said Suzie, blunt as ever.

"We cannot stop Lilith," Gabriel said calmly. "But we can make it possible for you to stop her."

"How?" I said.

"You could not destroy her, even with our help," said Baphomet. "She was created to be uniquely powerful, and so she is. Even here, in the material world. But together we could weaken and diminish her, so much so that the harm she could do in the future would be much lessened."

"How?" I said.

"We understand that this is important to you," said Gabriel. "It is not necessary for us to know why."

"We can make you powerful," said Baphomet. "Powerful enough to deal with Lilith as she deserves to be dealt with."

"How?" I said.

"By possessing you," said Gabriel.

Suzie and I looked at the angels, then at each other, then we stepped back a little way to discuss the matter in private. Neither of us felt comfortable under the implacable gaze of their blank faces. And the unblinking light and the impenetrable darkness of their forms was wearing, on both the eyes and the soul. There was something about the angels that made you want to accept everything they said, unthinkingly. But because they couldn't lie didn't mean they were privy to the whole truth.

"We can't destroy Lilith," Suzie said reluctantly. "Whatever happens. Because if she dies here and now, you couldn't be born, John."

"The thought had occurred to me," I said. "But if we could seriously reduce her power, while she's still vulnerable . . . it might make it possible for us to deal with her, back in our own time. We know something happens to weaken her in the past, because soon enough her own creatures will band together to banish her from the Nightside. Maybe what we do here will make that possible."

"We're back to circular thinking again," said Suzie. "Hate Time travel. Makes my head hurt."

"But . . . if we can learn how to weaken her," I said, "maybe we can do it again, once we get back to our own time."

"If we get back to our own time." Suzie considered the matter for a while, then nodded reluctantly. "You mean, we could weaken her again, and stop her destroying the Nightside in the future. Okay. Sounds like a plan to me. Except that there is no way in hell that I'm going to let an angel or anyone else possess me. One body, one vote, no exceptions."

We went back to the angels. "Explain exactly what you mean by possession," I said. "And be really, really convincing that this is necessary."

"We will not be controlling you," said Gabriel. "We will merely inhabit your bodies to grant you our power."

"One of us, in each of you," said Baphomet. "Your human nature will carry our power into Lilith's city, and together we shall bring her down."

"You will enable us to carry out our mission. And afterwards, we shall leave your bodies, and return you to where you belong."

"How can we trust you to keep your word?" said Suzie.

"Why would we want to stay in a human body?" said Baphomet. "We are spirit. You are meat."

"To stay would be contrary to our orders," said Gabriel. "And in many ways, we are our orders."

I sighed heavily. "I know I'm going to regret this, but . . ."

"But?" said Suzie.

"You want to get home, don't you?"

She scowled. "You talk me into the damnedest things, Taylor."

It was my turn to look at her uncertainly. "Can you cope with this, Suzie? With having an angel . . . inside you?"

She shook her head. "You pick the strangest times to get sensitive. Relax, John. Even I can make a clear distinction between a spiritual and a physical invasion. I'll be fine. I think . . . I kind of like the idea of having an angel trapped within me, having to do what I tell it to do. I could dine out on that story for months, once we get back . . ."

"All right," I said to Gabriel and Baphomet. "You've got a deal. Baphomet; you take me."

Even then, I was determined to spare Suzie whatever pain and trauma I could. And I didn't entirely trust the idea of an angel from Hell inside Shotgun Suzie's body. Some marriages are definitely not made in Heaven.

"I would have taken you anyway," said the dark angel. "We are the most compatible."

I wasn't at all sure how to take that. Without any warning, both angels stepped forward and into us, like swimmers diving into deep water. Suzie and I both cried out, more in surprise than shock, and as quickly as that it was done. Baphomet was in my mind, like an idea out of nowhere, like a memory I'd forgotten, like an impulse from a place I normally kept heavily suppressed. And with the angel came power. It was like being plugged into the energy that runs the universe. I could see for miles, hear every sound in the night, and every movement of the air on my skin was like a caress. Suddenly I had other senses, too, and all the worlds within the world, and above and beyond it, unfolded all around me. I was drunk with knowledge, raging with power. I felt like I could tear the whole material world apart with my bare hands. That I could lay waste to any enemy, or dismiss them with a look. I knew that I could breathe life into dying suns, speed the planets in their orbits, dance the dance of life and death, redemption and damnation.

I was still me, but I was more than me. I laughed aloud, and so did Suzie. We looked at each other. We shone so very brightly, our flesh burning with an intense light, and massive wings spread out behind our backs. Our eyes were full of glory, and halos of fizzing static sparked above our heads. The world was ours, to do with as we wished.

Slowly, we remembered why we had done this thing and what we had to do. The slow, steady purpose of the angels beat within us, stronger than instinct, more certain than decision. Suzie and I turned as one and walked into the city Lilith had made. Once I was moving, I felt more like myself again. Action helped to focus me. Both Suzie and I blazed with a light that was brighter and more genuine than anything the city could produce, and the ground cracked and broke apart under the spiritual weight we carried. The tall towers and mighty buildings seemed somehow shabby under our light.

It didn't take long for our presence to be noticed. We were uninvited guests, the first the city had ever known. One by one Lilith's offspring came leaping and slithering and striding through the streets to face us. Some watched from alleyways, some flew overhead, calling out warnings, but eventually a crowd of them blocked our way, and we came to a halt. The monstrous creatures cried out in shock and anger, seeing the angels we carried within us. Their voices were harsh and brutal, when they could be understood at all, and they threatened us, laughed at us, demanded we surrender or leave. Like the baying of beasts in a new kind of jungle.

"Stand aside," I said, and my voice crashed in the air like thunder, like lightning.

"Stand aside," said Suzie, and the buildings shook and trembled all around us.

The creatures rushed us, attacking from every side with tooth and claw and barbed, ripping tentacle. They hated us, just for what we were. For our having dared to enter the place that Lilith had assured them was safe from outside interference. Huge and monstrous, fast and strong, they came at us, death and destruction made flesh, hate and spite and bitter evil given shape and form. They never stood a chance.

Suzie and I looked at them with the power of angels in

our eyes, and some of the creatures melted away under the pressure of that gaze, not strong or certain enough to withstand our augmented will. The flesh slipped from their bones like mud and splashed on the ground. Others simply disappeared, banished from the material world by our overwhelming determination. But most stood their ground and fought. They cut at us with claws and barbs, and mouths snapped all around us, while spiked tentacles sought to enwrap or tear us apart. We took no hurt. We were above that. We grabbed them with our strong hands and tore them limb from limb. Our fists punched through the hardest flesh and shattered the thickest carapaces. We crushed skulls and punched in chests and ripped off arms and legs and tentacles. More creatures came running, from every direction at once, spilling and bursting out of every adjoining street and alley. They outnumbered us a hundred to one, a thousand to one, living nightmares and killing machines of unnatural flesh and blood, every shape and form that darkness could conceive.

But Suzie and I had angels within us, and we were strong, so strong.

The street beneath our feet broke apart as awful things burst up out of the earth beneath the city. They wrapped around our legs and tried to drag us down. Bat-winged things slammed down out of the night sky, to tear and rend or snatch us up and carry us away. Suzie and I fought them all, our fingers sinking deep into yielding flesh. We picked creatures up and threw them away, and they crashed into elegant walls and brought down tall buildings. We walked steadily forward, and nothing could stand against us. The dead piled up everywhere, and the wounded crawled away, cursing and weeping and calling out for their mother. Wherever we turned our gaze or our hands, monstrous forms broke or faded away, and some splashed like bloody mud in the streets. Finally, the survivors turned and ran, disappearing back into the centre of the city, back to the dark heart of the Nightside, where Lilith waited for us to come to her. Suzie and I walked through the dead and the dying, the dismembered creatures and the splintered carapaces, ignoring the wounded and the weeping. They were not why we were there.

But still we smiled upon our work, and knew it to be just and good. I like to think this was the angel's thoughts, my angel's satisfaction, but I'm still not sure. I wanted to kill these awful things, these monsters who shared the same mother as I. I didn't want to think I had anything in common with them, but I did, I did. Angel or no, I was as much a monster in what I did then.

We followed the retreating creatures, all the way into the heart of the Nightside, and there was Lilith, sitting on a pale Throne, waiting for us. Her surviving offspring crouched and huddled around the Throne, and at her pale feet. She didn't look at them. All the power of her dark gaze was fixed on Suzie, and on me. The buildings were very tall, impossibly heavy and impressive, and I couldn't tell of what substance they were made. They just were, drawn out of her mind and stamped onto reality by her will, in this place that was not a place, hidden within the real world like a parasite deep in a man's guts.

Lilith watched unwaveringly as Suzie and I stepped unhurriedly into the courtyard and approached her throne. A dozen kinds of blood and offal dripped from our hands. Lilith's gaze was steady, her dark mouth unmoved as her wounded offspring surged restlessly around her feet, crying out for vengeance. Suzie and I came to a halt a respectful distance before her, and Lilith gestured sharply with one long-fingered hand. The clamour about her fell silent. She gestured again, and the creatures slunk away, fading into the dark shadows of the surrounding streets and alleyways. Until there was only Lilith and Suzie, and me.

"I see angels in you," Lilith said calmly. Her words came clearly to me, perhaps because they were filtered through Baphomet. "You carry Heaven's and Hell's restraints within you. I should have known they'd find a way to sneak into my perfect paradise. All I wanted was a world to play in, one world for my very own. A fresh start, I thought, but no; we have to follow the old ways, even here. So, which of you is the snake and which the apple, I wonder? Though I've never seen that much difference, between Heaven and Hell. Both so certain, so limited, so . . . unimaginative. Just bullies, determined to make everyone else play their depressing little game.

"Still, it doesn't matter. You've come too late. I have made a new realm, separate from both of yours, and what I have done here can never be undone, except by me. And you have no power to force me to do anything any more. The very nature of this city limits and diminishes you, while I . . . have designed this body to be very powerful indeed."

I could feel Baphomet boiling and churning within me, enraged by her words, desperate to unleash its power and follow its programming. But I was still in charge and pushed it back. There were things I needed to ask, needed to know.

"Why are Heaven and Hell so concerned about this place?" I said, and my voice sounded very normal to me. "Why do they see your little city as such a danger?"

Lilith raised a perfect dark eyebrow. "That isn't the angel talking. You're . . . human, aren't you? I've seen your kind, in visions. What brings you here, so many years before your time?"

"Is it the concept of true free will they find so threatening?" I persisted. "Why are they so scared of a place where freedom is more than just a word?"

"Your thinking is very limited," said the angel Gabriel, through Suzie's lips. Her mouth, its voice. "We do not care about Lilith or her city. It is the creatures and powers this freedom from responsibility will someday produce that are our concern. They will be more terrible and more powerful than the rightful inhabitants of this world were ever meant to have to face. Humanity must be protected from such threats if it is to have its fair chance. Unlike Lilith, we take the long view. She has only ever cared about the here and now."

"Here and now is certain," Lilith said calmly. "Everything else is guesswork."

"She must be destroyed," Baphomet said suddenly, forcing the words through my lips.

"That is not what was agreed," said Gabriel, through Suzie.

"Lilith is here and at our mercy," said Baphomet. "And we may never have a better chance."

"Our orders . . . are more important than any local agreement," said Gabriel. "We must destroy the outcast while we have the opportunity."

And just like that, the two angels changed our deal. Using all their strength and will, they pushed Suzie and me aside, forcing us into the back of our heads so they could take control of our bodies and complete their mission. They were supposed to stop her, not destroy her; but their nature would not let them miss the chance of disposing of such a notorious enemy of Heaven and Hell. Lilith didn't move. I could sense the weakness in her, her strength drained by how much of herself she'd had to put into creating her Nightside. I could have sat back and let the angels kill her. I could have watched her die, knowing it would ensure the Nightside's safety in the future, even if it meant my own death, through not being born. I could have. But in the end, I had to do something. Not only for me, but for her. I couldn't let her die because of something she hadn't done yet and might never do. Humanity had to have its chance, but so did she. Making decisions like this is what Humanity is for.

I surged forward in my head, taking Baphomet by surprise. I forced my hand out towards Suzie, and her hand came jerkily forward to grab mine. And together, inch by inch, we took back control of our bodies. The angels raged every step of the way, but there was nothing they could do. I smiled at Lilith, and spoke with my own voice again.

"I have to believe in hope," I said to her. "For you, and for me."

You cannot defy our authority, said a small voice in the back of my head. *You have no power without us.*

"I'm just exercising the free will I was given," I said. "And you two are more trouble than you're worth."

Defy us, and Heaven and Hell will be at your back and at your throat for the rest of your life.

"Get in the queue," I said. "You only possess us by our will, and by our consent. You broke the agreement. And this is the Nightside, where you have no authority at all. So, get out."

And like that, Suzie and I thrust Gabriel and Baphomet out of us. They shot up into the night sky, great wings flapping frantically, then they shot up like living fireworks, fleeing the city before it destroyed them. They couldn't risk being destroyed before they could report what had happened there, in that spiritual blind spot.

Losing the angel's power was like having the heart ripped out of me. It felt such a small thing, to be merely human again.

Suzie quietly let go of my hand. I nodded, understanding. And then we both looked at Lilith, still sitting in state on her pale Throne. She considered us, thoughtfully.

"So," she said finally. "Alone at last. I thought they'd never go. You are humans. Not quite what I was expecting."

"We're what humans will be," I said. "We're from the future."

"I thought you must be," said Lilith. "Without the angelic presence to mask it, you're dripping with Time. Thousands of years of it, I'd say. Why have you come such a long way to be here, speaking a language you shouldn't be able to understand, knowing things you shouldn't know?"

Suzie and I looked at each other, wondering how best to put this. There really wasn't any diplomatic way . . .

"I envy you your travel through Time," said Lilith. "That's one of the few things I can never enjoy. I had to imprint myself so very firmly on your reality, in order to exist here . . . and even I dare not risk undoing that. Tell me— what dread purpose brings you here, from so many years ahead, to murder my children and destroy my pretty city?"

"We came here to stop you from destroying the Nightside, in the far future," I said.

"The Nightside?" Lilith cocked her head on one side, like a bird, then smiled. "A suitable name. But why should I wish to destroy my realm after I've put so much of myself into its creation?"

"No-one seems too sure," I said. "Apparently it's tied in with me. I am, or will be, your son."

Lilith looked at me for a long moment, her face unreadable. "My son," she said finally. "Flesh of my flesh, born of my body? By a human father? Intriguing . . . You know, you really should have let those angels destroy me."

"What?" I said.

"I have put too much of myself into this place to be stopped or side-tracked now. By emissaries of the great tyrants of Heaven or Hell, or by some unexpected descendant from a future that may never happen. The Nightside will be what I intend it to be, here, and in all the futures that may be. I will do what I will do, and I will not accept any authority or restriction over me. That is why I was made to leave Eden, after all. You may be my son, but really all you are is an unexpected and unwelcome complication."

"You have to listen to me!" I said, stepping forward.

"No, I don't," said Lilith.

She rose suddenly out of her Throne and surged forward inhumanly quickly to grab my face in both her hands. I cried out, in shock and pain and horror. Her touch was cold as knives, cold as death, and the endless cold within her

sucked the living energy right out of me. I grabbed her
wrists with both my hands, but my human strength was
nothing next to hers. She smiled as she drained the life out
of me, and into her. Smiled with those dark lips and those
dark, dark eyes.

"I gave you life, and now I take it back," she said. "You
will make me strong again, my son."

I could no longer feel anything but the cold, and the
light was already fading out of my eyes, when Suzie
Shooter was suddenly there. She stuck her shotgun right
into Lilith's face and let her have both barrels. The shock
of the blessed and cursed ammunition at such point-blank
range drove Lilith backwards, jerking her hands off my
face. I fell to my knees, and didn't even feel it as they
slammed against the ground. Lilith cried out angrily, her
face undamaged but blazing with rage. Suzie knelt beside
me, her arm around my shoulders to stop me falling any
further. She was saying something, but I couldn't hear her.
Couldn't hear anything. I felt cold, distant, as though inch
by inch I was slipping away from life. And all I could think
was, *I'm sorry, Suzie . . . to have to do this to you again.*

She shook me roughly, then glared at Lilith. Some of
my hearing came back, though I still couldn't feel Suzie's
arm around me.

"How could you, you bitch! He's your son!"

"It was easy," said Lilith. "After all, I have so many
children."

She beckoned with one pale, imperious hand, and from
all sides her monsters came creeping forward again, crashing and slumping out of the streets and alleyways from
which they'd been watching. There were lots of them, even
after all those Suzie and I had killed, more than enough to
deal with two foolish humans. I fought to keep my head up,
watching helplessly as the monsters circled slowly around
Suzie and me, laughing in their various terrible ways, forms
hideous and powerful beyond hope or reason, monsters

from the darkest pits of creation. Some of them called out, in awful voices I could still somehow understand, boasting of the terrible things they would do to Suzie and to me for the destruction of their kindred and because they could. They promised us torment and horror, and death so long in the coming we would beg for it before they finally chose to release us. They would hurt us and hurt us until we couldn't stand it any more; and then they'd show us what pain really was.

And I thought, *Not Suzie . . . I'll die first, before I let that happen . . .*

She drew a slender knife from the top of her boot, and made a long shallow cut along the inside of her left wrist. I gaped at her stupidly, and she slapped the cut wrist against my open lips. Her blood filled my mouth, and I swallowed automatically.

"Werewolf blood," said Suzie, her face close to mine, her voice sharp and insistent, cutting through the fog in my head. "To buy us some time. I can't save us, John, and there's no-one here to act as the cavalry, this time. Only you can save us. So I'll fight them, for as long as I can, to buy you time to come up with some last throw of the dice. A miracle would be good, if you've got one about you."

She put the knife away and stood up to face the crowding monsters. She held her shotgun with familiar ease and sneered at Lilith, back sitting on her Throne. Suzie Shooter, Shotgun Suzie, stood tall and defiant as the monsters surged forward, and I don't think I've ever seen a braver thing in my life.

And maybe it was the werewolf blood, or maybe it was her faith in me, but I stood up, too, and looked at Lilith. For the first time she looked surprised, and uncertain. She opened her mouth to say something, but I laughed in her face. And using the very last of my reserves of strength, I forced open my inner eye, my third eye, my private eye, my one and only magical legacy from Mommie Dearest;

and I used my gift for finding things to detect the familial mystic link between me and Lilith. The very same link she'd used to draw my life out of me. And it was the easiest thing in the world to reach back through the link, seize her living energy, and haul it right out of her. She cried out in shock, convulsing on her Throne as the strength flowed out of her, and back into me.

The monsters stopped their advance at Lilith's horrified cry and looked around, confused. My back straightened and my legs grew strong again. My head cleared, and I laughed again; and something in that laugh made the monsters draw back even further. And still the power roared out of Lilith, and into me, for all her struggles. Suzie grinned at me, her single blue eye shining. Lilith cried out again, in rage and horror, and fell forward from her Throne, sprawling inelegantly on the ground before me. Her monstrous children were silent now, watching in shock at their powerful mother brought low. I smiled down at my helpless, thrashing mother, and when I spoke my voice was every bit as cold as hers.

"One day," I said to her, "all your precious monsters will get together and turn on you, banishing you from your own creation. When that happens, do remember that I made it possible, by weakening you here and now. They'll throw you out because, deep down, the only freedom you believe in is the freedom you dispense to others. You could never allow anyone else to be truly free, free of you, because then they might some day grow powerful enough to have authority over you . . . You'll lose everything, and all because you never could play nicely with others."

She looked up at me, with her eyes darker than the night. "I will see you again."

"Yes, Mother," I said. "You will. But not for thousands of years. In my time, on my territory. Still, here's a little something, to remember me by."

And I kicked her in the face. She fell backwards, and I

turned my back on her. I looked at Suzie, and she grinned and pumped one fist in the air victoriously. I grinned back, and using the power I'd drained out of Lilith, I broke Time's hold on us, and we rocketed back through history, all the way back to the future—and the Nightside, where we belonged.

EPILOGUE

Back in Strangefellows, the oldest bar in the world.

She said, "So, what do we do now?"

I said "We put together an army of every Power and Being and major player in the whole damned Nightside, and turn them into an army I can throw at Lilith's throat. I'll use my gift to track down wherever she's hiding herself now, then . . . we do whatever we have to, to destroy her. Because that's all there is left, now."

"Even though she's your mother?"

"She was never my mother," I said. "Not in any way that mattered."

"Even with an army to back us up, we could still lay waste to most of the Nightside, fighting to bring her down."

"She'll do it anyway, if we don't do something," I said.

"I've seen what will happen if we don't stop her, and anything would be better than that."

I didn't look at her scarred face. I didn't think of her half-dead, half-mad, come back through Time to kill me, with the awful Speaking Gun grafted where her right forearm used to be.

"What if the others don't want to get involved?"

"I'll make them want to."

"And end up just like your mother?"

I sighed, and looked away. "I'm tired, Suzie. I want . . . I need for all this to be over."

"It should be one hell of a battle." Shotgun Suzie tucked her thumbs under the bandoliers of bullets that crossed her chest. "I can't wait."

I smiled at her fondly. "I'll bet you even take that shotgun to bed with you, don't you?"

She looked at me with her cold, calm expression. "Someday, you just might find out. My love."

Coming October 2005 from Ace

For Those Who Fell
by William C. Dietz
0-441-02167-1

The new novel of *The Legion of the Damned* that's "a genuine adrenaline rush," from the bestselling author of *Runner*.

The Great Tree of Avalon: Child of the Dark Prophecy
by T.A. Barron
0-441-01308-2

The peaceful world of Avalon is in danger—and only the wizard Merlin's true heir can save its fate.

Also new in paperback this month:

Age of Conan: Scion of the Serpent
by J. Steven York
0-441-01336-8

Sebastian of Mars
by Al Sarrantonio
0-441-01337-6

Dragonfly
by Frederic S. Durbin
0-441-01338-4